Mildred

Raising the Ante

Steve from and enjoy Toni Kief

Toni Kief

Mildred

Raising the Ante

Toni Kief

The Writers Cooperative of the Pacific Northwest
Seattle, Washington 2019

The Writers Cooperative of the Pacific Northwest
Seattle, Washington 2019

ISBN: 9781092651578

Toni Kief's website: www.tonikief.com

Cover design: Heather McIntyre, www.coverandlayout.com
Cover photos: Dice © blickpixel; Poker chips © Cristi Lucaci; Woman © Axel Bueckert

Interior design: Heather McIntyre, www.coverandlayout.com

This book is dedicated to Friday Night
Happy Hour at Collectors Choice.

Special thanks to Rosie Kuhlman,
Joe Kurke, Barbara Vericker, and Tyler Davis.

A special Thank You to Susan Brown.

Mildred

Raising the Ante

Toni Kief

– Contents –

— 1 —

Depositions

Mildred was early for the deposition and waited in the parking lot. It had been over a month since Elijah Walsh, the pimp, was shot at the casino. Listening to the radio news, she pondered her surprise that this story had stayed under the radar. There had only been a second-page mention of a shooting and no information on the victim or the accused shooter. Elijah Walsh was a mean old piece of work, and Mildred suspected he was part of a sex trafficking ring. One of his prostitutes and wife, Nadiya Kovalchuk Walsh was accused of the shooting, but they could find no witnesses or video of her action. Mildred had arranged for her friend, Tim Selkirk, to represent Nadiya and her sister Galena, who was being beaten by the victim at the time of the shooting. Mildred was a little ashamed that she privately thought the world was better with brutes like Elijah Walsh gone.

Ten minutes early, she entered the attorney's office. Mildred scanned the offices; everything was exceptionally professional.

She continued to scan the offices as the receptionist led her to a large meeting room with an oval table.

The young woman brought Mildred a cup of coffee as she settled into a seat at the foot of the table, nearest to the open door. Mildred sipped as she surveyed a stack of files at the other end, then silently checked her telephone and waited.

The coffee had cooled when Mildred started to hear a heated discussion in the next room. No matter how she tried, there was no way to discern what was being said. Only a word or two at a time drifted in. She was certain they were discussing this case. The voices changed, and it was clear the negotiation had ended. Mildred watched as the men moved to the hall; she could see her reflection on the glass walls looking at the three men. One was Tim Selkirk, her friend and attorney for Nadiya; the second was the lead prosecuting attorney, and the third was an unfamiliar but well-dressed young man. Mildred started to become anxious as her curiosity piqued.

Tim turned toward her and simply shrugged his shoulders. She could read frustration on his face. After goodbyes were exchanged and the other two men had left, Tim came to the conference room. Mildred was always surprised at how handsome the attorney was. She knew him best as his alter-ego, Penny Dumple, but there he was in an expensive three-piece suit, oozing masculine professionalism.

"I'm so sorry for the wait. That was the state prosecutor and an attorney from Baltimore. We worked out a plea agreement for Nadiya. I haven't seen anything like this before. You can go. There won't be any legal action, all charges were dropped, and Nadiya Kovalchuk is to be deported."

"What about her sister?" Mildred spoke louder than she expected. "This whole thing seemed to be the result of Walsh forcing both of them into prostitution and his brutality."

Tim pulled out a chair next to Mildred and sat down. "They based it on no eyewitnesses to her action. There was only questionable forensic proof of her pulling the trigger. I spoke with Nadiya and she assured me that she would gladly move back to Croatia. And here is the topper – they gave me a check to pay for a non-disclosure agreement, so Nadiya can afford to take Galena."

Mildred tried to let the information sink in before responding. "What? They are dropping the charges and paying her to leave? I have never heard of such a thing. Not even on television."

"I know," said Tim. "I have all kinds of suspicions, but my client is packing and saved from a murder charge and a sex-trafficking ring. I can't wait to talk to the prosecutor alone. I hope he digs further. That young attorney was really slick; seemed to have a lot of power, and I'm not sure where his involvement came from." Tim stood, signaling it was time to go. "I have to get back to a divorce and two child support hearings."

Mildred stood to leave, shook hands, and as she exited, turned back. "Tim, let me know if you or Penny wants to meet for dinner soon."

"Darn tootin'." Tim held the door for her as she came face-to-face with Perry Block, the other undercover security agent hired to work with Mildred after the casino expansion.

Perry looked at Mildred. "Darn tootin' – is that a thing?"

"It is now. The depositions are canceled. Let's go." They laughed as they entered the elevator and walked to the cars together.

She was about to start her car when Perry tapped on her side window. "Have you heard about Arnie? Is he out of the hospital yet?"

"He gets out today. Bud is going to pick him up since we had the depositions."

Perry winked at her. "Let me know if he needs anything."

Mildred smiled. "I'll tell him. See you later tonight."

"Shouldn't be busy, so if you need to help him, don't worry about it." Perry clicked his key fob and his car unlocked and started. "Darn tootin'."

— 2 —

Going Home

Bud Moses was called to the front window. "Excuse me. I'm here to pick up Arnie Arneson. He's supposed to be discharged today."

The clerked clicked a keyboard. "Yes, sir, he is on his way down to the front lobby. He told them someone was already here."

Bud Moses rushed to the main lobby and arrived just as the nurse wheeled Arnie from the adjacent elevator. "Hey, Arneson, about time you stopped lying around and got back to work."

Arnie laughed. The hospital had kept him a couple of extra days after his emergency gallbladder surgery. The nurse waited while Bud went for the car. She helped load Arnie into the passenger seat and put a bag with his personal belongings on his lap.

"Thank you; I appreciate everything your team has done for me." Arnie pulled the door closed. "Now, all the nicety is done. I'll be glad to get home to my own bed, and back to work. I didn't expect the boss to be my chauffeur. Where's Mildred?"

Bud answered, "As you know, Belinda is out with the new babies, and we are short-handed. With your surgery, we are all pulling double duty."

Bud started the car to exit the busy parking lot. They rode quietly when Arnie noticed that they were going to the Ivory Winds Casino.

"So, you're taking me in for a shift already? I'd like to get a clean uniform."

"No change necessary. If you are in the surveillance room, you don't need a uniform. Aw hell, the nurse said you can walk. We'll put you on patrol." Bud kept staring at the road and didn't see Arnie nod his head in agreement.

Arnie thought only for a moment before he responded. "I could do a short shift if you need me."

Bud wasn't sure if Arnie was calling his bluff but remembered how he refused to take time off with the recent death of his father. "No, you don't, big talker. The doctor said a couple of weeks off. I need to pick something up on the way to your place. Then you officially remain on sick leave. There are more interviews lined up, and we have an ad running for security. Even if you were there, we need more help with the expansion of the casino."

"Question: if you find new security officers, won't you have to train them?" asked Arnie.

"Oh, please, your job isn't that hard. We might just bring in a couple of dogs." Bud pulled into the front circle drive. Chef Mike from the buffet was standing at the curb. They stopped and within minutes, several carry-out boxes filled the car with enticing aromas. "Sorry, I didn't want you to starve to death during recovery."

Arnie rode along toward home. As happy as he was to be out of the hospital, exertion was exhausting. It was only minutes when they pulled into the driveway. Bud had to wake Arnie to walk him into the house and then helped him sit down in the living room. Bud ran back out to the car for the boxes of food.

Arnie sat quietly, still waking up when he noticed a huge white cat had jumped into the chair next to his. It took a moment for it to register. "What the hell! Popcorn, what are you doing here?" He immediately scanned the room. "Mildred, Mildred Petrie, are you in my house?" There was no answer, a black kitten joined the first cat and then climbed onto Arnie's lap. "Louie, is your momma here?" He continued to search the room.

A voice came from the kitchen. "Hold it down out there. We don't want to bother the neighbors."

"Mildred, my Bunny, you are here!" She walked into the living room with a soup ladle in her hand. Arnie struggled to stand, as she walked a few steps and he wrapped her in his arms. "I miss hugging you."

Mildred pulled away gently. "Settle down; you just had surgery. I don't know where I can touch and not cause any additional damage."

"I'd tell you if there is anything, but it was just a simple incision." He started to pull up his shirt.

"STOP! Can't you two restrain yourselves while company is here?" Bud stood in the doorway and visibly shuddered. "I can smell you've been cooking. I picked up some dinners to help keep him alive. I need to get that lazy piker back to work." Bud set the boxes on the coffee table.

"Thanks, Bud, that's so thoughtful." Mildred smiled and accepted the boxes.

Bud looked at Arnie and continued, "I've got to get back. I'm leaving him in your very capable hands, Mildred. We have you covered for tonight, so don't worry. Please don't break him."

Mildred led Arnie back to the chair and moved the cat. Once he was seated, the kitten jumped back onto his lap. Bud waved goodbye and walked out the door.

Mildred could see the questions on Arnie's face as he turned toward her. "You have no idea how happy I am to see you."

"I'm glad to see you too. Are you hungry?" Mildred smiled and started back to the kitchen.

"No, my Cinnamon Bun, I just want to look at you and talk to you." Arnie relaxed back into the recliner as Mildred went over to the adjacent chair and sat down.

"You scared the heck out of me, Arnie Arneson. I saw the video, and you were just fine, grabbed your chest, and dropped to the floor. Thank goodness Robin noticed and called for help." Mildred wiped a tear from her eye. "We all thought you had a heart attack. I don't know if I can forgive you yet."

"Scared me, too. I didn't know that your gallbladder would act like that. But I'm back on my feet now."

"I'm not blind; you are only tentatively on your feet. Luckily everything is turning out alright." Mildred paused. "It is, isn't it?"

"I've got to take it easy for a little while, but I'll be back to work in a few days." Arnie nodded. "Now what kind of soup do I smell? I could eat."

"Chicken vegetable, and homemade cornbread from a box." Mildred stood. "And don't you think for a moment that I won't check the computer for your recovery time."

"Perfect. Oh, have I mentioned that I love you, but especially with soup?" Arnie laid his head back, and it was obvious that he was exhausted.

Next time he opened his eyes, there were two TV trays next to him with food and a stemmed wine glass. Mildred was watching television even though the sound was muted. "Oh, I'm sorry; I didn't mean to doze off."

Mildred smiled. "Don't worry about it; you were only out a couple of minutes. The soup should still be hot." She unmuted the sound, and they contentedly watched the news and then reruns of *The Big Bang Theory.*

Arnie ate everything but resisted second helpings. He picked up the stemmed glass and toasted toward Mildred; she tapped his glass with hers. They both sipped, and then he coughed, causing a slight spill. "What the hell is that?"

Mildred sipped her glass and looked at him. "Apple juice. Do you really think I would give you alcohol the day you get out of the hospital? We've only been a couple for a few months, and I'm too old to bury another man. I truly don't want you to die." She set down her glass and winked. "Yet."

Arnie faked a pouty face. "You have apple juice, too?"

"Are you kidding? I have all of my internal organs and a box of Chablis," said Mildred as she took another sip. "I don't have to work tonight, so let me know when you want to go to bed.

Arnie took a sip and leaned back. "I'm doing alright, but I could lie down."

Mildred helped him up, but he was able to go slowly up the stairs on his own. She helped him undress and hook up his CPAP machine. He turned on the television, and she started relaying the story of the depositions and the plea agreement. He was asleep early into the details. Leaving the television running, Mildred went back downstairs to clean the kitchen, feed the cats and dip the litter box. It was nearly an hour later when she carried the cat bed to Arnie's bedroom. He was deeply asleep, and she undressed in the bathroom and slipped on her newest flannel nightgown. Mildred gathered the remote control from where he had dropped it on the floor. After sliding into bed, she turned the volume down and picked up her book from the nightstand.

Arnie rolled to face Mildred. "I remember when you came to the hospital, and you agreed to marry me."

"You were drugged up. Maybe that didn't happen." Mildred leaned over and kissed him gently.

Arnie smiled. "Maybe it did happen. I'm holding you to your promises."

"This is a dream. Go back to sleep. We'll talk later." Mildred flicked off the television and pulled the blanket over her shoulders. "Good night, my dear man."

– 3 –

Liars, Cheats, and Chips

Mildred walked through the main doors of the Ivory Winds Casino, muted her phone and tapped a message.

G-ma on the floor.

There was an immediate response. **OK – Starting to get busy.**

She had just put her phone into her pocket when it buzzed again. **This is Bud; meet me in interrogation.**

On my way.

Mildred turned and walked immediately to the isolated room behind the card rooms. She arrived at the same moment Bud Moses exited the stairs. "Well, boss, what's up?"

Bud opened the door to the empty interrogation room. "Couple things. First, how is Arnie doing?"

They both took seats at the metal table and Mildred smiled. "He is doing much better today. He slept about ten hours last night, but he was up and watching television with the cats when I left."

"Good news. Don't let him come back too soon. I want him to work for years more, and complications won't help. With Larry and Perkins, the swing shift guy, we are handling it."

"I met Perkins, but just once. Seemed nice enough. What else is going on?" Mildred asked.

"We found some more counterfeit fifty-dollar chips. They are really good work, but the color and weight are slightly off. They have been turned in, usually in trays or large deposits. I need you watching the gaming tables." Bud started to dig into his pocket and flipped a sample to her. Mildred examined the bright blue token; then Bud handed her another one. "Look in comparison."

"WOW, I can tell when they are next to each other, but only when I know to look for a difference. Which is the real one?" asked Mildred.

"The second one is authentic. Look at the gold in the logo," Bud said.

"Okay, I can see it looks painted and not as sharp. The edges are identical." Mildred continued to handle the two chips. "How the heck did the cashiers catch this?"

"It was Dolores; she has been with us since the beginning of Ivory Winds. She has handled thousands, maybe millions of chips, and she noticed something being off. It was in a tray; she took it down, and found a dozen counterfeits."

Mildred continued to inspect the chips. "A dozen at fifty a throw... that is getting up there."

"Those were just the ones we caught," said Bud.

"I hope Dolores got a reward or a raise. This is an outrageous catch. Do we know which trays? The ones dealers turn in or the ones they put together?"

There was a knock at the door. Bud answered and it was Perry Block. Mildred waited while Bud brought him up to date and shared two more chips. They sat around the metal table studying the chips.

"Usually security and pit bosses would have been all over this when they first appeared, but they didn't catch these. Last night it kicked up higher. Since this was discovered by accounting, everything is complicated by all of the new employees and being unsure where the fake chips have come from. I need you guys watching too. I went to Sam Langley,"

Perry interjected, "The new CEO?"

Bud shook his head yes and continued. "And he is having Human Resources review the initial background checks on the newer employees. I need you two, my tried and trues, working on this. I'm not sure who to trust otherwise. Keep it quiet. We will continue to go through the videos from the past couple days."

"Any idea which games?" said Perry.

"New or old sections?" asked Mildred as she handed back the chips.

Bud slid the counterfeit chip back to her, "Hang on to it for reference, and here is one for you, Perry. I'm concerned about a combined effort, not sure of anything. I'm thinking in the new section because there are more unknowns in that area." Bud scratched his chin. "I really don't know."

Perry continued. "It actually depends on how busy things are. I'll work through the game section, so in about an hour and a half we can move again. Let's keep in touch by earpiece – they don't tolerate phones in gaming."

"Change your earpieces to channel six; it's seldom used," Bud added. "It will only be the three of us. I'll update Larry when I leave. No one else needs to know at this point."

They had all changed the settings when Perry spoke. "This sounds like a plan to start, but we will have to keep it fluid and adapt as necessary."

"Deal!" Mildred stood to leave. "Hopefully we'll get a rhythm before Friday when they have the big floor show they advertised." She turned back. "Bud, do you have Robin to spare?"

"Sorry, I've got her on cameras, and she is actually working as the surveillance room supervisor tonight and over the weekend."

Mildred looked startled. "That was quick; she is a relatively new hire."

"Thanks to you, she has more than proven herself. Maybe we need to train everyone on the floor with you, Mildred."

Mildred giggled. "Gunfire in the parking lot does weed out the lightweights. Speaking of which, there will be no more legal action on the shooting."

"What? What happened?" asked Bud. "I was going to meet with the new head of the legal department on this."

Mildred gave him a quick review of the meeting while Perry left to start the patrols. It only took a few minutes and Bud simply rolled his eyes. "I wonder if we will ever know what happened?" Bud stood. "Now get to work. I need you on the floor."

They left the room, moving in two different directions. In the short time she was away from the floor, the activity had increased. Mildred went to the gaming area in the new addition. She decided to plop into a seat and watch a variety of games. Not putting any money down, she was ignored. Mildred appeared to be watching the players, but was more aware of the dealers, security, and the pit bosses. The hour dragged on; she was so used to the constant movement that her back started to ache.

Her ear bud crackled. "Trade? Finishing the north patrol, on my way over."

Mildred answered, "10-4. Which way is north again? I'll head to the hotel." She stood quietly and looked around the gaming area. It was getting busier by the minute. "We can weed out the lower betting games." With a leisurely turn to the south, Mildred started the usual patrol. It took nearly forty-five minutes to walk through the gift shops, hotel, spa, half the slots, and four restaurants. *Thank goodness Perry had taken the north end.* She tapped the earpiece, and whispered, "Just arriving. I'll stay an hour unless anything changes."

"10-4, G-ma. Agreed." Perry signed off.

The night continued, and they both signed out a little after two a.m. The games had slowed when the nightclubs shut down. Mildred saw Perry walking out with the last of the club party crowd.

While leaving the casino, she said, "Como, meet me at lot G, my car."

"Perfect timing. On my way."

A different voice interrupted their conversation. "This is Larry. Do you need me too?"

Mildred smiled. She had forgotten the line was monitored. "No, just wanted to reassess while everything is fresh. Did you catch anything on the cameras?"

Larry said, "Call you right back. I'll check with the crew."

Mildred saw Perry walking up. He was hard to miss. Well over six-feet tall, his silver hair reflected the lights and showed off his good looks. He approached as if searching for his car. "Over here." Mildred unlocked the car doors and sat in the driver's seat.

He slid into the passenger side and shut the door. He spoke first. "Do you have any suspicions?"

"Nothing yet. I've had several ideas of possibilities, but no real suspects. I'm drawn to watching the pit bosses and security as they carry the chips and cash for the fills."

Perry pondered. "I can't disagree. I thought that for customers to pass counterfeits, they'd have to hand off to employees so that it might be a team of sorts."

Both earphones vibrated. Mildred spoke, "Larry? You have anything?"

"No one noticed anything obvious on cameras, but I'll leave a message for the morning supervisor to check with accounting to see if anything was turned in. You guys go on home and get some sleep. Tomorrow is Friday and you know it can be crazy, with the events added to the mix."

Mildred and Perry spoke in unison. "Agreed."

Perry continued speaking to Mildred. "I'm following orders, but I'll write up my report tonight and get it over to you."

"Perry, do you want a ride to your car?" Mildred asked.

"No need, I'm about two rows over. By the way, how is Arnie doing?"

Mildred smiled; no secrets in the Casino. "He is doing well, slept a bunch, but feeling pretty frisky when I left today."

"Tell him he's missed." Perry got out, as Mildred watched him almost skip to his black, shiny car.

Damn, he is obviously an ex-cop. Clean-cut and his car looks like it was taken in a high-end drug raid. Mildred pulled away from the nearly empty parking lot. *I hope Arnie is sleeping; all of the focused attention tonight was exhausting.*

She turned toward home before suddenly remembering that she was staying at Arnie's house. Mildred made a left turn at the exit and drove the few miles to his house. She pulled into the drive. The place was ablaze with light. The giant white cat sat in the front window, watching. She had expected the house to be quiet, but when Mildred put the key in the lock, she could hear music playing. The door opened to the warmth and the smell of something baking.

The two cats met her as she walked in. Popcorn weaved back and forth between her legs. The kitten, Louie, simply meowed for attention. Arnie stepped out of the kitchen with a towel wrapped around his waist. "Welcome home, Bunny. I timed it perfectly." He started to dance. "I made brownies for you. Just a little snack before I sweep you off to bed." Arnie approached and engulfed Mildred in his arms.

"Careful, Arnie, your incision." She pulled back.

"Please don't worry. If it hurt, I wouldn't hug. I feel great, and we have warm brownies."

They walked into the kitchen, and he had a platter he was filling with still warm treats. He had also set up her laptop computer, and it was open to a blank document, waiting for her password. Arnie held the chair for her, and once seated he went to make two cups of Sleepy Time Tea.

"I thought you would be asleep; you're still in recovery." Mildred took a large bite of the surprise treat. "Oh my, your mother would be proud of you. Is this her recipe?"

"No, sorry to say. I got the recipe from a dear friend from my youth, Duncan Hines." Arnie's face was flushed and smiling. "We went to school together."

Mildred was surprised. "Really? You know Duncan Hines?"

"No, you must be tired. I'm not even sure if he's real. I remember his baking mixes when I was a kid."

Mildred nodded and put the rest of the brownie in her mouth, sipped some tea and looked at him lovingly. "Your assignment tomorrow is to learn about Duncan and report to me. But for now, let me crank out this report, then I'll be up."

Arnie stood at the kitchen door and said, "I'll leave you to it. You can find me in the bedroom." He winked at her very suggestively, stuffed an entire brownie into his mouth and walked away. The kitten followed him up the stairs.

It took only a half hour for her to type the report and email it to Bud. She noticed Perry's report in her inbox but decided to read it in the morning. Mildred put a bowl over the remaining brownies to keep the cats out, moved the two cups to the sink, locked the doors, and shut off the lights. Finally, picking up Popcorn, Mildred whispered quiet messages of affection to the cat as she climbed the stairs to bed.

They entered the dimly-lit room. Mildred could hear Arnie's CPAP machine running softly, but he was still awake. He took off the mask as she entered the bed. "That was quick. How was work tonight?" They talked about the counterfeiting at the casino and the usual gossip until they both fell asleep.

— 4 —
New Day

Mildred slept well and when she woke up around noon, Arnie was already gone. It was hard to believe that he could move so quietly. After a long hot shower, Mildred walked downstairs. He was puttering in the kitchen and she could smell fried ham.

"Hey, Romeo, how are you doing today?"

He continued to cook as he responded. "I'm great, and how are you, Madam?"

"I haven't had emergency surgery any time in the last twenty plus years." Mildred poured a cup of coffee and topped off his cup that was sitting next to the stove. "I'm supposed to be here helping take care of you, and it has reversed in less than two days. Shouldn't you be doing recovery stuff?"

"I'll tell the truth. I feel good most of the day, but I do get tired easily. I need to be active and the waiting around all night for you is asking too much."

Mildred blushed. "Sweet talker. Why don't you sit down and I'll finish breakfast?"

Arnie handed her the spatula and took his cup to the small table against the wall. She noticed he looked pale as he put two slices of wheat bread into the toaster. She divided the ham onto the two waiting plates.

"What's the egg order, Mr. Arneson?"

"Any way is fine. Just be sure mine is cooked."

She turned to see him grimace and she made a mental note, *runny egg issues*, as she cracked four eggs into a small bowl and scrambled them. Within a few minutes, they were seated across from each other with the hot and hearty breakfast.

"I like this, a team effort with an edible reward."

Arnie smiled as he buttered a piece of toast, handing it to her. "I told you we were good together."

"No, you didn't. You must still be on pain pills."

"Check the bottle. I haven't had any since I left the hospital. I'd rather be in pain than gonked-out in the recliner." He continued to eat. "I remember more than you give me credit for. I could hear you leaving with Bud the night after the surgery. I'm still waiting for an acceptance to my proposal. Since you are here, I'll take that as a yes. So, we have some planning to do."

"You keep bringing this up. You were groggy and talking nonsense." Mildred kept her head down, focused on cutting the ham. "This is too soon. We have only been on a couple of what you called dates and ah…"

Arnie pretended to cough, "Bullshi…" and wiped at his nose with the napkin. "I can see you are asking for time, but how old are you?"

"You know how old I am. I'm seventy-two. You were at my birthday party."

"And I'm sixty-three. I'll give you time, but not much. Let's be real, there is only today that's guaranteed and I'm not going to let you get away. I've truly loved two women in my life and I stalled too long for the first. Never going to make that mistake again. Go ahead and think, but, Ms. Petrie, I expect you to confirm the yes any day now." He looked at her deeply and then went back to eating. "Do you need more coffee?"

They laughed together and he allowed her the escape. Together they cleared the dishes, and he loaded the dishwasher while she wiped the counters. Mildred walked out to her computer to check email and reports from the night before. There was no indication of new developments or new problems. Arnie turned up the stereo and put on a Bruce Springsteen CD before retiring to his chair. When she finished, Mildred noticed he was asleep with a black kitten on his lap and the giant white cat, Popcorn, in the chair next to him. She felt a warmth recognizing that this was her newest family, and how lucky her life has been.

"I'll get it." Arnie released the recliner, coming back to a seated position.

Mildred reached down and moved it back in place. "Stop right there. I'm here to take care of you. Now, what do you want?"

"Yes ma'am. I'd like some iced tea, unsweetened."

There wasn't any made. So Mildred filled the pot and put it on the stove. She filled the washer and removed yesterday's load from the dryer. After hauling the clothes to the living room couch, she went back to brew the tea. There was a large pitcher and Mildred set it to steep.

She called back to the living room, "Tea is almost ready, anything else? Maybe a brownie?" She heard a sound and assumed it was agreement. She delivered the glass and plate next to his chair. "This is how it is supposed to be. Think you can allow me to help?"

Arnie looked better than at breakfast and agreed that she could help. Mildred moved to the couch and started to fold towels while they watched the news. It was surprisingly comfortable.

It was during the commercial when Arnie brought up work. "I've got some thoughts about the counterfeiters at the casino."

"Stop it. You are not involved in this until the recovery is complete. When do you go back to the doctor's office?"

"Monday afternoon, but I'm doing really well," Arnie said as he picked up the brownie.

"I'm going in early tonight. We have so many new people, and with you and Belinda still out, looks like a late night." She stood to put the towels away. "I can't make any promises. Please don't wait up."

"Aren't they doing the midnight showing of that Rocky Mountain Horror movie?"

Mildred shook her head. "That is the Rocky Horror Picture Show. No mountains involved. That starts at midnight, so it will be well after two for them to clear. I'll leave if Perry can handle it. Security knows I have a valuable patient to attend to."

"Don't worry about me. I'm okay and I'll do what I want."

Mildred sighed. "That much I know. You have those dinners Bud brought. I'll set one out before I leave."

"You don't have to worry. I can microwave with the best of them. There is no issue with my incision.

It's healing up like a champ." Arnie lifted his shirt and poked at the bandage.

Mildred said nothing and left the room shaking her head. *He is impossible; it is as if he is unaware of how horrifying it was to see him collapse and be taken away. Caring about someone new is hard enough to adapt to, and then he doesn't help.* She continued to put away the laundry she had folded last night and called from the upstairs linen closet. "If you want me to love you, better take care of yourself. Do you hear me?"

Mildred heard a muffled answer that sounded like "Yes, ma'am."

By five-thirty, Mildred had the house in order, laundry done, food plated in the refrigerator. She woke from her nap and found Arnie was in bed next to her. "When did you come up here?"

"When I heard you snoring from downstairs, I felt it was a welcome."

Mildred cuddled next to him. "I don't snore."

"Okay, if you say so." He pulled her even closer and winked. "You don't have to be at the Casino for awhile, do you?"

"Right, Romeo, but no hanky-panky until you have the stitches out and the doctor gives the okay." Mildred held him a little tighter, kissed him deeply, turned over and got up. "I have liars and cheats to catch."

Mildred was on her way before seven. As she walked from the car to the Ivory Winds, Mildred tapped on her phone, **G-Ma on the floor.**

Welcome – already busy. Good luck.

I'll be on the headphone tonight.
10-4 – channel 6.

Mildred silenced her phone and stowed it in her rear pocket as she walked through the main entrance. A regular patrol was in order since the plan was to focus at the gaming tables, hotel, gift shops, slots, and restaurants. Since she had eaten a little with Arnie before she started, it had thrown her rhythm off. Accustomed to enjoying the buffet as a break, she murmured, "Damn it, Italian night too." Her mouth watered for cannoli. Maybe she would pick up a couple later to take home.

When she reached the gaming room, her phone buzzed; she took it out for a look.

Como in-house.
10-4 – G-Ma is in.
Where?

Mildred stepped to a quiet corner to not disturb the players with a phone. **G-Ma at new blackjack area. Not busy.**

Her earpiece ticked and she answered, "Perry?"

"Yes. Should I do a north or south walk through, then the original gaming area? I'm Harold tonight."

"Oh, what fun. I don't know Harold. Maybe go north and upstairs. I'm Mildred, but I'll pick up a new sweatshirt later. I need to go home tomorrow and pick up a disguise."

"How is Arnie doing?" Perry asked.

"He acts like he forgot the surgery. I left him and the cats with the TV remote. Hopefully, he stays down."

"Good to know. I thought I saw his truck at the rear loading area."

"Aw, hell no. We have enough to worry about tonight. I can't have him out of that recliner. I came in early to get established," Mildred whispered.

"Don't worry, I'm probably wrong. There are a lot of ten-year-old pickup trucks."

They heard a third voice interrupt on the secured line. "There aren't that many old pickups. He's here."

Mildred answered immediately, "Larry? Please, don't let him do anything. Send him home."

Larry chuckled heartily. "I'm sorry, G-Ma, but you know we can tell him things, but not much. He will do what he wants. I plan to keep him on a screen, and Robin is babysitting. If he gets tired, I'll drive him home."

"You are right about our control of that cantankerous old coot. Thank you. I need to get moving. We have the Rat Pack show that pulls in the older folks and then the midnight movie." Mildred clicked off. She swore under her breath as she walked back to the action. In the few minutes they had talked, the tables were noticeably busier. She strolled through blackjack, looking for another seat where she could watch both the dealers and the pit boss. After trying several angles, Mildred settled between the crap tables. There was a lot of action so early in the evening – a sign of what was to come as night took over.

From past experience, she knew that she couldn't sit still for too long. She had started to check for the next vantage point when her earpiece ticked and Perry's voice came through the constant din of games and slots. "Time to swap; I'll take gaming if you go south."

"Agreed."

Half hour to patrol the two largest slot areas, a couple of bars. It was still early for the nightclubs, a walkthrough should be sufficient. Mildred checked her watch and started when she noticed a conversation between a security officer she didn't know and a pit boss. It wasn't possible to hear them, and they had plenty of reasons to interact. For no particular reason, she made a mental note to watch them. Once away from the gaming tables, she took out her phone and texted Perry.

Watch security and boss.

Her phone buzzed immediately. **Which one?**

Main desk, and ginger guard, she answered.

A text from the security office came in. **Got them on camera.**

Mildred tapped an answer, **Who is this?**

Security – got your back.

She was about to tap in a response when she saw a tall, balding man approach, so she put the phone back in her pocket. He walked directly to her, and then turned and stopped next to the cash machine. He nodded at her, and then she realized that it was Perry. Mildred lined up behind him and took out her debit card. "Nice no-hairpiece, Harold."

He smiled and tapped on the cash machine. "Your gal Ruby over at Glamour Gals worked this up."

"Seems you have been seeing a lot of her. Do I need to worry about you two?"

Perry shook his head slightly. "Please, it's all professional. I'll have a beard by the first of the week. I've been signing over my social security checks to her. Can you tell me what you saw?"

Mildred started to dig through her purse. "Nothing really, it was just a security guard and a pit boss whispering. I didn't hear anything – it's a gut feeling. They both were scanning around the room and up the stairs."

"Yeah, I heard." Perry took his card out of the machine and put it back in his wallet. "I didn't have anything. It sounds like it's busier in the new addition. Switch in about an hour."

Mildred stepped up past him to the machine. "Make it an hour and a half; then we can reverse patrol rotation."

Perry spoke as he walked away. "By then the show will be in progress and the nightclubs will be cranking."

"Check in before we rotate." They both ambled away in opposite directions through the acre of slot machines.

Mildred Raising the Ante

− 5 −

Long Night

Mildred meandered through the tables on her walk to the main showroom. She appreciated that they had set up the theater similar to the New York and Vegas clubs that the Rat Pack had entertained in for years. The crowd was older, the only demographic familiar with the stars of those long-ago years. The Sinatra impersonator looked like old Blue Eyes, but the singing was an obvious imitation. The Sammy Davis Jr. was excellent. *That guy can not only sing, but dance like the real deal.* She walked around the outer edges of the tables − the uniformed security covered the exits and she was confident they could handle this show. After all, people this age could run, but neither fast nor far.

The main stage was adjacent to the original gaming, so Mildred took a stroll through and then settled at a Queen's Consort slot machine, giving gave her a view of the roulette and Big 6 Wheel of Fortune. These games moved a lot of chips and there were crowds around them with constant noise. There was a palpable energy, completely different from the slot machines. That had been one of her surprises when she had started, how everyone playing slots appeared hypnotized as they bet and punched the buttons and stared at the rolling lights. Even when they won, they often hid that fact as they continued. The constant drone was programmed to keep them in their seats and it worked. For Mildred, they offered a chance to sit for an extended period and it was a good cover. She could make minimum bets and fake easily.

Mildred noticed someone weave and then staggered a couple of rows over. She immediately stood and was walking that direction when the middle-aged man hit the floor. Mildred knelt next to him. "Are you alright?"

He was flushed and gasping for breath. Mildred tapped the headphone. "Need medical at..." she stopped talking for a second to check the location, "end of the slots between main stage and roulette." His choking increased and he couldn't breathe. Mildred elevated his head onto her lap. He couldn't talk, but pointed up to the ceiling. "I don't know what you need. Are you having a heart attack? Are you choking?"

He struggled to raise his hands. A security officer ran toward her and she made a short prayer for the medical crew. Mildred didn't know why, but she put her finger into his mouth, and he bit her, but the panic in his eyes told her she was on to something. The uniformed guard joined her on the floor. "I think he is choking. Help me sit him up." The guard got behind the man and held him while they forced him into an erect position. "Do you know the Heimlich thing?"

There was no further conversation when the officer gripped the man from behind and jerked back and up violently, an unidentifiable glop flew out, and hit Mildred on the forehead. "Damn, it's a churro."

The emergency medical nurse on duty arrived and was able to take over. Mildred slipped away to the restroom to call Perry. "I need to move on — too much attention. I'm going to go out to my car and change shirts and maybe add a hat. Let's trade in ten minutes."

"What happened?"

"Some guy has tried to destroy my love of churros, and I have to wash it off my face and hands. Explain later."

Larry answered, "We watched you saving lives again. Did he bite you?"

"Yeah, I forgot about that. I was too upset about the churro."

"Get over to the clinic. Make sure you don't need rabies shots or something."

Mildred answered, "Rabies, Larry? That's a pretty low regard for our dear customers."

Mildred could hear Perry laugh in the background while Larry spoke, "You know what I mean — that other shot."

"I had a tetanus shot last year in the ER. Now that I think about it, Perry, be sure your shots are up-to-date. Something about this job."

"Yes, G-ma, I'll do that, but I can't chit-chat. I'm working here."

They all disconnected. Mildred went to a gift shop, purchased a casino sweatshirt and a gray beret, then traded her sweater in the adjacent restroom. She was back on the floor in ten minutes and walking through the Mozam-Beat nightclub. The band hadn't started yet, so she moved to the Sahara. The canned music was blaring, customers were drinking and starting to dance. Everything looked to be progressing as usual. She took a spin through the original gaming section.

It wasn't as busy as the new addition. Mildred noticed some action at the rear crap table, so she strolled over to join the crowd. Everyone was watching a thin young man handling the dice. He was on an extraordinary run. Mildred was watching the chips and the dealer. The handling of chips for this action moved quickly. They would rake them in and make a quick payment in stacks. There was little time for inspection; everything was rapid, adding to the tension. If the chips came from customers, it would have to be on a busy table so that there was no time to notice.

Her headphone beeped. "Dammit woman, go get your finger checked."

Mildred rolled her eyes and stuck her tongue out at the camera over the table. She mouthed, *I'm working here.* She looked at her finger. It was scraped and slightly swollen, but there was no evidence of blood.

After another rotation, the audience for the midnight show started to arrive. Many were in costumes from the characters in the *Rocky Horror Picture Show.* She whispered a message, "Perry, new crowd arriving. Do you need me to cover while you put on your Dr. Frank N. Furter's bustier?"

"Nice, Magenta. I only wear that at home."

"With Ruby from the beauty shop?"

"You don't give up. Are you bored or something? It's busy over here."

Mildred responded, "I'm just surprised this movie is well over forty years old, and it still draws a crowd. I'll stay a little longer and follow up later for the switch."

"Okay, gotta go."

"Mildred, this is Larry. Before you sign off, we have someone coming down for the movie. So, you can go back to regular patrol for now."

She scanned the crowd to see if there was a face she knew when suddenly she saw an older man in an electric wheelchair with a blanket over his legs. "Oh, no. Arnie!"

He rolled past her, saying, "That is Dr. Scott. Everett Scott."

"How many times have you seen this movie?"

"I spent the end of the seventies hiding out at the theater. What is your excuse?"

Mildred tapped the earphone. "Well, Larry, at least you got him to take it easy."

"He had it all planned when he arrived. He even brought toast and we had the chair. Now back to work."

Larry disconnected, and Mildred walked toward the upper-level sports betting and high limits card rooms, so she could be back down to end of the Sinatra show. Making a turn to the restrooms, Mildred noticed a line for the women's room, so she joined in, listening and watching.

In the midst of the changing crowd, she swapped out with Perry and the night continued. It was nearly two when the excited crowd departed the movie venue. After decades, that bizarre film still thrilled the masses. The nightclubs were closing at the same time. Mildred and Perry both walked out with the crowds, came back in through the hotel and walked out again. A large group in grotesque costumes went to the buffet and a couple of the snack bars that stayed open for the event.

Mildred passed Perry on his way out for the third time as she turned to come back in. "Going to be a late one, watching the dealers closing their trays."

Perry said, "I didn't see anything. Pretty busy, but it's calming down now. Did you see Arnie?"

"I saw him early, haven't since. Wonder where he got that horrid mustache?"

He chuckled. "I asked. Apparently it came out of Robin's hairbrush."

"Oh, my good grief! Gross."

Perry continued, "You're in charge of him and not doing a very good job."

"I'll go find him. Why don't you go home? Most anything tonight has happened. It's clearing out fast."

"You aren't the boss of me." Perry added, "You pick up that old man and I'll finish. I want to watch the dealer cash-ins."

"I am the boss of you, Mr. Block. Hopefully, you are the one man that will listen to me. Now go," said Mildred.

Perry saluted her and made a turn to the C lot.

Mildred tapped into her cell phone. **G-ma here, where is A A?**

Her phone responded almost immediately, **A at buffet. Handicapped table near the desserts.**

Thanks.

Mildred made a pass through the gaming area. It was finishing up so she walked straight to the buffet and slipped in through the exit. There he was, with a Columbia and two Riff Raffs. They were all animated and having a great time. Mildred sat directly in his line of vision at an empty table near the edge of a closed section. It took a few minutes before he noticed her. He rubbed his nose and threw her a kiss. One of the men handed Arnie a card. She watched him pick up a to-go box and roll toward the exit. Mildred followed him out and, once on the quieting gaming floor, she approached him. "You ready to go, James Bond?"

"Yep. It was a great night, but I'm tired."

She could hear the exhaustion in his voice. "Take that gross mustache off. I'm driving. We'll get your truck tomorrow."

"Cool." Arnie took the chair over to customer service and stepped out of it while she walked outside and sent her text ending the night. **G-ma and bad boy A out.**

Night – we've got it from here.

Arnie walked to catch up as she exited the main entrance and handed her the to-go box. "A little something for my Bunny."

Mildred waited until she was in the car and opened the gift. "A cannoli! How did you know?" *Damn him; he knows how to work me.* "You make it darn difficult not to love you." She hummed all the way home.

It was a short ride, but he was asleep when they arrived. Mildred went into the house, turned on the lights and put the cannoli next to the computer. Once back at the car, it was difficult to wake him. "Okay, Romeo time for bed. Lean on me, and...."

Arnie sat up. Even though he was groggy, he walked in on his own, going straight to the recliner. He turned on the television and Mildred took the remote from him. "Sorry, you have already done too much tonight. It is bedtime. I'll help you upstairs."

"No need. I'm fine." Arnie got up and went to the stairs. "I'll see you in a few." He wiggled his eyebrows and winked.

Mildred waved off his suggestive wink and went to the computer to prepare her report. Feeling much more interest in cannoli and sleep, she rushed through. She crept up the stairs and silently prepared for bed. Without a sound, she slid into bed and heard his machine whirring. He was sound asleep. The two claps to shut off the light didn't disturb him. Mildred scooted closer and kissed his shoulder goodnight.

He stirred and pulled her into his arms and through the sleep mask she heard, "Pwease stay, I truwy lub you."

Daddy's Boy

Rocky was a tough kid, but you couldn't tell it by looking at him. He was slim and small, with an innocent demeanor. His dad was in prison for murdering his mother, and some other charges that were never explained. The foster home was hell and Rocky had walked out shortly after arrival. So he raised himself on the streets of Baltimore, determined to be more than a statistic. He dreamed of a better life and was smart enough to know that education was the only way out.

His dad's associates gave him small jobs in the company. The work helped him earn just enough to survive as he fought to stay in school. It was mostly errands and questionable deliveries for the Boss. Rocky had learned almost from birth to keep his mouth shut and they trusted him. The wise guys would tease him about being an egghead lawyer, which pleased the old man, who seemed to like the dedication. They all encouraged him, in an offhand manner, to continue with his education. His slight build and youthful appearance was a plus, so the jobs became more complex, and the money improved. Rocky could walk right through a crime scene and the cops would simply send him home. Every day he worked toward his dream, saving and studying. In June he went from punk to high school graduate. No one attended the ceremony.

Well aware that he was the old man's favorite, he was smart enough to play straight and get the work done. As a graduation gift, the Boss promised Rocky a life-long job with the company, but the kid wanted much more.

Rocky first saw Celeste at an evening computer class. He was bowled over, gobsmacked, blindsided by her dark sparkling eyes and her sassy intelligence. His first thought was to grow old with her, confident she was the Forever One. He wanted desperately to deserve her. He went back to his room at the shelter that first night and filled out an application for the university.

He was surprised at how she liked his air of danger and rough exterior. With her, he wasn't homeless. He could be somebody and have a life that would change the world. She called him James. No one ever called him by his given name. He called her Sweet Cookie because there is nothing better.

They were both accepted to the university and he vowed to leave the past for the promise of a shared future. He told the Boss about being accepted to college and a future engagement.

The old man was clear: Rocky always had a job with him. He again gave Rocky a push to go into law and he could pay back the company by serving them. James spoke honestly, telling the Boss about Cookie and their plans for a life of service. The *conversation didn't end as he expected; the old man was angry at his ingratitude and left no room for discussion. This was when James realized there was no leaving the Boss. He knew too much and owed everything.*

Mildred Raising the Ante

– 6 –

Longer Day

"Mildred, phone."

Mildred stirred. It took a moment for her to register where she was and to sit up. She called out, "Arnie, where is my phone?"

"It's down here. I plugged it in next to your laptop."

Mildred shook her head and vowed to herself to do better about charging the phone nearby as she stumbled down the stairs. "I'm here. Who is it?"

Arnie was standing at the sink, filling the coffee maker. "Bud needs to talk to you about last night." He spoke into the phone, "Here she is, lovely as usual."

"Hello. What's up, boss man?" Her voice was gravelly and it was obvious she had just woken up.

"Mildred, we had several thousand dollars of the chips turned in. We are going to go through some video, and I hoped that you and Perry could join us. The more eyes, the fewer things we'll miss. We were going to start at one, but I'll make it closer to two if you can come in."

"Have you talked to Perry yet? We both pulled a long night." Mildred's head cleared, and she recognized the importance. "I'll pull myself together and plan on two. Let me know if he can make it."

Arnie interrupted, "I can ride along and pick up my truck."

"Arnie said he could...."

Bud answered, "I heard him. The more of us, the better. I'll call Perry and Robin and get back to you with details. Thanks."

Mildred replaced the phone on the charger. "I'm going to go lie down again. Hopefully, I can get another hour. Saturdays are the toughest night. It looks like the counterfeiter has stepped up the action."

"I'll hold off making breakfast until one. How does that sound?"

"We can pick something up. Or better yet, let's go over to the buffet at one. The Casino has that brunch thing until two. I could use the treat and there would be no dirty dishes."

"Deal. Let's both go lie down." Arnie put the coffee on a timer and they went upstairs together.

Mildred's body ached for sleep. When she came out of the bathroom, Arnie was already in bed and grinning. The CPAP sleep machine was pushed aside. His eyes were closed, but she could tell he was faking. Mildred slipped into bed and he scooted next to her. It was clear he wasn't interested in the nap Mildred needed. "You're naked! I can't, Arnie, not while you have stitches. I insist on an okay from your doctor – I will not bury another man."

He stuck his lip out in a pouting expression. "I wasn't asking, but I desperately need to feel your skin against mine and to hear your breath while you sleep."

Mildred shook her head and rolled her eyes. "Okey-dokey."

"Really?" he asked

"Really." Mildred removed her nightgown and kicked it to the floor. They drank in the warmth of each other's body and the comfort of unexpected love.

It wasn't easy leaving the warmth, but after an hour of spooning, they had to get ready to go. With no consideration of being seen together, they laughed when Mildred came from the bathroom. She wore extra make-up, sunglasses, jeans, a jacket and one of her new hats. Arnie stood looking at her, wearing a double extra-large Ohio State sweatshirt and he had combed his hair straight forward. On the way out the front door, he grabbed one of his dad's baseball caps from the front closet.

It was nearly one-fifteen when they walked into the buffet. Arnie stopped Mildred from going to her usual surveillance table and led her to a small two-seater in the center of the room. "Hiding in plain sight?" she asked.

"You betcha. Now go fill your plate; I'll hold the table." Arnie settled in the seat facing the rows of servers.

She was back with a plate of quiche and hash-brown potatoes. Arnie was up and off before she was completely in the chair. While she had been going through the line, he had ordered two coffees and they were delivered before she took a bite. Mildred relished the first sip. *Damn, this is delicious.* She leaned back into the chair and cherished the bitter bite of the steamy brew.

Arnie returned as she started to eat. His first plate was heaped with fruit, the second had eggs and what looked like prime rib. On a third plate was a cinnamon roll about the size of his face.

"Look Bunny; I found your sister." After he sat down, he ran his finger through the frosting. "She is sweeter, but not nearly as toasty."

Mildred stared at him, and she could feel the red creeping up her neck and covering her face. "Stop it, Arnold. My half-sister is older and in a nursing home. An eighty-year-old cinnamon roll would be a bit crusty."

He looked satisfied and continued. "By the way, Chef Mike busted me."

Mildred was concerned. "Oh no. We got to know each other from the robbery last year. What did he say?"

"Don't worry about Mike. He said that he has more respect for me now, seeing I have such good taste in women." Arnie started eating quickly. "We have a meeting in thirty minutes. Eat up and stop gossiping."

As they finished Mildred texted in. **G-Ma and AA here.**

It was a few minutes before the answer came through. **Meet old security room. All here.** They finished their plates and went to the almost invisible door behind the gaming area. Arnie held the door for Mildred to enter the hall. She held the door for him into the private room. Bud was the first to chuckle, "Oh, Arnie, old man, you need to work on your disguises. Where did you get that shirt?"

"Don't you all shop in the lost and found?" The room filled with laughter. He started to greet everyone.

Robin interrupted. "We have to get to work. I'm on tonight, and my nap is calling. Remember it's Saturday, goofballs."

Bud went directly to the computer and the large screen lit up. "Robin is right. Arnie, thank you for coming. Maybe the more of us watching, the more it will help. I have brought Detective Hampton up to date. He is out of town until Wednesday."

The date and time lit up showing the new gaming area. The door to the office opened and Detective Elton Block from the police station entered.

"Sorry to be late. I knew Hampton was out of town, and since I was off shift, thought I'd fill in." He nodded to his dad, Perry, and then moved over to the back of the room and stood against the wall.

Bud continued. "Glad you're here. I'll bring you up to date after the meeting. We have mostly established employees in the original gaming area. Accounting thinks that the problem is in the new section. They aren't absolutely sure, but we are considering coding the racks. That would help identify in what section the counterfeits are being passed."

Mildred was quiet for a second, and then asked, "Who else knows about this problem? Anyone, that is, outside of accounting and security? I'm worried about employee involvement."

Bud stopped the video feed. "I've had the new casino attorney check in. He had the accounting supervisor's report. It's supposed to be just her and the long-term employee who discovered the counterfeits. As for security, just us."

Mildred continued, "Is this attorney going to nose in on everything we do?"

Bud shrugged his shoulders, but it was obvious he wasn't happy about it. "I'm hoping accounting kept this quiet and didn't spread the problem."

Larry had been quiet, tapping into his tablet, "Good point. Looks like the accounting supervisor isn't on over the weekend. I've got her home number. I'll contact her after the meeting and try to see who else we need to talk to."

"Hope it hasn't spread too far in that department," said Robin. "Do you have a copy of the incident report? The employee's name should be referenced on it."

Bud slid a file folder crossed the table. "It's in there."

"I'll follow up today," said Robin.

They all sat quietly watching the streaming video. The room felt tense as everyone watched for any suspicious move. After nearly an hour, Mildred spoke.

"I am a little suspicious about that red-headed security officer. I didn't see anything, but he seems close to the pit boss. See the little guy on the left? I watched them whispering in the pit."

Perry spoke up. "Mildred flagged me about them, but I haven't seen anything obvious. I kept half an eye on them, but didn't catch anything. The pit boss continued with the fills and transfers. He is in a position to be prime for a switch. I didn't notice any funny business behind the counter."

Bud made a quick call to the officer on duty. Mildred could only hear a mumbling. "Damn you, Arnie, if you didn't look like a broken-down sports fanatic from Ohio, I'd send you down."

"Boss, you know I have a locker behind the good detective over there. What do you want?" Arnie stood and walked to the locker, waving Detective Block to his chair.

"I want you to go to the central station and do an inspection. Look for anything suspicious," said Bud.

Detective Block added, "Also anything that could be a hidey hole."

"Hidey hole? Is that an official police term?" asked Arnie as he pulled out a pressed uniform shirt. He changed shirts and put his jersey and hat in the locker, running his fingers through his hair.

Mildred blushed as several seemed to notice an obvious surveillance photo taped to the inside of the door. She kept quiet, but couldn't help but wonder if she had been sleeping with a stalker.

Block continued. "Keep your mind open and pay attention to every detail."

Arnie clipped on his badge. "Is the suspected boss working now?"

"No, he comes on this evening," answered Larry.

Arnie stopped at the door. "How new is he? I don't remember him, and I pretty well know all the night crews."

"This guy was a transfer from one of the closed Trump casinos." Robin was flipping through the paperwork in the folder. "He worked a few months on a day shift before he was vetted to be a pit boss.

Here it is, his name is Paul Clanton. There's a photo on the copy of his driver's license."

"Got it. I'm heading down," said Arnie.

"Stop. Do you have an earphone?" Mildred opened her bag. "Take mine. We can watch you on surveillance. That way we can all go together."

He put on Mildred's earphone and tapped it on. "Testing and I'm out of here. Let me know if you geniuses come up with anything else."

Larry brought up one of the original surveillance screens that was left in the office and started clicking cameras to find the best vantage. "There's our mole. He just came out to the floor."

The detective pulled up closer to the screen. "Can he hear all of us or just you?"

Bud turned on the speaker system and the constant noise of the casino filled the room. "Larry, does this screen cover the new section?"

Larry was busily tapping at the computer keyboard. "I'm not sure... I need to access. Yes, I've got it."

Mildred stood and patted Larry on the back. "You are filling in for Belinda. Great. It is a shame you aren't as cute."

Larry smiled. "I think I miss her most of all. We need a directive that none of the security management team can have children. Can't wait for those twins to go to college. No one can replace her." He continued to scan from camera to camera, finally zeroing in on the station as Arnie walked up. "I think he just gave us the finger, but he is waving over the pit boss."

Everyone hushed and listened as Arnie spoke. "I'm the Director of Security. We are doing a spot check."

The team couldn't hear exactly what was said due to the background noise. The group watched as the pit boss unlocked the three-quarter door and walked over to the blackjack area.

Bud spoke. "Keep watching this guy, looks like he is doing a set up for a new dealer."

The pit boss dropped off a cash box and unlocked the dealer drawers.

"There's an opportunity for a switch, but only if they are first-rate magicians," mumbled Perry. The entire room nodded in agreement.

The room stayed silent as they watched Arnie inspect the space. He finally spoke. "Excuse me, Boss, can you come over when you have a second?"

They didn't hear the response, but the pit boss approached. "Sure, what's up?"

"I'm sorry, I missed your name." Arnie read the name tag. "Tom, we're going through some of the support areas to make things more efficient. I figured you were the best person to speak with about potential changes. What can we do to make the pit more efficient for you?"

Tom answered, "I hadn't thought about it." He stepped back and rubbed his chin. "We do have some wasted spaces and the alarm button is problematic."

"How so?" Arnie reached over and picked up a pen and a drink coaster. He looked at Tom. "What do you suggest about changes? Maybe we should start with what works."

Tom pulled out a tablet and started sketching his suggestions. "Even though there is a lock on the drawers, I'd like them to be further away from the counter."

"I see, so that no one can reach over," said Arnie.

"Yes, exactly. I'd also like the door to be over here. Right now it blocks some of our view of the floor if we are sitting."

Detective Block whispered, "I assume that the casino layout was done by a committee of officers and an architect, without involving the workers." Bud nodded in agreement with a visible grimace.

A quarter of an hour later, Arnie came back to the meeting. He had a sketch and a list of suggestions on remodeling the space. "I think we need to meet with all of the pit bosses on both floors and all shifts. These are some good suggestions."

"At the same time, you can feel out each of them and if you think they could be involved," said Perry.

It was clear that Arnie was jazzed over the investigation. "I'll go back on each of the shift changes and do the same thing. I'm known so they shouldn't be suspicious."

"Unless they are guilty." Mildred went on, "In addition, Officer Arneson, you are on sick leave. You still have stitches, so settle down."

"Each of these visits takes a half hour if they are busy, and I'm not lifting anything besides a piece of paper." Arnie reached over and patted her shoulder. "This is who I am and consistency is important. I'd like to quote a well-known operative, 'You aren't the boss of me.'"

Mildred grimaced at how her own words kept coming back on her. "I am your boss, Mr. Arneson, so that statement is false. Time to listen up."

Bud stepped in. "It would be appreciated, Arnie. With you and Belinda both out, it would be helpful. Larry and I would have to pull the duty and it is tough with the new employees."

"Besides, Ms. Petrie, I only have six stitches." He looked around the room. "She thinks I had open heart surgery. They come out tomorrow afternoon."

Mildred folded her arms across her chest. "Tomorrow is Sunday. The appointment is for Monday. You act like I have a vote. Do what you are going to do."

Robin came back into the room. "I was able to find our bookkeeper who discovered the bad chips. I learned that accounting planned to meet on this Monday. I've instructed her to stay quiet until further notice, and to keep her eyes open. Right now, she has only spoken to one other in the department and the supervisor."

Larry stood up, "I've got the supervisor's contact information. Hold on, I'll go call right now." He stopped at the door and looked back. "Do you know when and where the meeting is going to be? I could be there if I miss her."

Bud said, "Go ahead and I'll call. If we have an issue, most any one of us can attend the meeting. It will be good to update them."

"Might be the time to have a representative at their meeting anyway if you guys don't need us anymore. I have to work the shift tonight, and I need to get home," said Mildred. Perry and Robin agreed, and they all stood to leave.

Arnie answered, "I need to pick up my truck, go ahead without me. I'll do the shift changes at five, five-thirty and six, and then I'll be home."

They all broke to different directions.

Rocky

When he left the old man's office, he called Cookie, and she didn't answer. With a desperate feeling of foreboding, Rocky raced to her. Their plans seemed to dissipate with each tear on his face. He knew there was no escape from the crimes of his father and the men around him. When he arrived, he saw her bloody body tossed into the yard. He was stunned to learn her parents also had been hunted down and executed. Rocky laid down in the pool of her blood and held his Sweet Cookie. The need was desperate to hold her escaping soul. He clung to her cooling, lifeless body, trying to release his spirit to cross over with hers. His grief blocked out the sound of the police vehicles screeching, the yelling and confusion as help arrived too late. Where were they today, before this horror happened? Where had they been when he was still a kid? He heard nothing and demonstrated no discernible movement, wrapped in his indescribable grief.

He jerked back into his body in the emergency room, angry with the rude interference into his privacy. They cut off his bloody clothing, and he heard the nurse's bewilderment as they found no injuries. They were oblivious to the mortal wound he had been dealt. Rocky was numb as they helped with a backless hospital gown, a prescription and turned him over to the police for questioning.

Several detectives interrogated him. They all blended into one cheap suit with a cacophony of voices. Confused by time and the waste of energy, it was seventy hours later before a Captain Petrie drove him back to the shelter. The cops seemed sympathetic, but Rocky knew he was a suspect. He had never trusted them, no matter how many condolences and sandwiches they handed out. He had worked close enough with the company to know they couldn't be trusted. In reality, Rocky just wanted to lie down in the numbness and wait for the sweetness of death. He took two of the pills, then four more, and surrendered.

The dreams were erratic, offering no answers, and he awoke confused in complete silence. There was never silence in the shelter. He didn't realize until that moment how much comfort the background noise had offered. Rocky looked around a large room he hadn't seen before. Convinced it was all a nightmare, he took another pill. Cookie was with him and he could feel the comforting warmth of rain. They held hands and ran with laughter and peace. She stopped and looked deep into his eyes, and he watched her lips move.

"You are my one and only love; I will never need another." Her urgent eyes glistened as she said, "You will live for us both from now on. I'm confident you will do what is right."

He reached for her as she faded away. He reawakened to the stillness.

Rocky felt a throbbing in his head and knew he must face the life he was struggling with. There was a deep hunger, but the bathroom was first. He saw a diffused light creeping through the drapes and spied his meager belongings stacked near a closed door. He staggered into the bathroom, dumped the rest of the pills, and watched them swirl away with the flush. Rocky removed the hospital gown and took a long hot shower. He had left the bathroom, a thick towel wrapped around him, when he noticed the blood on a bag of rags. That was Cookie's blood and the ache returned. At that moment, he became aware of the Boss. The old man sat in a chair by the window. They studied each other and the kid waited to see the next move. Rocky had been around the old man enough to know that everything was a chess game.

The Boss spoke calmly in reassuring tones, and Rocky gazed at the lying lips. This was no accident; there were no unknown intruders and it was not a coincidence. He heard the old man's promise to find the truth and invited Rocky to stay here, in his home as long as necessary. The sound of the old man's voice grated, as Rocky imagined him practicing this line of crap in the mirror, looking into the eyes of the real murderer. Rocky's hard-scrabble life had honed his intelligence. He knew how to survive. He was not the broken boy the old man thought he saw. Rocky was not fooled by the invitation. Fully aware that he was no guest, but a captive, he listened with quiet tears to the bullshit about other girls and how he would love again. Rocky played the part as the drone of fake concern continued and the vow to help fell on the floor at his feet.

The tears convinced the old man that Rocky believed him. The old bastard had decades of working his men and this was just a kid. The Boss was certain it would work the way he wanted; everything always did. The confidence was obvious on his face and Rocky knew who he was up against. The Boss seemed to have forgotten that this was Frank and Miriam's kid.

Rocky knew there was only one person he could trust and that lying ass had taken her away. He decided at that moment he would live in this room and the company could pay for college. A ghost of a smile crossed Rocky's lips as he watched the two-faced liar speak. The old man rose, pulled the drapes and Rocky looked through the large windows onto an expanse of gree. He knew justice moved slowly. The plan wouldn't be for revenge; the losses were too great. He alone would see that the Boss and all of the company paid; he silently vowed to his mother and Cookie that he wouldn't disappoint them.

– 7 –

Sunday

G-Ma on the floor.

Welcome back. Call me.

Mildred stopped just outside the main door. "Hello, who is this?"

"This is Bud."

"Don't you have a home?" asked Mildred.

"This is my home, but it should get better soon."

She could hear Bud chuckle as she answered, "Okay, what's up?"

"Wanted to let you know, Perry is coming in later, so hopefully you can leave early."

"Great! So I'll do a general patrol and some gaming time. Do you need me to hit the shows?"

"I think we have them covered. Does it sound like a plan? Robin is coming in to relieve me any minute now. She will be your contact. We have a mixed crew and a couple of new floor guys. Just a heads up."

"Don't worry boss; this will all even out soon. I'm heading in."

Mildred stowed the phone and pushed the walker of her redheaded Delilah disguise through the door, thanks to the help of the valet on the circle drive. She activated her earpiece, turning toward the hotel. There was an Indie Author's conference on and Mildred, having been so focused on the gaming tables, hadn't paid much attention to hotel events. On her walk through, she noticed that they had presentations, writing assignments and book sales. The lobby was quiet and the chairs by the fireplace were full of guests reading books. Mildred didn't recognize any of them, but then realized Stephen King would probably be the only author she could recognize from a book jacket. Not the usual conference. Mildred walked to the hotel lounge. It was full and Mildred couldn't find a seat, but she noticed the room was subdued with quiet conversations and only one boisterous table. A silver-haired woman was wearing a Tee-shirt that said *Write Drunk, Edit Sober – E. Hemingway.*

Mildred walked back to the casino through the gift shops and past the restaurants. She couldn't help but notice the smaller cafés were full, but the more elegant places had empty tables. Halfway through the gift shops, Mildred turned around and went back to the conference booths. It took only a few minutes for Mildred to discover that there were no romances that spoke to her, but there was a women's fiction and a thriller for Arnie. The authors autographed them and she stowed them in the small basket on the front of the walker. Mildred straightened her bright red wig and continued back to the patrol.

It developed into a usual Sunday night, busy initially, then clearing earlier than the other weekend nights. Mildred spent some time in the gaming area, but she was sure it wouldn't be a visible catch. Whoever was passing the chips wasn't going to be a fool. She kept moving, steady and slow. She finally settled into the Hungry Hippo slot machine with a generous view of the original gaming area and into one of the sports venues.

Como in-house.

OK

Just in time. G-ma is going to Pizza Leone.

FYI G-ma, I'm Willy Cane.

My fav.

Mildred rolled over to one of the new cafés and had a quick meal. As she was about to leave, Perry showed up in his little old balding man disguise. "Hey doll, you come here much?"

"You make a creepy old man, Willy," Mildred answered as she was gathering herself to pick up her patrol.

"Hard to miss you with that red hair. I was strolling through when I saw you. How's the food?"

Mildred smiled, "I hadn't come here before, but I'll be back. They have a pizza on injera bread and it is something like I've never had before."

Perry nodded. "I'll give it a try, maybe this week. Back to work. Have you had any action tonight?"

"No, I did a walk through at the conference center. Author conference, they are a quieter bunch. Which side are you working now? I'll go the other way."

"We don't have to worry about events, mostly older high-end shows."

"DJ Spin Doctor on tonight?" asked Mildred. "I'm sure it is on the schedule."

Perry pulled out his phone and searched through the apps. "You are right, they are at the old showroom. Shoot, we are both too old fogy chic for that."

"You're darn-tootin'. Neither of us has any outfits that don't make us look like geezers. If necessary, I have other clothes in the car. I'll change out or dump the walker and wig," said Mildred. "I know we have to pay close attention to party drugs with the kids."

"I noticed some stuff sounds harmless, and then it isn't." Perry put his phone back in his fanny pack. "I was watching the news. There are some new ones and some old favorites are more intense than back in our day."

Mildred stood to leave. "All the previous rules are off. Sometimes I cuss at science. I'm heading to the upper rooms. If the way is clear, I'll drop off the walker in the office. Catch up later." She went directly to the elevator. When she turned back, Perry was standing at the order window for the Pizza Leone Palace.

As she made her way past the high roller card rooms and horse betting, she stepped aside to call the office. She tapped the earphone. "Anyone there?"

"This is Robin. What's up?"

"I'd like to drop off the walker in the old office. I'm on the second floor."

Robin didn't hesitate. "I'll meet you at the door behind baccarat. I'll tap when I'm there and pick it up. Be there in a minute." It was less than a minute when the door opened and Mildred peeked in. "All clear, no one can see you."

"Great." Mildred stepped in, passed off the walker and dumped the wig. After a quick fluff of her hair, she reached in her shirt and handed Robin the two size EE water balloons she had used to fill out the shirt. "Little quick change. Thanks."

As the door closed, Mildred could hear the wheels creaking and Robin snickering as she walked away. Mildred noticed her reflection on the window trim. She went immediately to try and convince her hair to cooperate. By ten-thirty, she was in the DJ show skirting the outer edges, always watching. On a token walkthrough, Mildred noticed Melody, the narcotics agent she had worked with before.

Mildred slipped up behind the young undercover officer. "New hairstyle, different color. I like it."

Melody spun around initially on guard, but when she saw Mildred, she squeezed her hand before she turned away facing the mosh pit of sweaty dancers. "Always good to see you, old gal."

"Do you need me? Anything breaking?"

"No, we have three of us here, so I think we're good. No obvious problems." Then Melody started pumping her fist in the air in time with something like music.

"Okay, I'm outta here. Love you." Mildred couldn't help it as her body started to sway with the pounding rhythm as she inched to the exit.

Once outside, she heard her earpiece click with Perry's voice. "Heading to original section patrol. Time to trade."

"On the move."

Mildred was near the transition passage and walked around the north side to enter. She slowly made her way to the gaming area. While watching roulette and the transfer of chips she heard a familiar voice. After a quick scan of the main room, she noticed Arnie talking to the pit boss. Only momentarily distracted she saw him being allowed into the work area. She assumed he was using the same pretense and this time was carrying a tablet. Turning away, Mildred continued to the crap tables.

It was the usual Sunday crowd, but nothing suspicious. She walked past the Keno lounge and the blank stares as the players made their bets on the individual play cards. Since there was no major exchange of chips and everyone seemed focused on the game board and the flashing numbers, Mildred carried on. A seat was available off to the side of the blackjack tables. Mildred settled in. She had a good view, and Mildred always enjoyed the energy of players at this game. A new dealer came in, and as Mildred witnessed the smooth opening of a new table, she felt a subtle tap on her left hand. She calmly looked, and Arnie was standing slightly behind her.

"When are you signing out?" he asked.

"The way it is going tonight, probably around one."

"Okay, I'll wait, heading to other side." Arnie walked away toward the original casino.

Mildred shook her head. *He is the worst taking sick time person I've ever seen.* She was about to walk away when she noticed the pit boss bring over a new rack of chips that had a small red mark on the holder. *That's new.* She walked to the isolated corner away from the action, where she could still see and tapped her earpiece. "Como, watch the chip racks. Just saw one marked in red. Let me know if you see any others."

"I'm at the Bill Banner Band in the showroom. I'll get back over to the games and let you know." She could hear the music start to dim as he moved. "Did you know Arnie was here?"

"I thought I saw him downstairs, but I didn't get a clear shot. I think he is using the premise from yesterday to check out the pit bosses and search the setups. Security. Gotta go." He signed off, and Mildred watched the pit boss as he walked behind the tables, checking in with each dealer. She couldn't hear any conversation.

Near the end of the night, she had seen the red dot on several racks, and when she rotated with Perry, there was a discreet green mark in the original gaming area. Mildred was sure that this was Arnie's doing, and had to admit it was a simple way to hopefully narrow the search by half.

She activated the earphone. "Perry, do you need me any further?"

"It's busy, but well behaved. No big shows and those writers are a weird group that turned in early, so I've been watching for little colored dots."

Mildred answered, "Such a simple way to help determine if this is a single section. Hopefully, it narrows down the investigation. If it is alright with you, I'm heading out."

Before he could answer, another voice came into the conversation. "You two done chatting? If so, I'll be right down. Meet you outside at the employee entrance."

"Good night, all. I'm going to finish the night at the floor games." Perry disconnected.

Mildred walked out of the employee door and Arnie's truck was waiting for her. "How about my car?"

They pulled away heading toward the retirement condos a few blocks away. Arnie said, "We will come back once I help you get some more clothes and you check the mail. I heard you mumbling in the bathroom."

"Thanks. Good to know that I talk to myself out loud and you were snooping on a private conversation," said Mildred.

He simply shrugged as they pulled into the parking space in front of her condominium.

The security light came on as they exited the pickup truck. Arnie put his arm around her. "Glad to see you are using the security system that the police installed for you last year. Now let's see if you locked the door."

Mildred opened the door and Arnie entered first, turning on lights while she punched in the code to close down the security system. He moved straight to the kitchen. Mildred went to pack extra clothes, gathering her Bambi Hunter, burned-out biker disguise. She could hear Arnie open the refrigerator. "Are you hungry?" she called.

"No, just checking things out. Do you want me to pack up the creamer and turnovers for the Tuesday meeting?"

"We will be meeting here; I have most of what we need. Could you please go to the laundry room and get the small bag of dry cat food and two cans of the wet?"

Mildred could hear him moving around. "We should take all of the bags."

Immediately Mildred knew that they had an issue. "No, Arn, I'm coming back here after your doctor's appointment." She thought about saying more but decided it best to keep it direct.

He was silent for a while but finally spoke. "You are wrong, Mildred Petrie. I'm not letting you go so easily."

"I'm your caregiver, not a hostage. You know I'm not ready."

"We'll talk this out later." Mildred heard the front door open and close. She picked up her sack of clothes and rushed to the door, just as he walked back in. "Bunny, what's the rush? I wouldn't leave you, not like you plan on doing to me."

She dropped her things and took him into her arms. Mildred kissed him passionately. "I like my home. It is mine and it's all I have left."

"Time to admit you have a new life." Arnie kissed both of her eyes and her lips. "I will never leave you." Contrary to her previously voiced plans, he moved her back to the bedroom. It was after three when they were ready to go back to Arnie's house. Mildred reset the light timer and the alarm. They started to leave when Mildred stumbled over the welcome mat. She caught herself and kicked the rug to the side.

Arnie was following her when he spoke. "Did you see this?"

Mildred stopped and turned. "See what?" He handed her a slightly soiled envelope. There was no writing, and it was sealed. "Do you think it is an invitation or secret admirer?"

"Only one way to find out." He unlocked the truck, and she held the envelope as she entered the passenger side, unsure of what to do next. Within a few minutes, he stopped next to her car, parked alone under the light in lot D. Mildred still held the envelope. "What's wrong?"

"I don't know. Is it alright if we look at it when we get to your place?"

"Sure, it's yours and up to you." He leaned over and kissed her cheek. "Leave your stuff here, and I'll follow you."

Mildred drove to Arnie's house; she convinced herself that her hesitation had to do with lighting. She was putting too much thought into a simple blank envelope. They walked in, with Arnie carrying her bag of clothes and the cat food. Popcorn met them at the door and wound her way through Mildred's legs with Louie passing judgment.

Arnie put the bags down and gathered up the kitten. "Bedtime, little fella. After that unplanned romp with your owner; I need my post-sex nap." Arnie went straight to the stairs and looked back at Mildred. "I don't know about you two, but we will meet you upstairs. Be sure to lock the door."

Mildred saw he had placed the envelope on the table between the recliner chairs. She turned down the lights, and double checked the locks. "We are on our way." Mildred put the juice in the refrigerator and picked up the giant white cat. By the time they were upstairs, Arnie was in bed with his sleep mask in place. "Guess there will be no goodnight kisses for either of us, Popcorn."

Rocky

The Boss acted like taking him in after the murder was a kindness for one of his soldier's kids. Rocky never had a choice and the click of the door that day told him the old man had him trapped. Initially, he just endured, but this street kid knew more about survival than any expert. Never one to talk much, Rocky was almost mute as he gained a cautious trust from the Boss and his soldiers. He went through the actions of grief and continued with college. There was no need to hustle the streets and he could focus on education, getting everything he could while that bastard paid for his demise. Rocky was accompanied everywhere he went. Smart enough to use a semblance of loyalty, he covered his seething hate with a plan. Mouth shut and ears open, he completed four years of college in three, revealing to no one that he was an unwilling houseguest. The old man pushed Rocky into law school with the repeated promise of a career with the organization. Rocky could see how that was the perfect path to make his vengeance possible, total, and paid for by his target.

As the days, weeks and years passed, Rocky knew the Boss better than anyone else. He stayed consistent and quiet while the old man thought he had put one over on Rocky as love and respect grew. Rocky trusted no one, especially the old man, as he gathered numbers, locations and names. As months clicked past, the violent and powerful old man became used to the kid and talked freely in front of him.

Rocky was careful that no one ever saw anything but Frank's stoic, heartbroken kid they had known since birth. The old man and Rocky's guards were unaware he majored in secrets. All of the information was coded and hidden in plain sight with his schoolwork. He knew there was enough to bring down the organization, but Rocky wouldn't settle for less than total annihilation of everything the old man held dear. The Boss needed to be left alone, humiliated and hopeless as he watched his life and power crumble. Rocky had been alone since he was thirteen when they had locked away his useless father for killing his mom. He had the drive to be more than his circumstances and rejected the blind allegiance he saw in his father.

Finally, it was the day. Rocky was ready for law school and packed his meager belongings and all of his precious books. Suddenly, the yard filled with black and whites and flashing lights. Damn cops could ruin everything, the timing sucked. Certain everyone in the house was secure in the hidden bunker; Rocky stood alone.

Accepting the circumstances, his mind reeled with scenarios as Rocky waved a floral pillowcase out of the window. He heard the weapons clicking, sure he wasn't ready to take a bullet for that bastard.

He prayed for the time to teach the Boss that Karma is spelled J-A-M-E-S.

"If you don't surrender, your next conversation is gonna be with the dead." The negotiator had an odd way of encouraging cooperation.

Rocky's wasn't scared, he was terrified, but not of the cops. He knew too much, but he felt he didn't have that last bit of information to turn on the old man. No longer running errands, Rocky was too well-known by the police since the day they had pulled him off of Cookie's dead body. He crept to the window and peeked. All he could see were police cars and guns, all aimed at the house. He couldn't imagine why they were out there now. They knew plenty about the Boss, but they left him alone. He had too much power in unknown places.

He laid spread-eagle on the floor. Rocky's heart pounded as he listened to the SWAT team move from room to room. He heard the varied proclamations' of "clear." Escape options tumbled through his mind, and survival trumped the risk. He didn't want a bullet from some nervous rookie. He had too much invested. Rocky realized he wanted to live for the first time since Cookie's death.

– 8 –

Finally, a Monday

Mildred slept late, even for a night worker. When she awoke, Arnie was already up and gone. Mondays were the usual day off. Mildred was lazily enjoying the warmth and sunlight streaming through the window when she heard Arnie come up the stairs.

"Lazy Bones, I have an hour to get to the doctor's office." He entered the room with a travel mug of coffee and a piece of wheat toast, smeared with a large amount of peanut butter.

Mildred grabbed the coffee and rolled out of bed. "How far away is this appointment?"

"Ten minutes, tops."

"Good. Time for a quick shower. I'll be ready soon." She turned back, kissed him, took the toast, and then disappeared into the bathroom. A half hour later, she worked her way down the stairs. Arnie's face lit up when she came into the room. His expression made Mildred feel loved and beautiful. "Ready to roll, old man?"

They arrived a few minutes early. He teased her with tickles, which kept Mildred continually embarrassed and started to make her angry.

"*Arneson, Arnold Arneson,*" came over the speaker system. A nurse opened a door and looked for him.

Arnie stood and took Mildred's hand. "Please, come with me."

"No. Even though you aren't acting like it, you're an adult."

"I am not. Please." She could resist his pout, but the embarrassment motivated her to leave the waiting room. She walked in with him. Mildred found a chair near the back of the examining room and they waited for the doctor.

Arnie threatened to pull out his own stitches seconds before the doctor entered. "Mr. Arneson, how are you doing?"

"I'm doing fine. I feel great."

Mildred sat holding a *People* magazine, trying to disappear, but also listening to their conversation.

"Have you been following the diet?" the doctor asked.

Note to self, find out about the proper diet for gallbladder. She focused on the magazine as they removed the stitches from the small incision. Mildred heard that Arnie had healed well and could return to normal activity, although the doctor suggested another week off of work.

That was when she heard Arnie ask, "Doc, what about sex? My wife doesn't want to risk anything, and, well, you know?" Mildred could feel the embarrassment return as it crept up her neck and take control of her entire being. She raised the magazine to cover her face completely.

The doctor looked directly at Mildred. "You're fine. Just don't get too wild. You could sprain something."

Mildred put down the magazine and looked sternly at the two men. "You two think you're funny, but you are not." Her announcement made them think they were even funnier. She left the exam room followed by laughter and returned to the waiting area.

Mildred found a seat. She scanned the room and noticed most everyone seemed to be her age, if not older. There were canes, walkers and hunched backs. With a realization that her job, genetics and good luck kept her mobile, she sent gratitude to the universe.

Arnie joined her a few minutes later. "I scheduled a regular physical and the doctor was thoroughly impressed that we were, you know..." He made air quotes. "Active."

Mildred shook her head as the flush returned to her face. "This trying to embarrass me in public must stop. It isn't funny. It is degrading and I won't tolerate it. Why do you work so hard to embarrass me?"

Arnie put his head down. "It isn't work, but you are so beautiful when your face glows." She remained silent, but obviously even angrier with his excuse. He continued. "To tell the truth, I think I was bragging. I have this beautiful woman with me and I was showing off. I promise you, that from this exact moment..." He looked at his watch. "I will never do that again. Never." He took her hand. "Come on. I'll buy you lunch anywhere you want."

When they got back to Arnie's, Mildred had laughed until she was weak. It was as if darkness had lifted. It was obvious that the surgery weighed heavily on both of them, and the relief of his understanding her boundaries became joyous. She dropped him off at the front and, after she parked, she went in the side kitchen door. Mildred could hear him humming as she walked into the living room. He was sitting in his recliner chair completely naked and ready for action.

"Arnold A. Arneson! I thought you said you were an old guy?"

"Get over here, please, and we can discuss my age more intimately." He captured her arm and pulled her into the chair. The cats stared, yawned in tandem, and left to check their food dishes.

Mildred reached for the fleece blanket on the back of the matching recliner chair and covered them. Arnie nuzzled her neck. "Still not ready for nudity, my dearest one?"

"I'm cold."

Arnie chuckled. "Okay, whatever you need." He pulled the other part of the blanket over his body. "Do we have any plans for this evening?"

Mildred cuddled into his shoulder. "I don't work tonight, so thought I'd make us a late dinner and we can take it easy. Maybe watch a movie." She kissed him on his shoulder and said, "I'm going to go put on my pajamas, then I'll be right back." She pulled the blanket to wrap around her, and the envelope fell to the floor. Arnie watched it fall but didn't say anything. "Guess this is as good a time as any to see what that is." Mildred picked up the envelope, settled in the adjoining chair and tore it open.

She could feel Arnie's eyes on her as she read the short note. Mildred simply stared at the cream-colored paper. There was no expression on her face. Slowly the first tear crept from her eye, followed by another. Finally, she sighed and looked at Arnie. She stood and he took the note from her hand as she left the room.

I have info on Captain Petrie
please message me at
alone@me.net
CR

Arnie put the note back into the envelope and returned it to the table. He knew there were no words that would help at this moment. He got dressed, fed the cats and simply allowed Mildred to have whatever time she needed.

It was a couple of hours before Mildred came back downstairs. Arnie was in the kitchen making egg sandwiches and had started a tray for her. "I'm so sorry," she said. "It was the timing that knocked me down. I felt guilty because of the joy I felt with you."

"Mildred, I can't say I know what you are going through. I can't. What I can do is be here and listen. Do you want mustard on this sandwich?"

There was an audible sigh as Mildred walked to him and wrapped her arms around his waist. "Thank you, and yes, mustard and some pickles would be great. Is there anything I can do to help?"

"You have done enough right now. Maybe get two TV trays out and we can eat in the living room. That music show is coming on shortly and we can watch it. Just remember I'm here for you, any way and any time you need." He turned and placed the fried egg on the waiting toast and added a handful of chips. She took one of the plates and walked away.

He called out from the kitchen. "What do you want to drink? We have soda, juice, milk, and wine."

Mildred asked, "What kind of wine goes with egg sandwiches?"

"A nice pinot, of course." Arnie smiled, hearing the sass return to her voice.

She came back into the kitchen with two glasses from the dining room buffet. "Wine for two it is." She left the glasses on the counter, picked up the second plate and turned back to the living room. Arnie followed her with the wine bottle and the chip bag. She was in the second recliner and had lit a candle. "I'm sorry."

Arnie looked directly into her eyes. "Don't tell me you are sorry. There is nothing to apologize for. We will talk about it later, but now we need to enjoy my gourmet dinner before this gets cold."

"I love you, Arnold Arneson."

"You should," said Arnie. Mildred savored the smug smile on his face, as they settled into the chairs, and he turned on the television flipping through the channels until they found her show.

It was after midnight when they went to bed. Arnie hadn't mentioned the note. They snuggled together under the electric blanket. Mildred clapped her hands, and the light went out.

Arnie whispered, "I'll buy you a clapper for every light if that is what it would take to make you stay?"

"I have no intention. I bought this one because Amazon had a sale and I want complete control of lighting in this room."

"One of these days you won't be so shy around me." He pulled her close before he reached for his sleep mask.

"Don't be so confident. I hide from mirrors too. Time and gravity are a couple of bitches."

Arnie sighed. "For me, too. Good night, my Cinnamon bun."

They kissed and laid quietly. As he was about to doze, Mildred spoke. "I did message that Lone guy. I haven't heard back yet."

"I knew you would. But please, be careful and don't do anything without me."

Mildred said, "I'll meet with him first, and then if there is anything to it, I'll call."

It was quiet for a few minutes before Arnie spoke. "This is your business, and I have no right to interfere, but please don't meet him without me. You have no idea what may be going on."

"I'll think about it."

James

They inched toward him with not a clue what brought them here on this day, but one wrong move could destroy everything. Finally, the locks on the outside of his door clicked and the door was kicked open. An officer moved in, stepping around Rocky, sweeping the room. Then he approached and barked, "OK, kid, on your feet."

Rocky whispered, "Cuff me. For God's sake, cuff me."

The officer jerked him to his feet and led Rocky outside, ignoring his request. Secured in the backseat of the police cruiser, Rocky watched the continued search until the old man's attorney arrived to inspect the warrant.

Finally, a detective approached the car. "Hey, don't I know you?"

Rocky turned his head and didn't respond. Little did the police know the old man had expected them for years and there were many layers of security. Nothing of value would be found. Rocky stayed silent as they hauled boxes of books and papers from the Boss's office.

An officer came back and stood next to the car. Rocky leaned out of the window. "I'm supposed to be leaving for law school this afternoon. Can I go back and get my suitcase and schoolbooks?"

The officer snapped, "We aren't a moving company."

Rocky said nothing more.

Another officer spoke briefly into his radio as they pulled away. Relief washed over Rocky in the realization as the fear started to dissolve. He had a long-term dread of being seen with police for any reason. Rocky knew to remain diligent and trust no one because some of these cops worked for the old man. There must be some way to make this mess work into a plan. He worried about his research and Rocky decided to continue the strategy of the last three years of silence and feigned indifference.

Hours passed as he waited in the interrogation room. Sporadically, detectives came in. Rocky could see the different schemes were to wear him down. The memories were as intense as the last time when he was accused of Cookie's murder. Rocky knew that pain would never go away. He used the intensity of his loss to steel his emotions and stay true to the revenge.

It was nearly four in the morning when the detective woke him for another round. Rocky was positive that they were the ones wearing down and that they were starting to believe the kid they had was ignorant about the old man's business. Rocky had years of playing this game. He knew if he didn't talk, he couldn't contradict himself. He continued to mention the locks on the outside of his door, and he used that fact to support his ignorance.

Through the elongated hours, Rocky studied the detectives and mentally cataloged who could be trustworthy for a future connection.

Released twenty-six hours later, it was Captain Petrie who offered him a ride back home. Rocky refused and called Jacko, his old driver. He stood outside and prepared his speech of indignation. The number one task was to get back to the old man's house for his suitcase, books, research and his only picture of Cookie. He breathed a sigh, knowing that once he had his things he could move to the room at law school and Phase Two could begin. He waited, exhausted and exhilarated.

− 9 −

Untypical Tuesday

With the night off, Mildred and Arnie were at her place with plenty of time to prepare for the Tuesday meeting. Bud arrived early, as usual, and brought a huevos rancheros casserole that was large enough to feed the cast of The Ten Commandments.

Arnie reached to help Bud with his things. "Damn, boss man, one more egg and we would have to borrow a forklift."

Mildred put the fresh turnovers on a platter while the two men tried to put the casserole into the still warm oven. It wasn't possible to completely close the oven door, which filled the kitchen with warmth and they all laughed. They poured cups of coffee and Mildred finished frosting the cherry turnovers. She could hear them setting up the dining room for the meeting.

There was a knock on the door, then Detective Hampton stuck his head in and called out. Mildred stopped for a moment, recognizing how this odd group of people had become a family through all of the stress and challenges.

"Hey, Brian, nice to see you. How did your trip to meet Q's father go?"

The tall, handsome detective blushed like a nun in a strip club. He glanced around then handed her one of several envelopes. "Please wait until Qaseema arrives. I promised her we would talk to you together."

Mildred held her finger against her lips, signaling silence, followed by a hug. Luckily, the other two were dragging chairs into the dining room and didn't hear. "I would expect a police detective would be better at keeping secrets."

"I am with other people's secrets, just not my own."

He picked up the dishes and went to the dining room. There was another knock at the door and she heard Hampton greet the other security members. Mildred called for Bud to help her take the casserole out of the oven; it was too much for her to lift alone without a running start and a back brace.

Everyone filled their plates and settled into the business at hand.

First, Bud agreed that Arnie's marking the racks of chips for the different centers had helped. "We've already met with the head of accounting and we agreed to keep all actions secret. She guaranteed that after they finish with the weekend's haul, I would get a report. Hopefully it will be today."

Second, Robin presented two reports on stolen credit cards.

Mildred sighed. "This is a problem that pops up frequently."

"No investigation as yet. They came in over the weekend. One in the east slots cash machine and the other in the Cape Town Nightclub. So no real trend."

Robin continued, "We are double-checking some video. I'll keep you posted."

Arnie added, "Also check the cashier lost and found. Solved about half of those complaints."

There was a quiet tap at the door, almost indistinguishable. The detective moved his chair back to get up, but Mildred beat him to the door. "Welcome, Dr. Q. I haven't seen you in a while. What's up?" As they walked into the meeting, Mildred noticed Detective Hampton was passing out the envelopes he had brought.

Arnie was the first to have his open and he turned to Brian Hampton. "You dog! Did you get married? I thought you were going to ask her dad."

"He approved of me. He's unhappy that I'm not Muslim, but he approved. I think he was worried Qaseema might be an old maid and she would move back home," said Hampton.

"Oh, you are teasing me." Qaseema covered her shy giggle with her hand. "As soon as Father said it was approved, I flew to meet Brian in South Carolina. We were married at the Mosque so my family could be there."

Bud was the first to speak. "Congratulations, Hampton. You married above your league. Then you saved a lot of money, with bypassing the big to-do."

Arnie stood to shake the detective's hand. "I feel cheated. We better see some cake in the near future. Congratulations, Dr. Q, I wish you all the happiness you deserve." He hugged her and patted her on the head.

After coffee and donut toasts, they began to break up the meeting. Everyone started cleaning and clearing. Mildred approached Hampton. "Can I speak to you for a moment?"

"Sure." He followed her into the living room.

Mildred, once they were away from earshot, she pulled out the note. "We found this under my welcome mat. I want to arrange a meeting."

He took out his phone and took a photo of the note. "I don't know Mildred. Elton has kicked up your husband's death investigation. This is suspicious. I'll talk to him. Wait for him to call you before you do anything. Please give us a couple of hours?"

"I have kind of already messaged the writer. No answer yet," Mildred said.

Hampton looked exasperated. "Don't agree to anything." He proceeded to text on his phone and Mildred assumed it was to Detective Block. Still tapping at his phone, he walked outside with Dr. Q and didn't come back.

Soon afterward, the rest of the crew were packed and ready to leave. Mildred addressed them, "Team, what are we going to do? Have a wedding party or what?"

Bud stopped and looked at Mildred. "You're right. I'll get a hold of Belinda. We'll need to work something around her baby schedule."

"How are the twins doing, anyway?" Mildred said. "I haven't seen them in weeks. I've been so busy with a big baby's surgery."

"They are doing well, getting fat and sassy, just like that one over there." Bud pointed at Arnie. "If I know Belinda, she will put together something much nicer than most of us can think of to celebrate."

Arnie answered, "Like the last event. She did such a nice job for my dad's funeral and then decided to have those babies. Guess she wasn't getting enough attention."

Mildred turned to face him. "Yeah, that was it. You were getting so much attention, she decided to squeeze two human beings out of her hoo-ha in a cemetery."

Arnie shrugged and went back to the kitchen. Mildred's phone beeped with a message as the team finished the goodbyes and were walking out. She waited a moment to respond, **Waiting for you.**

"Arnie, you get busy. It looks like we will need another pot of coffee. Detective Block is coming over."

He answered back from the kitchen. "Good. I hope you told him about the note."

"No, but I told Hampton. He took a photo and then rushed off. I assume he has already reported everything to the head honcho."

Arnie started loading the dishwasher. "I'll leave the food out and get another pot going. Do you want me to duck out so you can talk? I can come back and pick you up when you're finished."

"No, you can stay. I don't want any secrets and I may need your support." Mildred walked over and wrapped her arms around him and nuzzled his neck. "I'll make the coffee. Your coffee is sub-par."

As they finished the clean-up, there was a single knock on the door. It squeaked open and they heard "Yoo-hoo. Are you decent?"

Arnie went directly to meet Elton. "Yoo-hoo? Is that any way for a cop to enter a home. Where is the door kicking? Where is the gun? We citizens pay taxes and have expectations."

Mildred listened to them banter as they walked to the dining room. She smiled at Elton and handed him a mug of coffee. He spoke right away. "Where is that note? Why didn't you call me immediately? Tell me everything and in order."

Arnie spoke first. "I found the note peeking out from under the welcome mat. When I picked it up, there was nothing on the envelope. It looked raggedy, like it had been there a while."

Elton made notes. "Show me." They walked to the front door, as he took photos Mildred stayed at the table. "How about the security system we installed last year?"

"I had the alarm on, Arnie made sure of that. I didn't get any notice of it going off. He found the note and brought it to me."

"Do you still have the envelope?"

Mildred had kept the note in the envelope. She took it from her apron pocket and handed it to him. He opened a plastic bag for her to slide it in, then marked it with a date, time and location. "I'll have this processed. How about the outside video?"

"I forgot about that," said Mildred. "I haven't checked it."

"Since we don't know how long it was there, it may have recorded over, but I'll take it and arrange for a tech to reinstall. Aw hell, I don't know how it works." Elton picked up his phone and called, asking for a tech to come out. "I wonder why you didn't notice it before?"

"I haven't been here in the past week."

Arnie interrupted, "Mildred has been staying with me while I recover from my surgery."

"I noticed that the cats were MIA. I'm concerned that someone knows who you are and where you live. We don't know if this is a set-up or what. Now explain to me how you responded. Was it on your phone or computer?"

Mildred handed him her phone. "I used my personal line and sent, ah, here it is. Just a simple response to the note. It went out after work last night."

Elton continued to make notes and then took a photo of her phone screen. "Don't do anything without me. I got the ballistics back on the bullet that killed Captain Petrie. It was from a similar make and caliber, but it didn't come from his gun. I want to apologize that no one had taken his death seriously. It just fits so many officer suicides. Looks like a pro the way everything had matched up."

"Not just the police. I was so stunned and stressed; I simply assumed, too." Arnie handed her a paper towel to wipe her eyes. "Nothing we could have done would have brought him back."

"True, but we will get him justice now," said Elton as he stood to leave. "I'll call as soon as I have anything, and you better too, Missy. Contact me on my private line."

Arnie walked him out and Mildred could hear them talking softly. Once back inside, Arnie took her into his arms and said, "Elton thinks you should continue to stay with me. You know, for safety's sake."

"Bull, Arnie. He did not." Mildred unwrapped herself from his embrace.

Arnie continued, "He would have if he thought of it. I'm helping with the details and safety is my department."

"You know I don't live in fear. Now that you're better, I'm moving back home."

Arnie pondered then responded, "Okay, Bunny, I'll sell the house and move in here."

"Your timing is the worst." Mildred started the dishwasher, gathered her things and walked out the door.

Arnie set the alarm and followed her.

— 10 —

Personal Calls

"Detective Block is away from his desk. Please leave a message with your name and return number. BEEP..."

"Hello, Elton. This is Mildred Petrie. I have had a response. He wants to speak to me. He gave a number and I'm to call at eight p.m. Please call when you get in."

Mildred went back to packing her belongings and chasing cats. They had made it clear there was no desire to get into the pet carriers. After a run through the house, she finally tricked Popcorn by rattling a bag of treats. Louie had climbed onto Arnie's lap and was watching every move. There was no cooperation from the cat or the man. Arnie was pouting in his recliner chair with a baseball game at full volume on the television. He had made it clear he would not help her move back home.

"Alright, I will leave Louie here."

Arnie sounded shocked. "You can't separate the two of them, that's cruel." He stood up and left the room, taking the kitten with him.

Mildred continued to load her belongings and one cat into her car. She came back inside, stood at the foot of the stairs and called out, "Arnie, everything is loaded. I'm heading out. I would like to kiss you. Goodbye." There was the sound of movement, and after counting to thirty, she called again. "This isn't the end. I have things to do and I need to go home."

He appeared at the top of the stairs and started down, carrying a backpack and the kitten wrapped in a towel. "We're ready. Are we taking one vehicle or two?"

"Two would be best." Mildred shook her head but was secretly happy that his bad mood was ending and he had accepted her need to go home.

"I'll meet you there. Most of our groceries are here, so I'll pack some things and be right behind you."

Mildred answered, "I'm going to drop off my load and head over to Glamour Gals. Maybe for tonight, there is a pizza coupon on the counter at my house; we can call for a pie."

"That will work. I'll grab the rest of the salad from the fridge and see you when you get there. I'll bring the cats' food too." She heard him sigh as Arnie walked to the kitchen, turning off lights as he went.

When Arnie arrived, Popcorn met him at the door. Mildred had cleared a spot in the closet and was ready to leave. He freed the young cat as he took the bag into the bedroom. Arnie unloaded his truck and put a bottle of wine in the refrigerator. He opened a bag of cookies and snuck a cookie, or maybe two.

"Call when you're done, and I'll order dinner." Arnie handed her the cell phone. She gave him a quick kiss and ran out the door.

Mildred chuckled. With all of the changes and demands, she hadn't thought about her hair until this morning. *Sometimes aging is humbling.*

She walked into the beauty shop fifteen minutes early and saw Ruby talking to a young woman, apparently a new hire, near the chairs. She waved at Mildred and pointed to the usual station.

Mildred grabbed the hairstyle magazine and started searching through the pages. As she waited, Mildred decided it was time for a change. *Maybe shorter, maybe a color, maybe, maybe, maybe...* With no idea how long, she looked at the pictures when there was a sudden realization, she didn't have enough hair to make half of the choices.

She was startled when Ruby began to run her fingers through her shaggy mane. "Hey, Millie gal, miss you around here. I've got a little something for you before you go. Now for this mop, do you have anything in mind?"

"Hell, I don't know. I was looking at the pictures, and they don't seem to work for me. What do you suggest?"

Ruby kept running her fingers through Mildred's hair. "Do you trust me?"

"You know I do," said Mildred.

The chair spun around, so there was no view of the mirror. Then the scissors, pokes, tugs, caps, chemicals, and chatter began. Mildred couldn't let the connection with Perry Block and all of his amazing disguises slip past. An affair was quickly ruled out, with a snort and laughter. The women's long-term friendship grew deeper.

Over an hour later, Mildred walked into the condo and snuck up behind Arnie as he stood searching the refrigerator. She kissed his cheek and he was the first to speak.

"You didn't call. Do you still want pizza?" He turned to face her. "What happened to you? You look sassy and twenty years younger."

Mildred flopped into her chair and simply shook her strawberry blonde head yes. Then she reached into a bag and pulled out a white curly wig and slipped it on. Arnie started to laugh. "How can you represent two generations and not leave the room?"

She immediately took off the wig and put it back on. With a quick explanation, Mildred started to talk about her ideas for a new disguise. They continued to laugh as he opened a bottle of wine while they waited for the large pizza to arrive. Her cell phone rang, and Mildred's eyes widened. She held up a single finger, indicating a minute. It was only a few seconds when she hung up and went to the kitchen. She looked Arnie directly in the eye.

"It was him!"

Arnie's face lit up. "What did he say? Funny how I assume it's a him."

"True enough. He/she says they want to meet. He will call me tomorrow at eight a.m. and give a location."

"Eight o'clock! That's the middle of the freakin' night? I think you better call Detective Block now."

"We could go to bed in the p.m. instead of the usual a.m. habit. I'll get up a little before the call." Mildred was keying in a message to Elton. She pressed enter and the phone rang. Arnie got out fresh wine glasses, staying close trying to hear everything, but not interfere with her conversation. Mildred hung up and put the phone back on the charger. "Elton said he would clear his morning and I'm not to go anywhere without him."

"You listen to that man, Cinnamon Bun. It took too many years to find you and I don't want any risks." Arnie opened the refrigerator and pulled out a second wine bottle from a nearly empty shelf. "I was going to save this for after the pizza, but I think now is the time."

Mildred took a deep breath and looked into his eyes. "You know I have to do this. It has nothing to do with you."

Arnie nodded and popped the cork of the wine. He poured each a glass of the deep, rich liquid. "I know. I know you would do the same for me."

Mildred was shocked. "I forbid you from dying." She grabbed his shoulders as he faced the counter and held him tightly. "You understand what I'm telling you?"

"So I can be stabbed or take a bullet, but no fatal wounds. Do I have that right?"

Mildred snapped back, "No. You can trip over a cat or tip out of your recliner chair, but nothing more. Do you understand, Mr. Arneson?"

He started to answer, but she turned him around. "Do you understand?"

Arnie bowed his head. "Yes, ma'am. Loud and clear. The same goes for you." He returned her hug, and whispered, "If we were younger, I'd carry you off to bed about now. Except for a fear that the pizza guy would arrive about the time we started to figure things out."

Mildred giggled, shook her head, picked up the wine glass and offered a toast. "To a long, lusty life." They were still laughing when the pizza arrived.

It was ten o'clock when Arnie shut off the television. He tried to pick Mildred up and carry her to bed. After several minutes of wrestling around, he had her over his shoulder and dumped her on the bed, falling next to her. "Well, that didn't turn out as I envisioned."

Mildred rolled toward him. "Nothing ever does. We usually are at work this early. Do you think we'll be able to sleep?"

With a big sigh, Arnie responded. "We didn't nap for step one and I have a plan to wear us out first. I took a pill."

Mildred clapped twice to turn the light out and scooted to her side of the bed. She melted into his arms and started to undress him. This time, Mildred took the control and kissed his scars and asked for details as he laid back. There were two round scars on his shoulder. She kissed each one and whispered, "Measles or bullet wounds?"

Arnie answered, "Umhum."

Mildred decided it wasn't the time or place to ask for details. She whispered, "You know I love you, right?"

"I know." He started to say more, but Mildred hushed him. She proceeded to slowly engulf him in her exploration. It was nearly eleven when Mildred slid out of bed and left to take a shower with the hope that warm water would help her sleep. She slowly turned up the heat, when she heard the door open, and the light went out. Mildred appreciated that he respected her modesty when the shower door opened.

Arnie peeked in. "I might still have part of a pill in my bloodstream."

Mildred laughed quietly as she answered. "No need, Romeo. I'm completely satisfied with the first go around." He shut the door and as he left, the light came back on. Mildred started humming *Oh Darlin'*, an old Beatles song. She noticed her lover singing along in the adjacent room.

– 11 –

Bad Night's Sleep

They both slept until nearly two a.m. Mildred's mind kept imagining different scenarios of what had happened and what morning could bring. She rolled to her back with her eyes clenched shut trying to distract herself, but every time she dozed, the memories of over forty years with Dick Petrie interrupted. She noticed that Arnie's rhythmic snoring was silent when she heard him stir. It was a slow movement as Mildred inched out of bed. She crept into the living room. Once settled into her chair, with a throw blanket over her legs and the phone on her lap, she turned on the television and muted the sound. In the dark, silent home, she flipped through channels until she settled on the cooking channel as Popcorn curled up next to her.

With no idea how long, she watched precocious kids run, mix and bake; then do it all again. She suddenly jerked awake when the channel changed. She looked back and Arnie was in a chair with the remote and Louie. Comforted by his presence, Mildred continued to watch some guys in a canoe in complete silence.

It was seven-fifteen in the morning when her cell phone beeped. Mildred got up to check and saw Detective Block's message.

"Arnie, wake up. Elton is on his way over. He should be here in ten minutes."

Mildred ran to the bathroom and grabbed the clothes she had worn the day before. When she came out a few minutes later, the bed was made and the living room had no evidence of the difficult night. She looked into the kitchen, where Arnie was setting up the coffee maker.

"Romeo, I'll take care of that. You might want to grab some pants. He should be here any second."

He turned and looked at her. "So you are telling me you are ashamed of all this?" He ran his hands over his rounded belly and smiled. Then there was a knock on the door. "You might want to answer that." He ran to the bedroom and pushed the door closed.

Mildred answered the door. Elton Block was standing there with a bag of fast food. "Hope you have coffee."

"Good morning, Elton. You know I have coffee. It should almost be finished brewing." Mildred picked up the telephone as they walked into the kitchen. She took three mugs from the cabinet and poured two coffees.

Elton looked at the extra cup but said nothing. He set out the sandwiches and sat at the dining room table. Mildred brought her cup over and joined him.

"How much contact have you had from this guy?"

"Not much. Just the note and then I sent a few texts, but they all came back as incorrect address, then this short message. I hope we are going to talk today."

Elton opened his notepad. "Do you have any suspects?"

Mildred thought for a second. "No. You have everything I had when Dick died. I also gave you the note. I heard a voice, but it was badly disguised. In fact, Arnie pointed out that I really can't tell if it is a man or a woman."

"True. Oh, I wanted to let you know we reactivated the bug on your home phone."

Mildred smiled. "That is great, but the contact has come through my cell."

"Aw, nuts." Elton made a quick note.

"Watch your language, detective." Mildred shook her finger at him. "I'll keep you informed of everything as it occurs. I have the business and my personal cell connected."

"How did you do that?"

Mildred answered, "I don't know. You will have to ask Belinda at the casino. She's a tech wonder." Mildred heard the water in the bathroom, but no other sounds.

"Okay, my last question. Why are you carrying around your house phone if the call will be on your cell?" He looked at her expectantly.

Mildred looked blankly at the phone sitting on the table, the same one she slept with last night. "I don't know, Elton. Maybe we can blame sleep deprivation." At that moment, her cell phone beeped. "Here we go." Mildred reached over to the counter and picked up her cell phone. "Mildred Petrie." She was silent with only mumbles of agreement. She reached over for Elton's pen and notepad, and she wrote several barely legible notes. "Um-hum, at nine-thirty. I'll be there."

She looked at Elton with a smile. "That was a recorded message. Sounded mechanical."

Elton took her phone and punched in the redial. "Well, there is no information on the caller or numbers. What are the details?"

"Federal Courthouse at nine-thirty this morning. I'm to come alone and enter at the main door."

Elton nodded. "Good. This gives me an hour to set up. I'll be there along with a couple of others. See you later." He gathered the papers, an additional egg sandwich, and as he left, he called out. "See ya' later, Arnie."

Mildred didn't hear an answer, so she followed up. "Arnie, are you busy?"

"No, I'm finished dressing. Just giving you some space." He walked out of the bedroom and scanned the room. "That was quick. Where did Block go?"

"Have a sandwich. I've got an appointment to meet with the guy in a little more than an hour. I have to go alone, but Elton is going to have people there."

There was a knock on the front door, and Arnie reached out for her arm and stopped her. "I've got this, stay here. I've got a bad feeling about all of this." He waved her to the bedroom as he walked to the door.

Mildred could hear low voices, then the door closed and locked. "That was Elton. He gave me this Kevlar vest for you to wear. I guess I'm not the only one concerned." He put the vest on the bed and sat down next to it. "I'm going with you. No discussion."

Mildred picked up the vest and held it up to her chest. "Yes, discussion. You are not going. Elton will be there and I'm not afraid. Whoever only wants to give me something. You guys are scaredy-cats."

Looking shocked, Arnie answered. "I haven't been called that in over fifty years. We are concerned about your safety. You know that this investigation is deeper than the initial belief. After you found those boxes of cold cases, it seems to continue to become more complicated as time goes on."

Mildred rolled her eyes and walked into the closet as he continued to lecture. "Don't turn your back on me, Missy." Arnie continued, but she chose not to hear him.

"If you are trying to scare me, you are failing. I wasn't involved in any of the cases and I'm just a little old widow. Whoever it is doesn't want me. There is a different reason for all of this. Dick is dead and no one knows about the old cases besides you and the police." She walked out in a pair of gray elastic waist pants and a bulky black sweater over the bulletproof vest. "Come on, have a cup and a sandwich before they are ruined." She carried her new athletic shoes with her to the dining area.

"Well, I'm going over there now and find a place to hide." Arnie grabbed his jacket and started for the door.

"Stop it! They know where I live and very possibly have seen you. Besides, you're wearing a security jacket. Lurking around the Courthouse will only increase any potential..." She did air quotes. "... danger. I have this, and you will help me the most by being safe and protecting the home front." Mildred pulled out a drawer in the kitchen and started throwing all of the towels and napkins around the room. "I need you to take care of this mess."

He reached over and stopped her hand as she started to pull out the knife drawer. She could read the aggravation on his face. "Okay, I understand. You don't have to resort to violence. But you call me and keep me posted."

At exactly nine-thirty, Mildred started up the stairs to enter the Federal Courthouse. She was nearly halfway up the multitude of steps when her phone buzzed. With a quick scan around the area, Mildred stopped and saw nothing suspicious. She opened her purse and pulled out the phone. At this time, she saw one of the uniformed guards from the security stop at the entrance. He opened the door and looked at her. It was Elton Block. Mildred looked at the phone. The message was simple and to the point. **Bus bench in front.**

Mildred fussed with putting the phone away and turned to go back down the steps. She moved cautiously, out of concern, playing on her age. A few people were waiting near the bus stop. Taking her time to descend, a man in a suit with a briefcase rushed past her. She was relieved to notice it was Detective Hampton.

She stopped at the bench just as a bus arrived, and in the confusion of loading and unloading passengers, Mildred was able to score a seat. She kept alert and continually scanned looking for whoever was to meet her. It was a little after ten when it started to rain lightly; she reached over and picked up the folded newspaper. She lifted it over her head to protect the new hairstyle from the weather. A small piece of metal fell to the ground. Mildred immediately looked around, but she didn't see anyone paying attention to her. She reached down to the pavement and picked up a small, smooth key. Once it was in her hand, she knew that this was the message. After another few minutes, she rose and walked back to her car. Once in the car, she texted Elton and then Arnie.

Hampton was the first to arrive. He slid in the passenger side, obviously glad to get out of the increasing rain. "What happened? You pulled out."

She was just about to answer when Detective Block opened the rear door. "What's up?"

Relieved only to have to tell the story once, Mildred started the car and turned on the heater. "I got a text telling me to go to the bus bench." She held up the phone. "So I went down there. It was confusing at first, but the bus arrived, the crowd cleared and I found a seat. When the rain started, I picked up the newspaper on the bench to put over my head."

Hampton looked puzzled. "I haven't seen many newspapers. Were you suspicious?"

"No, not at all, but my head was getting wet, and I have this new do. I wanted to use it as a makeshift umbrella." Both men nodded but stayed quiet to let her tell the story. "When I picked it up, this fell out." She held up the small key.

She could hear Elton exhale. "No need to check it for prints now. Did you keep the paper?"

"I have it here." She handed him the newspaper. Elton took it. "Damn, this is wet. Probably nothing there, but I'll have it checked. Give me the key too, and we can try to search it."

Arnie entered the car and Mildred hid her aggravation. "No. I'll find out where it goes and keep you posted," said Mildred.

Elton was quiet for a moment. "Mildred, I can't allow that. I've got a team to help with things like this."

"Give me a week and I'll turn it over then. If I find what it opens, I'll call you before I use it."

"No, I can't do that." Elton held out an evidence bag.

"It was given to me. Five days and we have a deal."

They negotiated back and forth for a while, but it came down to the fact that it was evidence. Elton allowed Mildred twenty-four hours.

— 12 —

Seek and Find

When Mildred entered the parking lot to the condo, it was well before noon. Arnie had beated her there and was standing out front with an umbrella. She pulled into her designated parking spot and didn't have a chance to turn the car off before he was in the passenger seat.

"I'll buy lunch. Show me the key?"

Mildred handed it over and watched as he traced the outline on a piece of paper. "Where do you want to eat?"

"We have things to do, so how about a drive through?" She headed for a drive through restaurant while Arnie kept handling the key. He took his phone from his jacket and snapped several photos. "Looking at this, it's small and looks like a locker key. Did you notice this lettering?" He held the key out at an arms-length, squinting in an attempt to read it. "Looks like D11, or maybe that's a zero. We need a list of gyms and pools to check out the lockers."

He started tapping a search onto the internet app on his phone. Mildred ordered food, pulled to the designated area, and, once the chicken sandwiches were delivered, she immediately began to eat. They worked together as he searched for other possible locations.

"Bus and railroad stations, bowling alleys..."

"Post offices!" Mildred put the second half of her sandwich back into the bag and started the car. "I can't eat right now. I'm too excited and the clock is ticking."

Arnie took the last bite of his lunch and continued. "Calm down before you take off. Contact Perry to see if he can trade tonight for tomorrow."

"Great idea. I don't have to go on until after seven, but that only gives us six hours."

As Mildred made the call, Arnie started a list of new possibilities on the back of an envelope from some junk mail that was in the car. He scratched some abbreviated addresses. Mildred stowed the phone.

"Done! I'll tell you that tall drink of water is the perfect teammate. I'll owe him a day next week. Shouldn't be any problem at all."

"I can cover for you, too, if necessary."

"Arnie, I know you mean well, but you have worked at the Ivory Winds since they opened. There is no disguise alive that you wouldn't be recognized. So we will do the best we can. Which way first?" Mildred pulled up to the parking lot exit to the highway and stopped.

"I think we can hopefully rule a group out. Let's go to the Main Post Office at Market and Twentieth. It is the closest. They should be able to tell us if this looks like any of their boxes."

It only took a few moments to find out that the key looked similar to those at the post office, but they didn't have any similar numbering. They returned to the car as Mildred's phone began to buzz. "Hello, this is Mildred."

"Mom. It's me, Richie. You know, your oldest son."

"Yes, Richie, I know you. I was about to get into the car."

"I wanted to see if you could come over for dinner. Lindsey made lasagna."

"Oh, honey. I would love to, but I've got a lead on something on Daddy's death and I only have today to search it out."

"WHAT? You have what?"

Mildred stepped out and walked around to the passenger seat, and Arnie climbed over to drive to the first gym, as she explained what had happened to her son.

"Mom, where are you? I'm on my way. I have to be part of this. I can help." He sounded frantic. She heard him talking to someone in the background.

Arnie called out, "We are on our way to University Fitness on Fremont Street. We will be there in about ten minutes."

"I'll be there as soon as I can," Richie yelled.

"Richie, I have you on speaker, you don't have to holler. We've ruled out the US Post Offices – the numbering on the key doesn't fit. We will wait for you in the parking lot." Mildred ended the call. "Looks like we are going to have back up. Arnie, I think we can do this."

They were at the fitness club sooner than expected. Mildred was too anxious to wait for Richie, so Arnie waited in the car. She dashed in and learned their keys were larger. The manager helped when he suggested the YMCA. When she walked out, Richie was parked next to her car, and the two men were talking. He had his middle daughter, Amelia, with him.

"Hi, Grandma. Mom is putting the lasagna in the refrigerator for later. Dad and I are going to help. I'll bet Glory will be jealous. She can't do anything because she isn't back from the police academy until Friday." Amelia looked very smug as she stepped out of the car to hug her grandmother. "Can I see the key?"

Mildred held it out and Amelia took photos with her phone. "Me and dad will take the north end of town. You guys get the south."

Mildred saluted. "Ten-four, boss. Sounds like a great plan. Did you decide this or talk it out with your dad?"

"We figured it out on the way over. He said you only have a day to find out where it goes and there should be information on grandpa's murder."

"His possible murder." Mildred patted Amelia's shoulder. "I have no objection to your plan. It is better than our wandering street by street. We must keep in close phone contact. If you find where it belongs, we aren't to open it until the Detective Block is called." Mildred wrote his number on a scrap of Arnie's notebook, then handed it to Richie.

Amelia read the note. "I'll remember for him."

Mildred knew she could count on Amelia. Both cars pulled away, turning opposite directions.

Mildred was exiting the Hot Yoga studio after learning they didn't offer lockers or any storage areas when she received a text.

Grandma, check the mail stops. Mildred could almost hear her son in the background. **Daddy said people can rent boxes there.**

Mildred tossed her phone to Arnie as she got in the car. "Amelia just texted us with another angle." Mildred picked up the paper with the next gym. "She suggested we add mail stops. Could you please answer her? She pointed out they have postal boxes."

He tapped on her phone, then changed to a search on his own. "We need to turn on South Plantation at the next light. There is a FedEx store." He started writing more addresses. "If you see a store, can we stop?"

Mildred started to edge into traffic. "Sure, what do you need?"

"I need a tablet. The back of this envelope is insufficient to keep a proper log," said Arnie.

"Good idea."

It was nearly seven when their energy started to wane. Mildred pulled into a steakhouse parking lot. "I'll call Richie, see if they are hungry. We can decompress and compare notes."

Arnie sighed, "I love you. I didn't realize how much I needed a break."

He handed Mildred her phone when she parked and made the call. "Come on; they are about twenty minutes away. He sounded tired, but I could still hear Amelia talking in the background."

"We have been searching since late this morning. That's a lot of hours." Arnie gathered his notebook and added, "I'm going to run over to the gas station. Go ahead and get us a table and order me a great, big, giant beer." He left so quickly Mildred didn't have time ask about brands.

There was a short wait, but Mildred had barely sat down and ordered drinks when Arnie walked in with Richie and Amelia. The men looked worn out, but Amelia's eyes were still bright, as she chattered away. The beer and iced tea were delivered with menus.

Arnie took a large drink and then pulled out a map from his pocket. He also had a marker. He started clicking off the locations they had already visited in black.

"If this key fits anything in this town, we should have it figured out pretty quickly."

Mildred's voice was strained. "We have covered a lot of ground. I feel like we are missing something."

"I have been surprised how exhausting this has been. I've been strangely emotional." Richie put down his menu and drank half of his bottomless root beer. "At least we are doing something for Dad."

Everyone stayed quiet until Amelia spoke up. "Grandma, where did you get the key?"

"I think it was left for me at the bus stop in front of the Courthouse." Mildred pointed near the middle of the map.

Amelia pulled the map over toward where she was sitting. "You said it was in a newspaper. Do you know which newspaper?"

They all looked at her. Richie was the first to speak, "Honey, what are you thinking?"

"I was wondering if there were any clues in the paper and maybe..." She stopped as the server came to take their orders. "Daddy, I know I'm supposed to go to school tomorrow, but there aren't any tests or anything important. Can I help more?"

"I don't want you missing school for this."

Mildred reached over to pat her granddaughter's hand, laying on the map. "Richie, I think we need her. My girl sees things differently. Amelia, if he says no, tell him you have cramps." The two men shuddered. "Dads can't deal with that stuff, but you didn't hear that from me."

Arnie broke into a smile and looked at Richie. "That's your mother and daughter; I've nothing to do with them." He turned and looked at Mildred. "I'll get hold of Detective Block and see if they have any clues on the paper." He finished his beer and waved for another. "Once I talk to him, we will set out a new plan for tomorrow." He stood up and walked outside with his phone. By the time Arnie came back in, the food had been delivered. "Okay, team, the Detective said that it was the *Neighborhood Shopper*. He didn't see any markings except the sudoku had some numbers. You remember it was very wet. They haven't been able to determine if it was a message or not."

Everyone turned and looked at the sixteen-year-old girl. Richie spoke first. "Well, honey, what's the plan?"

"First, Dad, you can have a beer. Remember I have my driver's license." Richie's face perked up as he waved to the server. "I think we need to start at the courthouse and circle out. I am going to places that would have lockers, storage and the *Shopper*. Let's see if there is one of those paper machines near the bus. They have locks. Were there any cameras that cover the bus stop?"

Arnie continued to add to his list as she spoke. Everyone was silent as Amelia picked at her food, searching on her phone. She then reached over, took her dad's tablet and continued to click away.

"We are looking at this wrong. I think the person was trying to talk to you and give you clues. I keep thinking about the paper."

Mildred answered, "It was the little weekly paper that we see at the post office and the convenience stores. You know, all ads, coupons and local events." Mildred nodded at Arnie and as he added it to the list.

"They had them next door at the gas station. It could be the same issue since they only come out weekly," Arnie said.

"Was it the whole paper, or only part?" asked Richie.

Mildred could see her granddaughter's mind working. "They aren't very big, a few stories and mostly ads. It could have been the entire paper."

"Could you tell if it came from a particular section?" asked Amelia, as the men stayed quiet.

"No, I couldn't. It started to rain, and I picked it up to cover my head when the key fell out. I wish we had it; it would be great to try some of these locations and see if there were any messages."

Amelia continued to research. "I think we need to go back to the beginning and take it all apart. Dad said that this guy knew where you live and how to call you. I put your name on the internet, and your information came up, so that isn't a clue. They are working hard to be invisible, but they know that there was more to Grandpa's death than has been publicly shared. That tells me they are probably in law enforcement." Mildred was stunned, watching her granddaughter's mind working. Amelia continued, "I think we should start at the beginning. When does the Courthouse open?"

Arnie answered first. "Nine a.m. and then they start proceedings around ten. What time is it now?"

Richie answered, "It is almost nine now. I have to work tomorrow morning."

"I can pick up Nancy Drew a little before nine and we can go over there," said Mildred. Arnie shook his head in agreement. "There isn't much more we can do tonight and everyone is tired. I'll get a message over to the Detective and see if they have anything on your questions." They all passed on dessert. Amelia wanted to research more and the others wanted to rest.

Mildred had to wake Arnie to go into the house. She watched him stumble in and appreciated his support.

Once she had Arnie in and sent up to bed, Mildred

opened her computer and emailed a message to Detective Block with an update of their search and a change in strategy.

— 13 —

Personal Mystery

Mildred had another difficult night of sporadic sleep obsessing over her husband's life and death. She was used to late nights and late mornings, but the key had thrown her rhythm off. Up before seven, she made the requisite coffee and signed on to the computer. There was no response from Detective Block yet. She made a quick scan of Perry's report. There were consistent problems with the counterfeit chips, showing up regularly now. He was confident they could narrow the search to the green dot section. Their suspicions seemed confirmed about the new gaming block. It was a relief to Mildred to take her thoughts to the casino and away from the key.

At nearly eight o'clock, Mildred could hear Arnie moving around. They had planned to pick up Amelia at nine. She started to think about putting together a quick breakfast when a text came in from the detective asking for a call. Breakfast waited as she tapped his number in the phone.

"Detective Block."

"Good morning, this is Mildred. You wanted me to call."

"Yeah, I got your email from last night. I have what looks like a message from the sudoku puzzle in the paper. The tech team believes it may be a coded message. They have been translating the numbers to letters – it was obvious whoever left the paper wasn't playing the puzzle. Play, key, pick and pop, or some other combination."

"Hm. Was there anything else?"

Elton was quiet for a moment. Mildred could hear him riffling paper. "Not that we can tell. The paper was damaged."

"Thanks. I'll set my team on any clues you come up with." Mildred continued, "I have to work tonight, so we're going out early. Starting around the courthouse looking for places with lockers. You know, gyms, mail drops and storage."

Elton stayed quiet a moment. Mildred hoped he had a new angle. "Wait a minute. What time are you going? I might have something."

"We are picking up our teen-team leader at eight-fifty and will go straight over from there." Mildred felt a jolt of energy. "What do you have?"

"I don't know yet, but I'll meet you in the Courthouse parking garage. Let me know when you arrive." He didn't even say goodbye, simply hung up the phone.

Mildred poured a second cup, then called for Arnie to hurry. She fed the cats, put some frozen waffles in the toaster and tried to shove her feet into her shoes without untying them.

It was nearly nine when they pulled up in front of Richie's house. Amelia was standing outside.

Mildred noticed that she had a binder, her dad's tablet and a serious look on her face. As soon as she got in the car, Amelia started to talk about her research from last night and how it felt like Grandpa was helping her find his killer.

Mildred shared the new information and that they were to meet the detective in the parking garage. Amelia unfolded some pages she had taped together. It was a map of the blocks surrounding the Courthouse and she had designated possible locations. "Grandma, you said the words were key, play, pick and pop?"

"Yes, that was it. Detective Block said they were still working on it, but if there was anything else, the rain and my dropping the paper may have compromised it."

Amelia was silent for the rest of the ride, but Mildred could hear her tapping on the tablet. They pulled into the parking garage. It wasn't busy yet and finding a space on the main level was easy. As they waited, Amelia laid out her map and plan for the on-going search.

Within minutes, Elton Block pulled in and parked next to them. He was all business. "As you were repeating the words we found back to me I recognized the pick and pop as a basketball play. The courthouse has a small court on the lower level, and maybe, just maybe, a..."

Amelia squealed, "A locker room!"

He nodded at her and they bumped fists. "It's a private room now. But I got digging around and they still have lockers for the judges and attorneys to use." Amelia gathered her papers and started for the door. "Wait a minute, captain. We have to get prepared. I've got a call into the prosecutor to see if we can get in there. I wasn't sure if we would have access and we don't want to make any mistakes."

"Do you think it is a trap? Someone after my grandma?" Amelia looked ready to fight.

Detective Block smiled and measured his words. "I don't think that is what is going on, but since this could have to do with some of Captain Petrie's cold cases, we don't want to contaminate any possible evidence. I haven't had a call back yet, but let's go talk to the security guards."

Mildred and Arnie followed Amelia and Detective Block through the main doors and to the security station. Elton called one of the guards aside, showed them the picture of the key and they talked for a few moments. Amelia's excitement was obvious. Once the conversation was over, Elton whispered to the girl and she nodded. They both watched as Elton stepped away and started to make a phone call.

Amelia walked over to them. "Grandma, looks like we have found where the key goes. It was obvious; I can't believe I didn't think of this first."

Mildred put her arm around her shoulders. "Sweet girl, I never knew they had a gym here. We were all so excited; no one was thinking clearly, but we are here now." They all sighed and, as the energy coursed through them, Mildred broke the silence. "What is Detective Block doing now?"

Amelia answered. "He's calling the State Attorney's Office. He wants to be sure we move forward legally. Since we don't know what we may find, he doesn't want to make any mistakes."

Arnie added, "Darn lucky you are here, Amelia. I would have run right in there and jerked that locker open."

They were quietly laughing and in agreement that each one of them would have done the same thing when Elton joined them.

"Settle down, wild bunch. We have no idea what is in there, could be almost anything."

"Like a bomb?" asked Amelia.

"Or a cherry turnover?" asked Arnie.

"Or all the evidence we need to solve Grandpa's cold cases?" asked Mildred.

Elton rolled his eyes. "Or someone's old, sweaty, gym clothes. You had a message from an unknown person that was evasive and we don't know if this is evidence or a coincidence. So, the plan is to move carefully and protect any possible evidence. I suggest we go to the coffee shop and wait for the attorney to get here. He'll bring a search warrant and it could take a while."

It didn't take long for them to settle at one of the café tables in front of the kiosk. Three cups of coffee, three donuts, an egg salad sandwich, chips, and a coke later, Mildred watched her granddaughter as she questioned Elton. The enthusiasm was catching and her intelligence was obvious to everyone. Elton was completely engaged with Amelia, answering every question she had with sincerity. He explained he had gone into law enforcement because his dad had been a Deputy Sheriff and about the challenges of the police academy.

Mildred got a chill of premonition, knowing she already had one granddaughter training for service. "Amelia, don't you want to be an engineer like your dad or an attorney like your mom?"

Amelia shook her head. "I don't know what I want to do, but I'm sure I'll never be an engineer. Ack! That's so boring."

There had been more drink refills and some trips to the restroom before Elton's phone vibrated. While he spoke, he stood and started to gather the accumulation of debris from the table. Amelia swept away the rest of the garbage and tried to appear patient while she squirmed, waiting for Elton to speak.

"Okay, team, they're here. We are to meet the prosecutor and the bomb squad at the locker room." Elton turned to leave and Amelia was next to him. Mildred and Arnie could barely keep up as they rushed down the escalator followed by a staircase to the lowest level.

Mildred heard the commotion waiting at the entrance to the private gym as they approached from the dark stairs. Never expecting to find a work-out room and showers for court officials and attorneys, she scanned the area. The more she thought, it made sense and Mildred started to wonder what other surprises could be found in the massive old courthouse. They stayed behind Elton as a group of officers divided to let them through. Waiting next to the door was a middle-aged man in an expensive suit. Elton walked straight to him, his teenaged assistant at his elbow. The crowd closed around them and Arnie took Mildred's hand to keep her close.

Elton turned to Mildred and waved her forward. "Mildred Petrie, I would like you to meet William Hutton, the Assistant State Attorney. William, Mildred was the wife of Captain Richard Petrie. I'm sure you have been read in on the note and calls she has received suggesting evidence on his death."

"Yes, I'm aware. I was called in on one of the cold cases that Captain Petrie had stored." Hutton turned to Mildred. "Mrs. Petrie, I have a warrant and we brought the bomb squad to open the locker. Since we have no clues on the intent and the implications from his investigation, we want to move cautiously."

"Thank you, Mr. Hutton. Is it possible for me to go in when it's opened?"

"Sure, but only after the bomb squad clears it, then you can go in with me." Hutton waved to the uniformed officers. The apparent leader entered first to confirm it was empty, then waved in the officer with a heavily padded uniform and heavy helmet. He handed the key to the officer. Everyone held their breath as he started cautiously into the locker room.

It was only a few minutes, but Mildred felt every second of time ticking past. Finally, the door opened and the officer had his helmet off. "The locker is open and it is secured."

The officer held the door for the attorney to enter. Hutton seemed to grow in stature once they entered the locker room. It was dark, dingy and obviously as old as the building. The lockers were similar to the ones in Mildred's memory of high school, decades ago. An officer led them a few rows in, where a small, metal door stood open. Mildred stopped and couldn't move forward.

Elton handed her a pair of rubber gloves. "This may be the day when so many questions and misunderstandings could be resolved."

After a very deep breath, Mildred started forward, and Elton and the rest of the team followed. Unaware of how nervous she was, Mildred struggled to put the gloves over her sweaty palms. Arnie reached for Amelia and held her as they watched Mildred approach the locker. She found three books and removed them as everyone watched. One book was *The Fundamentals of Philosophy*. It had a tattered cover and folded pages. The second book appeared to be a math textbook with a discolored, aged cover. Some of the pages were loose. The last book looked new. It was a paperback of Mario Puzo's *The Godfather*.

Mildred didn't have much of a chance to inspect the books, or even open them. Elton took them from her hands one at a time and placed them in evidence bags. They were ushered out, as Elton called to the forensic team to enter. "I didn't expect books, Mildred, but we will be very thorough and I promise to keep you informed."

Flustered, Mildred asked, "Can I be there when they go through them?"

Attorney Hutton answered her question. "I don't think so. The FBI is coming in, due to some of the names that have shown up. They aren't particularly generous with their intentions."

Elton looked pensive. "I'll ask, but I have my doubts."

Amelia stepped forward with Arnie and she spoke. "Grandma, I have an idea. The books look funny. Tell them to look in the spine. Something isn't right."

Mildred nodded, and walked over to the detective, and whispered to him. He nodded in agreement.

"Come on, Cinnamon bun. We need to get this young lady home." Arnie and Amelia each took one of Mildred's hands and started for the stairs. Mildred was quiet and simply followed along. They settled into the car and had started toward home when Arnie asked, "Anyone hungry? I'm buying."

Amelia was the first to answer. "I'm hungry and thirsty."

The words snapped Mildred out of her malaise and she looked at Amelia, "You just ate?"

"Oh, Grandma, that was a snack and over an hour ago. I'm not ready to go home yet."

"I didn't eat, but I could now." Arnie made a quick right turn and drove directly to Denny's. "Oh, look, ladies, a restaurant."

"I swear, Arnold Arneson, you must own stock in this place." Mildred laughed and felt the tension melt away as they talked about the books and possibilities. Amelia believed that the titles of the books were part of the message. Arnie worked with her, breaking down the titles and anything else any of them had seen was cataloged. Her enthusiasm filled each of them with hope and energy.

— 14 —

Back to Work as Usual

G-MA on the floor.
10-4 Como at hotel.
I'll start at new section.
Meet first. Hotel lobby.
On my way.
She was still distracted by the activity of the past two days. Dressed as a little old lady with a little dark shadow under her eyes and her new, curly gray wig, Mildred headed for the hotel. It was when she entered the large hotel lobby Mildred noticed that she was surrounded by ghouls and fiends. *Damn, how did I forget this was the Horror-Con?* A glance around and Mildred was obvious as one of the few with no blood spatter. She had planned to review the schedule while on the first patrol. That changed as she moved toward the overstuffed chairs by the fireplace. That area was out of the frenetic flow and quieter with a full view of the lobby.

She was only there for a moment when what appeared to be a seven-foot green Frankenstein approached. "G-ma, glad you came."

"Jackson Pollock's mother! Is that you, Como?"

"One of the few times that standing out helps you hide in plain sight."

"I didn't recognize you. Who made the costume?"

Perry smiled. "I have skills. You act like I can't put together a simple costume." It looked funny seeing such a serious green monster smile so broadly. "If you must, Ruby at Glamour Gals has jumped totally into our disguises. I tell her what is happening, and she measures me then calls me just before the event."

"She measures you?" Mildred asked with a wink.

"Stop, not like that," Perry sputtered.

"Your reaction confirms my suspicions." Mildred started to hum. "Perry's got a girlfriend."

She had to look closely, but his embarrassment seeped through the heavy make-up. "Either way, you have found a goldmine of creativity. I was over there a couple of days ago. You haven't mentioned my new color and sassy cut." Mildred fluffed her hair and made a turn that a model would envy.

"Rockin' it, old woman. Now, back to business." He stretched out and she noticed his platform shoes and matching socks. Perry looked off toward the gift shops. His attempt at being discreet was lame. "I've got the Horror-Con, but I'm going to stand out in the casino itself. If we have any groups venture out, I'll tag along."

"This will work. I had forgotten about the events this weekend. I'll let you know if I need you." Mildred leaned toward the fireplace and continued to speak. "Have you talked to anyone in security?"

"Robin is on screens and she knows. But the main question is, how did it go today? Did you find anything?"

Mildred's face lit up. "We did! Found where the key went and it was in the courthouse locker room."

"Wait a minute, I forgot about that spot. Most people don't know about it. Brilliant. Did you find out if the locker was checked out to someone? What was in it?"

"Some books, but I don't know much. The attorney general's office sent one of their suits over. They're moving cautiously so as not to compromise whatever we found. I saw several large university books, a new paperback of *The Godfather*. We didn't get to see anything closely; they swept it all away. I'm sorry, I have to get back on task. Do I need to be concerned about any shows tomorrow or Saturday?"

Mildred stood and couldn't help but stare at the green mouth attached to the tall monster speaking to her. "You need to take a walk around. There are horror stars, panels, writers, costumes and fans, everything you can imagine."

"I'm surprised they are starting on Thursday. I just signed in, but we should expect the conference to bleed over," said Mildred.

Mildred knew it was Perry talking, but she was mesmerized by his appearance. "It's the two hundred-something anniversary of Mary Shelley's *Frankenstein* and around the ninetieth year since the first *Mummy* film, so this is a blowout. There'll be lots of bandages, gore and staggering. The south stage has classic films playing continually when there isn't another event."

Staying silent, Mildred took in all of the information as she watched two horrifying mummies and three werewolves walk past. It seemed even stranger hearing them chat and giggle.

"This could be crazier on Friday when it's full-tilt. I'll ask security for backup and we can decide later where to assign Robin." She watched the bolts in the massive green neck bob in agreement. "We need to keep in touch and plan as we go along." Mildred sighed and turned to go toward the gaming floor. "Okay, I better get staggering. Later."

She started back to the main casino and the show stages. This convention was even larger than the Elvis Convention last year. It was obvious they would need help wrangling ghouls.

She passed through the gift shops and restaurants when an idea came to mind. Mildred phoned her daughter-in-law, Lindsey. No answer, so she left a message asking about Halloween costumes. It was time the patrol got serious. In almost no time the convention took over much of the casino with an array of bizarre costumes and outrageous behaviors.

It was near midnight and the night had moved smoothly. Mildred sat comfortably between the slots and cards watching the chip racks. Suddenly there was a blood-freezing screech from the crap tables. Mildred bolted and turned towards the scream. It was a surprise how few people noticed the outburst in the constant din of background music, slot machines, and conversations. In a few seconds, Mildred could see a bloody hand at the end of the table still holding the dice. The security guard was rushing in, so Mildred scanned the area and saw a ghost and a zombie sneaking away through the crowd, trying to stifle laughter. Calmly, Mildred began to follow through the closest bank of slot machines. They were moving with obvious intent as the ghost floated to a series of empty machines. Mildred saw her drop a foot from under the shroud and the zombie kicked it under the seat in front of the Mummy's Quest slot machine.

Mildred tapped the earphone and whispered. "Bloody hand on the crap table and a ghost just dropped a foot at machine 398, next to the new gaming area. Still following."

"This is Robin, calling housekeeping. Security is stretched thin. Stay with them."

By two a.m. Mildred had followed a variety of monsters and fiends. The housekeeping toll totaled three heads, six hands, four feet, an arm and two legs. It was nearly three o'clock when Mildred arrived home. She was exhausted and only then did she start to laugh as she typed her nightly report. Still giggling when she laid down to sleep, she wondered what Friday would bring. Dozing off was the first Mildred thought of the key since she had talked to Perrystein.

— 15 —

Night Two

It was nearly eleven when Mildred woke to a beep on her phone. Picking it up, she discovered multiple messages from Arnie and Bud. Since Arnie should still be sleeping, she decided to call Bud first.

"What's up, Mr. Moses?"

"I was reading your report and I swear I haven't laughed this hard since Arnie proposed under anesthesia. Was this a team of freaks, or were they simply falling apart as zombies are known to do when they gambled?"

Mildred giggled. "I think, and it is just a guess, that this was an organized prank. It was small teams handing off to the next group with extra body parts. If we could find some trunks, we could rebuild a couple of bodies."

Bad answered, "I'd give them uniforms and stand them up in dark corners. We could use extra security. It sounds as if it was all good fun."

"Agreed. Hopefully, this was a one-night deal. I was watching for counterfeiters when the first bloody hand appeared. I didn't see anything. Do you mind checking the employment records of who was on shift the days that the counterfeit chips appear?

Mostly the heavy hits."

Mildred could hear Bud writing. "Sure, I already started along the same line. I have to meet with the new casino attorney on Monday. I'm working up if there are any patterns. I talked to the human resource supervisor, and she'll help. I don't want to flag any employees we don't need."

"I have to talk to Perry this afternoon to organize for tonight." Mildred continued, "Do we get Robin?"

"You do. Robin's excited and said she would talk to you about the assignment this afternoon." said Bud, "I'm calling in the part-timers for the rest of the weekend. Shoot, I've got another call I need to take."

"Later, boss." Mildred struggled out of bed and started her day knowing there would be a lot to prepare before the shift. She walked out of the bedroom with a towel still on her head and noticed a large box inside the front door. There was a note on top.

Mom, here are some costumes that may fit. I assume it has to do with work. Love you – Rich. PS Lock your doors.

Mildred rolled her eyes, and mocked her son then tore the box open. She found a cat, hobo, Raggedy Ann and finally toward the bottom there was a ghost. Not any old ghost, but one with flowing white and gray robes and gauze. There was also a pair of gray leggings and long sleeve turtleneck. Mildred sighed in relief as she gathered it up and held it up for size. *These are perfect! Check one thing off my list.*

With a scrap of paper, Mildred wrote *costume* first and checked it off. Next, she added *make-up*, *Arnie*, and everyone else she had to check in with, *follow up with Detective Block.*

The toaster popped and her English muffin was ready at the same time as her single cup of coffee finished brewing. Mildred sat at the breakfast bar and started her calls. Even though Detective Block was last on the list, she called him first. He wasn't in, so she left a message. Next Robin. They decided she would work at the conference and was putting together her costume. Next was Perry. He would represent the living human beings for the night since his feet were still aching from the platform shoes. They would meet early in the old security office to store back-up clothing and costumes. At the same time, they could run a quick update from night and day before.

It was mid-afternoon when she checked another item off the list as she returned from the costume store: more make-up, a pair of inexpensive ballet shoes and a gray shoulder bag for the Taser and pepper spray. She loaded it all in a rolling suitcase and left it by the front door. Mildred felt exhausted when she finally was able to contact Arnie. She learned he had worked until six in the morning due to the extra activity. After hanging up, Mildred laid down for a nap and realized it was wonderful to sleep feeling loved. Close to a half century had passed since she had felt the flush of a new romance and she was confident this would be her last foray into that risky emotion.

She had only been down for a few minutes when there was a knock on her door. Struggling to shake the drowsiness, she stumbled through the living room.

"Cinnamon Bun, open up it's me." Relieved to hear Arnie's voice. She opened the door, and he stood there with that goofy smile on his face. "Put on some shoes. Let's go eat."

"Arnie, I've got an extra-long night in front of me."

He wrapped her in his arms and said, "That's two of us. I need some time with you before clocking back in."

Mildred yawned. "We can eat here. I'm bound to have something edible."

"I want more than a frozen Lean Cuisine and a package of frozen apple turnovers." He started to dance her back toward the bedroom. "Now shoes. I need a big breakfast and you need sugar."

"You are right. I could eat. Then I wouldn't have to be at work so early. I have to meet Robin and Perry to organize and plot things out." Mildred shoved her feet into her still-tied shoes and ran her fingers through her hair. They left within a few minutes of Arnie's arrival. He rushed ahead of her to hold the door when he tripped over the suitcase by the door and fell backward into a seated position.

"Arnie! Are you alright?" Mildred rushed to catch up.

Reaching his hand to her, Arnie began to laugh. She helped him up and he shook his head. "I'm fine. Are you running away from your own home or is this a clever plan to stop murderers?"

Mildred set the suitcase back up and there was an obvious tear in her eye. "No, it's my costume set up for the conference. I didn't want to forget it. I'm sorry."

"Apology accepted, but unnecessary. All my fault, trying to be chivalrous and clumsy at the same time."

Mildred opened the door. "Well, next time, call first."

Within an hour Mildred was fed and back home, and still had time to nap. It was six when she gathered everything together, picked up the suitcase and went to work. When she arrived at the interrogation room, Robin was already there putting her things in the cabinet. Perry followed her in with three lattes and some energy bars.

"Ladies, looks like we are all early. From last night, I thought we would need everything possible to face the night." He put down the coffees and tossed them each a bar. Robin caught hers, and Mildred was bonked on the shoulder. They laughed as Mildred stowed her suitcase in the back corner, while Perry pulled up chairs.

"Let me start." Mildred opened her drink. "Last night we were busy in every freaking corner of this place. We had some good-natured pranks, but it was obvious the energy was growing. We had a particular problem with a perverted Mr. Frankenstein."

Perry snorted. "Monster, Frankenstein's monster, to be accurate."

Robin giggled and Mildred continued. "That is why Robin will pull the costume gig."

Robin murmured, "F Y I, it's called cosplay."

"Damn, I'm trying to act like a leader here. Maybe a little later you can explain what cosplay is, but right now, we need to plan. Robin, I noticed you brought clothing. Is that your disguise?"

Robin nodded and waved towards her stash of items. "Yes, I'm prepared, and I have more clothes as needed."

Perry spoke. "Thank you, I really couldn't go two nights in those shoes, but I'm ready to back up as necessary." He pointed at a large garbage bag under the table.

"Let's set our earphones to channel six. It's what we've been using and we really can't use phones. Now, I met with Officer Arneson this afternoon." Mildred saw Robin poke Perry in the side as they smirked. "He was here until after six this morning. He told me that after the bars closed, the place stayed active. They did have some pranks and the conventioneers seemed to have their own alcohol. He wasn't sure if that was all or if there were other mood enhancers. He wanted to flag us that we had some parking lot punks threatening some of the cosplayers." Mildred looked at Robin for approval. "They are putting out extra lot security and some of the part-time crew."

"How are we going to cover everything?" asked Perry.

"We don't have to. They also have a full contingent of security. We are to continue with our usual assignment of walking and watching. I'll work the floor with you, Perry. The counterfeit chips are expanding and the new casino attorney is getting involved. I'm especially worried about this weekend taking a big hit. They appear more often when we are busy and this is particularly distracting. Robin," Mildred turned toward her. "I brought a ghost get-up I can get into quickly if it's needed. Otherwise, I'll pull Saturday."

Perry spoke first. "I don't think we need much Sunday. The convention ends Saturday night and we will have mostly tired whipper-snappers checking out by eleven. We can split a shift. I also talked to Bud. It's clear from the coding that most of the counterfeit chips are coming from the new section, but there have been a few on the big games on both sides."

Mildred was quiet for a bit. "Do we have any suspects yet?"

"I've been watching on the cameras and haven't caught any obvious moves yet. I think you were right about being suspicious of employees. Those dealers are used to the chips, so somehow they are getting them under the counters," said Robin. "I've flagged all of the surveillance crew, but stayed quiet on new floor officers. Now, I need to get you guys out of here so I can get dressed." She wadded up her coffee cup and threw it at the trash can.

Mildred tapped her earphone. "Okay, but you forgot I'm the boss."

Perry rolled his eyes, gathered the trash and heaved a big sigh as he left. He said, "I'll start the upper-level patrol."

Their phones beeped. **Como in-house. 10-4**

Mildred gathered her equipment into her bag and turned back to ask, "Do you need any help?"

Robin turned back to face Mildred. "Now that you mention it, can you tie a hangman's noose?"

Mildred smiled. "Never thought I'd be needed for this particular skill again in my life. Luckily, I had sons. Where's the rope?" It took a few minutes; it has been decades since she learned the knot. When she raised her head, Robin was dressed as a cowgirl and was putting on zombie make-up and freckles. "That is great; I never thought of horrifying something I already owned."

Robin looked strange as she smiled through the rot and goo on her face. "Little notice and no time make for desperate creation."

"Good job, rookie, now to work." Walking out, Mildred tapped her phone. **G-ma on the floor.**

10-4

She started the lower level patrol with gift shops, restaurants and a couple of the lounges. The main speaker would end soon at the Horror-Con, so it was still relatively quiet.

Fifteen minutes later there was a text. **Shadow checking in.**

10-4

Mildred decided it best to check in further. **Any updates we need to know?** Her phone beeped with a call.

Larry started a quick report. "Nothing extraordinary yet, G-ma. The conference has a bunch of workshops and speakers today. They are also having a dinner so we will only have them heavy after ten. Extra security started checking in an hour ago."

"Good, pretty well nothing new from what Arnie had to say this afternoon. We have all three of us on channel six, hope that is alright."

Larry said, "We have been matching into one and two, we added six, but might be tough with the new guys."

"Don't worry, any emergency we will use channel one. Later, gator." Mildred tapped her earpiece. "Team, if we need official back up, use channel one or let me know and I'll tag the office."

Mildred heard a uniform response from the team. Mildred strolled through the slot machines and found one of her best vantage points was open. There was a relatively clear view of the crap tables, roulette wheels and the Big 6. It was early and the Casino was already busy. This would be a prime night for shenanigans.

It was nearly an hour later when she saw Perry walk into the gaming area. Mildred nodded and turned to do a patrol to the north for the sports venues and bars. Things were busy and, even with the welcoming event, there were still clusters of freaks patrolling the halls. Some of the costuming was brilliant and some guests were dressed as living human beings. The largest conference room had a sign, *Dark Market*, and it was filled with the vendors. The lighting was dim and each booth was decorated to pull attention. Mildred walked through and was fascinated with many of the bizarre items. She was partly through when she was bumped and pushed to the side.

Initially, it was a shock, but when Mildred turned, Robin was standing there. "Excuse me," she moaned.

It was clear that the event was under control, so Mildred made a turn toward the spa. All was quiet. Clearly, ghouls don't line up for manicures and facials. *Mental note, looks like it is all nightclubs and gambling tonight.* Taking the back stairs past the pool, she saw a couple snuggling in the hot tub, and no one in the pool.

Wait! Mildred stopped, looking through the steamed glass around the pool. Two lounge chairs had towels and toys with a tiny pair of sandals. She scanned further. The kid's pool was empty and she looked further, beyond the dividing rope. *It doesn't look right.* Mildred didn't decide to take a look. She simply took action.

The humidity of the indoor pool area struck her in the face as she tried to answer her unrealized question. The couple looked up at her as Mildred sped around the pool. There was a child-sized inflated ring floating in the deep end. That was when she noticed a very small movement and, finally, Mildred could see a Captain America bathing suit near the bottom. With no thought, she ran and dove in. She reached the patch of cloth and it was on a small child. He was limp and there wasn't any fight, swimming the boy to the side of the pool. As she tried to lift the child out, the man from the hot tub reached in and pulled them both to the deck.

Mildred was gasping and unsure if she had even taken a breath when she dove into the pool. The woman was screaming and sobbing as the deck filled with casino employees, working on the boy, and a crowd gathered. Even though Mildred was drenched, she inched her way out of the area while everyone focused on saving the boy. She heard the crowd cheer as she slipped into the dressing room. First, she called for medical assistance, then she leaned up against the hand blower, trying to dry off.

After a moment to clear her head, Mildred placed the emergency alarm for security, then called Arnie, but he didn't answer. Finally, she tapped the earpiece and Perry answered. "What's up?"

"Perry, I need some help."

"Sure, where are you?"

"I need dry pants and a shirt, maybe a ball cap," said Mildred.

She could almost hear Perry thinking. "Ah, ah, okay, I'll get on it. Where do I find you?"

"This is Larry. We heard on the video. I'll check out the lost and found, be right down. A women's small?"

"Okay, Perry you are off the hook. I prefer a women's large, but thanks for the compliment, Larry." Her exhaustion was evident, "I'm in the dressing room at the pool. There's a crowd and I can't leave."

"This is Robin. Are you the one that pulled that kid out of the pool? The word is spreading like a brush fire in a hayfield. I'm close by. I'll get you a hat and a Tee-shirt."

"No problem," Larry interrupted. "I've got stuff and I'm on my way now. I'll smuggle you out and over to the lost and found boxes."

All of the lines went silent.

— 16 —

Back on Shift

It was almost ten when she received the text. **Meet me in interrogation.**

After a quick rescan of the area, Mildred walked to the secret door. It was unlocked. Arnie was waiting for her with a garbage bag.

"I heard my gal was out saving lives this evening. I brought you some dry undies and stuff."

"Oh, my sweet man. I called, but with no answer, I decided not to leave a message. How did you know?" She started digging through the bag. Mildred was anxious to change from the lost and found sweatpants and *Kiss Me I'm Zombish* shirt. "I'm looking forward to being inconspicuous again. Does security have any update on the little boy?"

"No, but I'll follow up as soon as I get upstairs." Arnie sighed and watched as Mildred discreetly turned her back and changed into her dry underwear and a pair of elastic top pants. She could feel his eyes on her.

"Did you bring shoes?" Mildred continued to dig through the bag,

"You wore your shoes into the pool? I didn't think of them. I can sign in late and go get a pair."

"No need. I have some ballet slippers at interrogation. I thought these would dry quicker. Oh, you are the best. You brought make-up. How did you know?"

I've known you for a while and I noticed your face before."

Mildred couldn't restrain her smile as she pulled out the small sandwich bag of make-up. "Evidently, you don't know my face that well. Where did you get this lipstick?"

"Sorry." Arnie reached over and took the tube. "That's mine."

Mildred reached out to take it back. "Is not."

"You don't know everything about me." Mildred was about to answer when he continued. "It was in the middle drawer."

Mildred started looking at the other items. "Makes sense, that's my orphan drawer. After sixty years of make-up, some odds and ends appear from nowhere and last for decades."

"You should wear that color more often. It makes your face even more delicious." Arnie leaned in for a kiss and ended up with the same color on his lips.

Mildred packed up the wet and borrowed clothes and decided it was best not to tell him about the smear. "I have to get back to the floor. I owe you one."

Arnie opened the door and patted her behind as she walked out and watched her stop to text. She heard his phone beep with her message. **G-ma back on the floor.**

Her earphone ticked, and it was Perry, "I'm in the new gaming section."

"Do you have anything?"

"We have that pit boss and security guy you were wondering about. You were on to something."

"I'll continue the south patrol and check with Robin. Then I'll head to the upper level cards and sports betting. Let me know when you want to move."

"10-4."

Mildred started to walk when she heard the security code for the upper gift shops. As long as she was walking that direction, it couldn't hurt to hurry. Walking up at the same time as security arrived, she noticed Robin make an almost indiscernible nod to the officer and then slowly edge out to the main hall where Mildred was window shopping. "What's up, buttercup?"

Robin stopped to loosen her noose. Her lips barely moved. "Shoplifter."

Mildred answer was quieter than a whisper. "Good catch. How is the convention?"

"They are surprisingly well-behaved, and sincerely dedicated." Robin turned to leave. "I like them."

"You joining the horde?" Mildred watched the cow-*ghoul* stagger away with a dismissive wave and exaggerated foot drag.

Her earpiece beeped. "Head to high stakes, swap out in ten-fifteen minutes?"

"Perfect timing. I'll work that way." Mildred slowly turned back toward the grand staircase and ambled to the slot machines discreetly scanning the growing crowd.

Mildred's usual seat was taken. With a quick scan of the room, she settled on a new angle. There was a slightly obstructed view of the pit boss and several of the blackjack tables. The pit boss was dashing about from game to game as she watched the continual swap of chips. Slowly she ambled past him to read his name tag, *Paul C.*

The casino was full of players and even more spectators. There were some wins and a few more losses. She was a little embarrassed when each loss reminded Mildred that was what helped finance her paycheck. The chips were moving around at lightning speed and she noticed the tiny green dot on most racks. It appeared that there were a few not marked at all. She tapped into the earpiece, but the noise was too much to hear. Mildred continued walking toward the cashiers and a with a stop at the ATM. Mildred pulled a hundred off of her expense card and called again.

"This is G-ma. Have all chip racks been coded?"

Perry answered first. "I noticed three unmarked ones coming from maybe two different men. I've had security mark photos of them."

"This is Arnie. I missed that. The racks are supposed to be marked. I'll check with the video crew. Then I'll be down. Keep your eye on where the unmarked racks are going."

"Gotcha! Have to go. He's moving." Mildred tapped off and turned her head slightly in an attempt to watch indirectly.

She spotted an event flyer and used it as a diversion. The middle-aged man won a couple of hands, then moved on. That was an odd behavior, most stuck with a winning game. The ginger-haired security guard was on and Mildred didn't see Paul C., the pit boss he had interacted with before.

The suspect was moving to the closest roulette wheel when she heard a familiar voice. "One hell of a night. You can step off, I have him on camera and will follow." Mildred's nod was almost imperceptive. Larry continued, "We are watching to see if and where he drops the rack."

"I'm suspicious of that security guard. No reason why."

She walked away to the closest crap table plunked down a hundred bucks and was handed one fifty and five ten-dollar chips. Mildred made a small bet on the shooter who appeared to be on a streak. One throw and it was clear the guy's run was over. Mildred moved on. *Wait, a minute, that rack wasn't coded.* There was a reason to stay.

The monsters and freaks from the conference started to add to the busy tables. A quick wave at the camera, Mildred didn't see Arnie, but was sure he was nearby. Trying to clear her preconceived suspicions, she looked to the outer edges. She still had the chips in her hand when she noticed the fifty. *Damn, I need to compare this.* Mildred walked to the restroom, and there was a line. She waited for a stall, anxious to pull out the counterfeit she had with her. The women, as usual, were avoiding eye contact. Mildred moved slowly and opened her zipped pocket to pull out the counterfeit chip while putting the tens away. Once she had the two in hand, she couldn't tell. They felt the same. Stepping away from the line, she walked to the light at the sink and then to the exit. Barely out of the door, Mildred pulled out her phone.

G-ma need AA. West exit.

K

She stood over by the large pillar near the lot, trying to block any view. It was only a few minutes when Mildred received the text. **Where?**

Mildred stepped out and waved at Arnie, just as Perry came to join them. "This is perfect. I've spotted two racks of chips without the markers. At that side crap table, I was given this." She held up the two chips. "This one is the counterfeit that Bud gave me," Arnie took it from her and held it up to the light. "They are the same."

Perry reached into his pocket. "I have a couple of the fifties."

Arnie walked over to the corner of the building and pulled out his flashlight. He inspected the questionable chip with the others. "There is a difference in feel, but not immediately noticeable, but look at this, the gold is slightly off." Arnie handed the chips to Perry and then to Mildred. "Damn, amazing catch. I need to know which dealer gave you this."

Mildred repocketed the chip. "It was one of the new ones, young, dark hair, and eyes. He had a name tag that was Gerry or Jerry."

"I know who you are talking about. A good-looking guy. I think he's one of the new part-timers and fills in on weekends. I hadn't seen him tonight. Must have just come on for the late shift."

Arnie pulled out his notepad. "Notice if this guy buddies with anyone?"

Both Mildred and Perry stayed silent for a moment, with no answers. "I've got nothing on him other than the chip. I have gut feelings with the red-headed security guard and the night floor supervisor, but it is nothing of substance. They just whisper."

Arnie looked up. "That's Gordon. He's from that security school. He is pretty green. We will pay attention to him. Anyone else?"

"I noticed one of the cashiers," said Perry. "I saw her hand out an unmarked rack. Well, I thought it was unmarked. I couldn't get a complete view of it."

Arnie made a note. "We need to get back in there. Mildred, go ahead. We will follow in a few seconds."

Mildred made a quick call to Robin, but there was no answer. Had to assume that all was well. Mildred walked to the edge of the slot machines where she could see a couple of the tables and the Big 6 Wheel. She watched as Perry walked in and then a moment later was followed by Arnie. Perry turned to the bank of cashiers, seemed to ask a question and then cashed in his two chips. He was flagging his suspect. Mildred made a mental note to watch for an ID.

Her earphone buzzed. "Do you want to do a walkabout and I'll take over?"

"Sure. Have you heard anything from Robin?"

"No, she's quiet."

"I'll start north and circle down to the hotel. Keep me posted. We're busy enough to double up in this section."

Perry didn't answer, but Mildred could hear him talking to someone when he clicked off. Mildred played a couple pulls on the slot, and then wandered toward the buffet and keno.

— 17 —

Lasagna

Mildred woke up early, considering the challenges of the weekend. Her first thought was of Detective Block and the books that had been found with the key. It was almost nine. *Surely, he's in the office.* Instead of calling, Mildred hopped out of bed, showered, and loaded the bulletproof vest in her cloth grocery bag. It didn't take long and she pulled into the police parking lot by ten.

The desk officer waved her through. This was the first time she thought of Elton possibly working a different case. After leafing through a five-year-old *National Geographic* and a *Field and Stream* magazine, he walked in. "Well, G-ma, good to see you. Let me guess. You want to know what we've found?"

"Wow, Elton, you're good. Ever think about getting into investigations?" Mildred smiled as she stood. "No, I needed to return the vest. But in reality, yes. Have they found anything?"

"It was all thoroughly wiped clean. It doesn't appear to be a trap. You saw the philosophy book. It is an old standard textbook used at several prestigious universities. There are pages marked, but we are unsure if they are codes or class notes. Your granddaughter, Amy?"

"Amelia."

He nodded and continued, "Amelia was right about checking the spine. We found an old thumb drive. We're having a tech specialist go over it. We want to be sure that there aren't any malware or viruses. I was just there since... wait, this is Monday, right? I don't have more."

"It is mid-morning. Isn't this a priority?"

"Yes, my dear. There has been no other crime. This case is a priority to me, though, and I'll keep pushing. Do you want a coffee?"

Mildred smiled. "No thank you, I've got to get going and I've had the coffee here before. Almost made me a tea drinker."

Elton filled his cup. "This is how we break in the rookies. Toughens them up."

"I think it is the same pot we had when I worked here a decade ago." Mildred opened the door. "Please keep me posted."

Elton walked around to his desk chair. "You know I will. Now stay alert and take care of yourself."

Mildred went directly to her car and sat for a few minutes. There was no work tonight and it had been a tough weekend. She decided that it was time to make a payback and drove to Arnie's. Once inside, she noticed the house was silent. Creeping up the stairs she could hear the quiet whirring of his CPAP machine. Mildred slipped out of her pants and sweatshirt in the hall, crept into his room and slid into bed.

It was well into the afternoon when she woke up to Arnie staring at her. "I thought I was dreaming, but here you are."

"I guess we both had some sleeping to do after that weekend. I met with Elton this morning, but they have nothing yet."

"Check your phone. I heard it beep a couple of minutes ago. Maybe it was him."

Mildred rolled to her pile of clothes and purse to look at her phone. "No. It's Amelia. I'm sure she is asking the same questions." She listened to the message and looked at Arnie. "Are you interested in that lasagna dinner we were invited to last week?"

Arnie sat up, and he didn't need to respond. Mildred could see the yes on his face. "What time? I'm starved and I could eat lasagna for every meal, every day."

Mildred made the call, then she turned back to Arnie. "Good to know that about you. Can you wait an hour?" She bolted from the bed to the bathroom. "You are second, buddy boy."

He was gone when she came out all washed, brushed and dressed. It only took a few minutes to find him downstairs in the shower off of his parents' empty bedroom. The room was extraordinarily neat and dusty. Mildred made a mental note that lasagna was his biggest motivator. They were dressed and had time to stop at the bakery to take a tiramisu and a half dozen cannoli for dessert.

The usually-quiet Amelia was still excited by the investigation. Convinced her grandfather had been murdered, she had worked up several plots and shared presentations to the family. Izzie, the youngest granddaughter, was incorporated to hold posters and without direction added unplanned theatrics. It was wonderful to hear the studious Amelia share a laugh or two.

Even though the focus was serious, enough years had passed to allow the day to become light-hearted. As Mildred and Arnie were leaving, they agreed there were a lot of questions to answer. Mildred decided that she would call Detective Block daily and show up at his office if there wasn't progress.

– 18 –

Bribes?

Tuesdays seemed to come quickly as Mildred prepared for the weekly meeting. She put in three cans of Pillsbury cinnamon rolls and combined the tins of frosting into a small bowl. She had provided turnovers every week since the meeting had moved to her home. Arnie came from the bedroom and gave her a thumbs-up that the bathroom and bedroom were neat and tidy. Mildred had a quick thought that she would like a guest bathroom and not just the one off her bedroom. *Funny that I'd think a bath and a half as the height of luxury.* With a quick dismissal, she unloaded the dishwasher, leaving out mugs and small dishes.

Just like clockwork, Bud Moses arrived early carrying his usual breakfast offering from the casino kitchens. The members of security and the casino police liaison all were on time. Mildred listened to them talk and laugh, but felt strangely outside of it all. There was so much pressure and no progress that Mildred felt victimized by time. Taking out the cinnamon rolls, Mildred automatically finished the preparation, placing them on the small platter, drizzling frosting, and scraping the last of sugary topping onto her index finger. That was the moment the silence of the room brought her back to the present.

She looked up, and all of the team were standing around her in the kitchen, and it was Detective Hampton that broke the silence. "Cinnamon rolls? All the rules of the universe have been destroyed!"

Bud Moses continued faking a cough as he fell to the floor. "Nooooo, cherry turnover, come to save me."

Mildred came back from her unplanned meditations and joined in. "I thought you would be tired of the turnovers by now."

"But, G-ma, the... the turnovers are classics, no one could ever tire of the perfect frozen baked good," said Arnie as he picked up the warm cinnamon roll and stuffed the entire thing into his mouth. "Cinnamon Bun! Please ignore my previous comment. These are wonderful and they bring back such sweet memories. You are perfect."

The room broke into laughter and got to work on the week's reports and challenges. Everyone had suspicions on the counterfeiting, but no one had any solid proof. Mildred pulled out the big whiteboard from the bedroom closet and they started writing all of the ideas and brainstormed plots and plans with nothing substantial emerging.

Bud was shaking his head. "I met with the casino attorney on this. He seems to want answers and..." Bud scratched his head in obvious frustration. "No excuses. Please, folks, I don't know what to tell him. This Ivans guy seems more invested in the casino than the other board members."

Arnie took a photo of the whiteboard and all the scribbling and lines, then he spoke up. "If you can set it in the afternoon, I'll go with you to meet with him. If you want, together we can bring him up to date and both of us will show our dedication and that only a select few are involved."

Bud nodded in agreement. "I appreciate this, Arnie. I also notice that G-ma has been particularly quiet today. Anything wrong?"

"No, not at all. I'm just lost in this investigation into my husband's death. I involved Elton and now I don't have any of the information. I'm frozen on what to do next. I feel as if something is right in front of my face and I'm missing it."

Everyone was sympathetic about her frustrations. Hampton promised to step up to see what he could find and would help her catch up.

Arnie rose and started to clear the dishes and Mildred breathed a sigh of relief. Bud picked up his briefcase and held up his hand. "One more thing. We have received a letter from the mother of the boy Mildred saved. I realized that there are no words better than how she expressed her gratitude. So I had it framed."

He handed Mildred a simply framed and mounted letter and the team applauded her. Tears covered her face with the magnitude of the eloquent thank you. Mildred held the letter to her chest.

After everyone left, Arnie started the dishwasher and prepared the trash. Mildred heard nothing. She was sitting on the floor leaning against her bed and the tears wouldn't stop. The simple act of gratitude released all of her pent-up emotions. Arnie was nearly silent as he sat down next to her and whispered, "Mildred, what can I do?"

She choked on her answer, "I don't know. I feel helpless. It's as if Dick is begging me for justice and I'm a failure."

He made no answers and sat quietly for several minutes. "This information came from nowhere. There was nothing a week ago. You have to wait and we will do that together."

She sank into his arms and sobbed, still clutching the framed letter. An hour had passed when they both woke up still slumped on the floor. Mildred felt purged and her energy started to rebuild her strength. "I'm sorry, Arnie. My mood has nothing to do with you. There has just been so much and my mind is full of questions."

"Everything in your life has to do with me. I've signed on and promise to be with you for everything."

Mildred sat up and looked deeply into his eyes. "I promise to be with you too." She dipped her head slightly. "But right now there is only one thing that can help."

Arnie returned the sincere look. "Anything, just tell me."

"Can we go to Dairy Queen?"

Both faces lit up and they knew the worst was over. "Absolutely! Do you need help getting up? Because I know I do." Arnie rolled to his side and groaned as he had to use the footboard on the bed to stand up. He seemed to exaggerate the struggle and Mildred began to snicker as she waited for him to offer her a hand.

An hour later they walked into the police department with two large banana split and strawberry Blizzards and asked for Detective Block. The desk sergeant waved them through and Mildred handed him one of the ice cream treats without a word. They went directly to the office. Elton was on the telephone and surrounded in files and paper, looking frazzled, and Arnie took the drained coffee cup from his hand and Mildred slid in the frosty treat. His face reflected a surprised joy.

He hung up the phone and held the cup to his forehead with a sigh. "My dad used to tell me when I was a boy that when things are too much, ice cream will make it better. How did you know?"

Arnie was the first to speak. "You aren't the only one that needed help today. We were just wondering if you had anything on the material we recovered on Captain Petrie?"

Elton smiled. "Tech has opened the zip drive, and are finding a wealth of information on some big organized crime names. There are pictures of documents, notes on criminal actions and human trafficking." He used the red spoon that came with the Blizzard and savored the first large bite. "This is going to take a while. Forensics is working on the books themselves. I think the copy of *The Godfather* was an obvious clue. There are no markings or anything we can find on the book. I'm still waiting on information on the Captain."

Mildred stayed silent, so Arnie answered for her. "Do we have to take the ice cream away until you have some answers?"

Elton embraced the cup. "An angel brought this to me. Don't you dare touch it or I'll shoot you, and it will be justifiable."

Finally, Mildred spoke. "Arnie, he is doing the best he can." She turned to Elton. "Please let me know if there is anything I can do. I feel helpless right now."

"I do understand. I can't imagine being in your position. I have to be careful about what I release to you. After all, you are the victim in this." Elton set the cup down. "I have to get back on it."

Mildred and Arnie made their way home and he worked to distract her. Mildred watched him try hard to enjoy a romantic comedy movie and waited on her every need. They went to bed about one a.m. and Mildred couldn't understand why she was still so withdrawn. He moved toward her, and as he spoke, he sat up. "May I please give you a back rub?"

She could see him in the darkness. "Oh, no, but I'll do that for you."

He shook his head. "Nope, Mildred, this was my idea. Roll over."

He reached over to the drawer by his side of the bed as Mildred rolled to her stomach. He began to rub at her shoulders, kneading the stress and tightness away. He helped her take off her nightshirt, and she heard him applying lotion to his hands. As he rubbed, a coolness embraced her and then it began to get warmer, penetrate her muscles and bones.

"Arnie, what is that cream, it smells familiar?"

"Icy Hot. It was in the drawer." He continued to work her back deeply. She fell into a gentle deep sleep while he recapped the ointment and joined her in his dreams.

– 19 –

Twist and Turn

Mildred bolted awake. "Arnie, wake up! We are going at the counterfeiting wrong. The quality of the chips makes it clear they aren't just a couple guys and a paint brush. These are pros and are not going to make an amateur mistake. We have to look deep. I want fingerprints! We need research on photos, facial recognition. I think the suspicions are close but not on target. This crime is deeper than a dealer and a pit boss. They are freaking professionals."

Rubbing his eyes, Arnie struggled to sit up. "Oh, damn! I didn't wash my hands."

Mildred ran for a washcloth he could use to wipe the Icy Hot from his eyes. She watched while he ran the cool cloth over his eyes and face. His swollen red eyes appeared deep in thought.

"You are on to something. What time is it?" He picked up the message pad by the phone and started making notes. "I was going to gather prints on the notepads I used when I did the remodel tour but forgot. Guess I wasn't 100% recovered when I started back. I'll go in for follow up meetings with the night pit bosses and get prints. Can you think of anything else I should address with them?"

"Not yet. We have to remember these aren't amateurs, but they have to be at the casino to transfer the chips. It really must also be a regular guest that pass off some, but I'll bet most don't even get to the floor."

"True. I'll get on it and befriend that red-headed security guard. I'll get with Bud and Larry on other possible employees that could have access."

Mildred's excitement was palpable. "Don't forget that cashier Perry was concerned about."

Each had a list of tasks and Mildred made contact with Hampton in the morning. It was nearly ten when Arnie stumbled out to the kitchen and found Mildred working on the laptop. "Hey, Romeo, do you know how easy it is to get casino chips? They don't even have to be in production other than logo and paint details. I'm kind of shocked we haven't had this problem before."

He scratched his head and went straight to the coffee pot. Arnie shook his head in relief. It appeared that his Mildred was back. "Get the board. Show me what you have."

They sat together, Mildred in her dead husband's Tee-shirt, Arnie in his underwear. They went over all the details and brainstormed even further. When Arnie went to take a shower, Mildred set up appointments with Bud, Detective Hampton and Perry for lunch. Mildred rushed to get ready, then flashed the lights in the bathroom and called through the shower door to Arnie. "Sorry, no breakfast. I've got a meeting for lunch."

"I'll come too?"

"Nope. It's at the Nairobi Café, and you aren't supposed to know me."

"Okay. We have some sad leftovers. I'll survive." Arnie's exaggerated pout came through. "I'll take care of the cats, keep me posted with anything new. Love ya."

Mildred was there first and the server recognized her. Without asking, the server led her to the small private table in the rear. She had the realization that after two years at the casino and several meetings in this restaurant, she should be recognized. She was barely through the menu when two of the men arrived. Bud texted to let her know he couldn't make it. She ordered the big breakfast that Bud usually ordered for her. Surprised how hungry she was, the realization dawned that her dinner the night before had been the ice cream from Dairy Queen.

Mildred laid out the research folder and a list she compiled through the morning. She was convinced that they needed to back up and relook at everything. The answers had to be right in front of them, and they were missing it. Hampton agreed that he would have fingerprints processed quickly and Mildred gave him her counterfeit chip. Bud had not kept him updated on the suspicions. He liked to wait until there was proof and not just a hinky feeling. Hampton would be there on Friday and Saturday nights in plain clothes. Larry would get him a secured earphone. He brought the security guard's background check, but it didn't indicate anything questionable. Once they could get more evidence, Hampton promised an expedited investigation and handed them ten evidence bags and instructions on how to use them so as not to contaminate anything. They agreed to wear body cameras.

They didn't waste any time as Mildred finished the last of her breakfast. Detective Hampton had to leave and get back to work. He reached for his wallet, and Mildred waved him away. "I called you; I've got this."

While they waited for the receipt, Perry leaned in. "I was worried about you yesterday. I'm so glad to see your drive back."

"I've only been like that once before, and that was at Dick's funeral. I felt I needed to step back, but my body took over for me."

"I was a deputy for years, and you have the innate skills for investigation. I'm honored to work with you."

Mildred felt a lump build in her throat. "I'm not a hundred percent yet, so don't get me all *verklempt* again." She wiped a lone tear with her thumb. "Since Bud couldn't join us, I need to report to him."

"Good idea. Do you want me to go home and email a report?"

Mildred smiled. "You are a genius. I'll do it, but now I know that I can unhook my pants, take off my bra and kick off the shoes."

"Damn, Mildred, I don't need to visualize that. See you later tonight." Perry waved goodbye as he left the table.

She went directly back to the condo. Arnie's truck was still there. It was a comfort knowing he was waiting. Not rushing in, she sat in absolute silence, pondering the report and next steps. Retirement was supposed to be restful, and, as she looked at the complicated emotions of the situation, Mildred experienced a feeling of disloyalty to both her dead husband and her living partner. She sat stoically to search for words to understand the conflict, then vowed to allow the emotions to sort out on their own. She had no idea how long she had sat there when there was a gentle tap on the window. Arnie was standing there with a box of tissues and an inquiring expression. She shrugged and he left the box on the hood of the car and walked away with a full garbage bag.

Mildred went inside and stopped trying to manage the complexity of her feelings. She hid behind the door and waited for Arnie to come back from carrying the garbage. As he pushed the door open, she jumped out and hugged him. "Sorry. I'll be back soon. I'm just frazzled with everything."

"Cinnamon Bun, I can only sympathize. There is no imagining what you are going through, but I'm not going anywhere except the dumpster."

Mildred pulled him to the couch, and when they plunked down, she noticed the place had been dusted and the carpet had been vacuumed. "This place looks great. You didn't have to do all of this."

"It was dust or look through your underwear drawer. I just finished up, so you are home in the nick of time."

Mildred laughed and felt a weight lift off of her shoulders. "You have already seen my best underwear, so it is only downhill in that drawer."

"If you're done now, Elton wants us to come to his office." Arnie stood up and pulled Mildred behind him. "Go fix your face. I'll call him to be sure he is still available, then we're outta here."

– 20 –

FBI

When they arrived, Elton was standing behind the desk sergeant waiting for them. "Glad you are here. Come on back."

Mildred fought back emotions, wanting to be open and ready for anything. The electricity of excitement surged through as he opened the office door. The office was in more disarray than usual. Stacks of papers and old coffee cups were spread out on nearly every flat surface. The whiteboard was turned away. Clearly there was information on something he was hiding.

Arnie was the first to speak, breaking the tension. "Elton, brought you an iced coffee. Hope that is okay with you." He reached into his insulated carrier and pulled out one of the largest drinks available at the nearby coffee shop.

Elton's expression was more than enough thank you as he tore off the lid and took a giant gulp. "Mildred, if you don't marry that man, I will." He cleared some of the file folders to a stack, set down his cup, and pushed the board back closer to the wall as he started to speak. "The information from the locker was a mother lode. The detail had to be compiled by an insider. We don't have any clues on who. Our forensic tech team found some coding in the underlined, accented material. The FBI is taking over and will have an agent here tomorrow."

Mildred nodded and asked, "Is this why you wanted me today?"

Elton walked over to Mildred and whispered. "I wanted to tell you personally, they don't want any of this out. It seems almost cruel to leave you out of the loop, but it is for your protection. You didn't have to include us and thank God you did. There are powerful entities implicated. There may be connections in police, the judiciary, government, not to mention the street. Brass doesn't want me to involve you in any way. Sorry, I can't say any more." He leaned toward her and patted her hand. "I'll let you know if we have any breaks."

His phone rang, and he answered mumbling into it. "Hold on Mildred, the agent is here early; I'll be right back."

As soon as Elton was out of sight, Arnie was up and walked behind the board. "Let me know if you see him coming right back?"

"Gotcha!" Mildred walked over and stood by the coffee pot. Casually she looked at her phone. "You know anyone on the board?"

Arnie whistled as he walked back to his seat and stowed his phone. He looked toward the door and whispered, "Oh, look, we got a stereotype." She turned to look as Elton opened the door with two officers, looking like central casting had sent them.

Mildred snorted, stifling a laugh as Elton ushered in the officers. They stood in unison to welcome the agents. There were polite introductions and a brief explanation of her involvement. Moments later, Elton turned and spoke louder than usual; his aggravation obvious. "Well, there are no other questions. If you need anything, please call." He walked them to the door. "Thank you for coming in."

Mildred and Arnie stayed silent until they arrived at Mildred's condo. He shut the door, flipped the deadbolt and turned to her. "Do you remember their names?"

"I did, but only for a moment." They laughed together as she reached over and took his phone from his pocket. "How do I get the photos?"

They stood side by side and looked at the screen. Mildred strained, then finally asked, "Can we send these to my computer without it going through the office? I need to make them bigger."

"Bunny, you will have to hook up with a younger guy for the tech skills. I don't think we should put any of this on your computer. Those agents didn't seem like the forgiving type. If this is as dangerous as Elton suggests, we have to be very careful. I recognize several names toward the top from the news."

"Lawrence McCaffie, the good judge. There is just a side sticky note about the women. I thought it was his wives that were manipulating him. He lost his position and I think he is still on house arrest. His involvement was questionable on many of the cases Dick was researching," added Mildred. "I hoped the prosecutors followed up with his connections. I don't recognize the other names above him."

"I remember, you were instrumental in busting the Judge. There was some talk about his connections. It looks like it wasn't just his wives; he was deep into something. That top name is familiar, but I don't know how. McCaffie was on the casino board too. Do you think Elton or Hampton have more info on what happened?"

Mildred sat for a while before answering. "I haven't heard anything or seen the Judge since the kerfuffle."

"Kerfuffle! Damn, Mildred, life threats, kidnapping and, if it wasn't for Popcorn the wonder cat, who knows what else. Enough of the past, we have research to do and we don't know who to trust. This information goes deep and is dangerous."

Mildred went to her desk to power up her laptop. Arnie reached out and stopped her. "Let's run over to the library and do some digging. We need to be careful what's on your computer. Keep everything here as per the usual. We have to be clever."

With a nod, Mildred opened a drawer and pulled out a small package with a couple of zip drives, dropped it into her bag and walked to the door. "I'll do a report to Bud later. I'm ready."

Within minutes, they were walking through the library and settled on a computer facing a wall. He loaded the pictures, and they were able to study them. Mildred searched some of the names that were attached. Arnie tried to find an update on Judge McCaffie's status to no avail. Mildred ran her fingers over the monitor, showing a picture of her husband with lines drawn to unknown faces. With a sigh, she returned to digging deeper on some of the names higher on the board. Together they decided more time and privacy was necessary.

Arnie dropped Mildred off at home so she could nap and get ready for work. He took off to run errands and check on his house. He had been home less and less over the past weeks.

Mildred continued her usual schedule and was at work on time. After a couple of hours, she was clocked out for dinner at the buffet. Her mind was preoccupied with the list, but it was Chinese night and she rarely missed. She observed Arnie, in his usual security uniform, approaching. With an apparent focus on the slot machines near the entrance, she felt him touch her arm and slipped a note into her hand.

"Ma'am, you dropped something." Then he turned and was gone.

Mildred slid the note into her pocket and would find somewhere private to check it. After her first plate of General Tso, Mildred started to sort through her purse and slid the note from her pocket to the checkbook. Her mind wandered with the question of *Why do I still carry a checkbook? Everything is done with cards these days.* Luckily, she still had hers which worked as a diversion. She opened the note, and it was a simple receipt for an electronic tablet. There was no other writing, but she understood. They now had a means for research, unconnected to the casino's system.

It was a quiet night with only one bar fight and a reported car invasion. Neither event involved Mildred.

— 21 —

Unexpected Guests

"Old man, get up! We have guests." Mildred dashed to the bathroom, grabbing pants and shirt on her way. A quick call out to the door. "Just a moment, I'm almost there." More covered than dressed, she ran back to the door, doing a quick check on Arnie as she passed, but he was still sound asleep. "Wake up! Someone is at the door."

He sat up in bed, but she could tell he wasn't registering what she had said. Mildred repeated slow and loud. Finally, he shook his head and took a deep breath. He rolled to the side of the bed, then started toward the bathroom as she heard him mumble, "Not the usual girlfriend. What next?"

Mildred ran headlong to the door, hearing someone trying the knob. With a quick peek out the front window, she saw two large men in dark suits. With the door opened a crack one of the men announced, "FBI. We have a search warrant." They quickly flashed identification.

"Sure. Why didn't you just call?" Mildred was puzzled that these weren't the agents she had met, but it was like the FBI to take over.

The man's voice was gruff. "We need to come in,

now." Mildred opened the door to them and they flashed a folded official appearing paper. "We need to search the place and any storage facilities you may have."

Mildred led them inside, "Tell me what you need, and I'll give it to you. This is totally unnecessary."

The larger man looked at her. "We have our orders."

Mildred pointed at the front closet and said, "Start here, and then there is a larger closet in the bedroom. Laundry room over there, and I don't have any other storage. I'll put on some coffee. Are you hungry?"

There wasn't a discernable response, just a huff from the officer who had spoken before. She filled the coffee maker and then slipped into the bedroom. Arnie was still in the bathroom. Opening the door, she whispered to Arnie as he brushed his teeth. "I think you should go home, immediately. They say it is FBI, but they are different officers than the ones we met. I don't want them to see the photos on your phone or find the new tablet either."

The officers came into the bedroom just as Arnie picked up his uniform shirt from the night before. Arnie kissed Mildred passionately. She slipped the tablet into the front of his pants. "Call if you need me. Or, better yet, come on over when they finish and wake me the way I like."

There was a snort from the walk-in closet. Mildred walked Arnie to the front door. He whispered, "This doesn't feel right. I think I should stay."

"No, I've got this. I don't have anything here. I'll be over soon."

After closing the door, Mildred walked back to the kitchen and poured two mugs of coffee. She noticed that they were tearing everything apart, even into the water heater cabinet. "Here's some coffee. Now for breakfast. I can do some turnovers, bacon, and eggs. How do you like them?"

This was the first time the smaller large man spoke. "Thank you, ma'am; we won't be eating. I appreciate the offer."

Mildred smiled and walked back to the kitchen and poured a cup of coffee for herself. As she sat at the counter, she tapped out a text to Elton.

EB – why did the FBI get a search warrant? You know you can come over at any time.

It was only a few seconds when she received a response. **They didn't. Get out of there. I'm sending a car.**

Mildred took immediate action. She noticed they had taken her office laptop, so she gathered both cats into a single carrier and grabbed her bag. "Hey guys, that's my work computer. Take it easy. I have to take my cats to the vet. Be sure to lock up before you go."

She didn't wait for an answer as she ran to the car. The smaller man came out as she pulled away. He ran toward her. She noticed he had her family picture album. She waved goodbye with a smile and swore under her breath. Not driving very far away she parked on a side road near the bridge. A dark sedan pulled out of the parking lot within a few minutes of her leaving. Mildred knew better than to be obvious, but she was able to get part of the license number and the make and model of the car. She called Richie's house and luckily Glory, the oldest grandchild, was home from the police academy. She secured a promise to call if anyone showed up claiming to be with the FBI. They hadn't heard anything about a possible search.

With a quick call to Elton, he was on his way to her condo. She learned that the real FBI agents had planned to visit her in the afternoon too for a statement. Waiting outside, she was only there a minute before Elton and the real agents arrived. Mildred gave a short statement about what happened and Elton called in the forensic team to look for any clues about the two men. She gave him Richie's contact information, just in case. Elton stated it would take a while searching for evidence. He sent her to Arnie's, pointing out how she looked tired. They were gathering possible evidence and she would have to wait outside anyway.

Mildred walked to her car, then rolled down the window and called back. "Detective, don't forget the outside camera." He gave her a thumbs-up.

It was nearly one-fifteen when she climbed into bed next to Arnie. Louie, no longer a kitten, beat her up the stairs and was already lying next to his feet. The CPAP machine was running and Arnie seemed unaware of her presence until she kissed the bald spot on the back of his head. He nearly bolted out of bed. After a short recovery, he wrapped her in his arms, mumbled something unintelligible and went back to sleep.

Mildred laid awake for hours, re-running what had occurred, asking questions and building a series of possibilities. She searched her mind for any recognition of the men at the door, and there was nothing. As time ticked by, the scenarios became more sinister. She watched a sunbeam creep from the ceiling and down the wall. Popcorn followed the light trying to find a warm place to nap. With the clarity of daylight, she began to calm and finally wrapped in the warmth of Arnie's arms; her thoughts went silent.

When she opened her eyes, he was watching her. "Good evening, Cinnamon Bun. You are beautiful today."

She could see the love in his eyes and it puzzled her. "How long have you been watching me? This wasn't supposed to happen in my seventies, but here it is." Mildred didn't give him time to answer. "Do you want coffee, tea or me?"

Arnie's face almost split in two with his smile. He rolled to the side of the bed and slid open the drawer to the side table. "I'm opting for two out of three, and the coffee can wait."

By the time Mildred was showered and dressed, Arnie was back from the kitchen with two cups. After a deep lingering sip of the hot brew, Mildred agreed to Denny's for brunch. She had an unexplained feeling of peace that she hadn't felt for a very long time. She looked at this goofy man backing her up, supportive no matter the circumstance as a true gift of time and place.

A quick message to Detective Block and a casual meal at the usual diner helped her back from fear. Elton suggested she stay away for a day or so just in case there was a threat and to watch the camera for questionable activities.

– 22 –

Continued Investigations

G-ma on the floor. Is Bud in?
He just left; this is Larry.
Did he leave anything for me?
Not yet.

Her phone clicked and showed the office. Larry continued, "You are getting a computer upgrade. He is running a lot of searches and checks, concerned about hacking and viruses through your laptop. The casino attorney suggested we be extra careful after your theft. By the way, are you okay? Bud said you were there when it all happened. Who were they?"

"Whoa, Nellie, one question at a time. Yes, I'm alright. I don't know who they were. I thought they were officers, so I let them in. The laptop is protected with a password that was never shared with anyone, and no, it wasn't 1-2-3-4. I gave all of the info to Detective Block, and am waiting for the all clear."

Larry barely took a breath. "Did they get anything else? Aren't you afraid at home?"

Mildred couldn't help but smile about his concern. "No, I'm not afraid, but I will pay extra attention for a few days to be sure. I haven't been back in, so I don't know what else may be gone. As you know, I didn't have much there."

"You take care. If you need anything, let me know." He ended the call as quickly as it started. Mildred was tempted to make light with a joke, but decided that she would allow his concern and continued to listen.

Mildred started her early patrol, walking from the back entrance around to the hotel, restaurants and largest section of slots when she heard Perry sign in. He always came to the main entrance, so she went over to greet him. They wouldn't speak, simply a nod, and he would automatically know she was doing the walkabout. She watched him start to the north end, and she turned toward the gaming tables. The questionable security guard background was reviewed and cleared, so Mildred focused on her suspect, Paul C. She had searched through the employee records and confirmed his last name as Clanton. There are also two of the dealers in his section that seemed to take in more chips. Once Mildred was settled in at the end slot with a view of the floor, she noticed they were all working tonight.

As she fed the slot machine, she tapped the headphone on channel six. "We have a full crew of suspects tonight. Como, let's tighten up surveillance."

She was answered by a familiar voice. "I'll focus a camera; let me know which ones."

Mildred almost squealed at the machine. "Belinda! You are back."

"Yes, G-ma. I'm just helping with the swing shift for now."

"We need you tonight. Are you up to date on the counterfeit chips?"

Belinda responded. "Bud and Larry both have. We do have a couple of new cameras in for that area too."

"Let me know when you can lunch, dinner or whatever." Mildred tried to stifle her smile. "I've missed you. I want to hear about those babies."

"I'm pulling some evenings to coordinate with Brandon's schedule. Dinner, for sure. Later." Belinda ended the call.

Mildred had more confidence in Belinda than the entire security crew. Purposely avoiding the uniformed officers, her whole association was with supervisors. Mildred had built a true friendship with Belinda and Doctor Qaseema. With Belinda's maternity leave and Dr. Q's romance, they had drifted apart. Mildred made a mental note to get the women together for dinner, possibly tomorrow. She looked at her contact list and clicked on friends, and tapped out a text to both of them.

Dinner Friday? Ladies night.

There was an immediate response. **8:30 Hotel restaurant.**

RSVP 8:30 works.

Mildred was humming as she moved to a seat near the cashiers. She picked up a racing form and sat down. There was a line of guests when she noticed a rack go in, and cashed out. Mildred didn't see if there was a coded mark. She immediately tapped her earphone and held up the paper to hide her face. "Larry, cashier in the new section, third window, I can't see her name. I think there may have been a handoff."

"We are on it. Sending someone in now."

"No, don't. Let us continue to watch. This is more than a single cashier."

Mildred slowly folded the paper, went to the cash machine, then left. She noticed that the supervisor was walking in very quickly with a security guard. *I guess I'll have to wait.* The Hungry Hippo slot was available, with Mildred's favorite view of the roulette and crap tables. There was a small crowd, and she decided it wasn't busy enough for a handoff. These guys wouldn't be obvious.

She got a quick message from Perry. **Swap.**

Taking a slow turn, Mildred started toward the north end of the crap tables when she saw Perry come down the main staircase into the gaming area. She stopped and waited for him to walk past. She stood up and backed into him. "Oh, excuse me, sir. I didn't see you and would like to whisper with you."

He reached over and patted her shoulder. "I hope you are alright." His voiced dropped. "Go ahead, I'll walk you out. Better yet, I'll buy you a drink."

"To the MozamBeat, they're only a little busy." Mildred looked at Perry and batted her eyes as if she was flirting.

Perry shook his head in agreement and they went over to the club. They were able to get two seats at the end of the bar. Perry ordered a light beer and added, "And whatever the lady would like."

Mildred thought for a second and then said, "I'd like a vodka tonic, just like I like my men." The bartender looked at her questioningly, as Mildred continued to speak. "...Big and weak." She could hear him chuckle as he went to mix her drink.

Perry looked directly into her eyes. "Nice. If I didn't know that you were attracted to round and weak guys, I'd be offended. Now, what's up?"

She went on to explain her stop by the cashiers and the possible unmarked rack, and how she backed off with security rushing in. They both had started to pick up on some consistent faces and suspicions. "Don't forget Detective Hampton will be undercover this weekend. We need to have him brought up to date."

He shook his head. They decided if it was quiet Perry would leave early and submit the night's report, including their gut feelings. Mildred would ask Belinda to send over some video. They decided to kick up the use of disguises since they had been working on the gaming floor so heavily.

The nightclub was starting to get busy, and the band was tuning up. They planned to report in the parking lot before Perry left and he would handle Mildred's additions for a joint report.

They left and turned in different directions. That was when Mildred saw Detective Hampton in a polo shirt and pressed jeans. He walked past with his wife on his arm. She nodded and quietly said, "Genius disguise, but quit glowing like newlyweds." Dr. Q's giggle followed Mildred toward the gift shops.

When Mildred arrived at Arnie's, she didn't have much left. The sleepless night had caught up with her, and by two a.m. she could hardly stand. Regular security had the belligerent drunk and a domestic dispute well under control. Desperately she wanted to go home and crawl into her bed, but she didn't have an update from Elton. With not enough energy, Mildred couldn't deal with anymore hassle tonight, so she drove to Arnie's. It was a welcome relief to be greeted at the door by Popcorn winding through her legs and Louie's little meow demand for attention.

The next thing she remembered was Arnie kissing her forehead, waking her up gently. "Bun, let's go to bed." Mildred had been asleep in the chair, still holding her purse and completely dressed with both cats cuddled on her lap. "I didn't know if you would be here when I got home. I'm happy you are."

Staggering up the stairs, holding onto the railing Mildred sighed. "For the first time, I'm kind of afraid to go home."

"You are safe here. I'll go check the locks and be up in a minute."

"My hero." Mildred couldn't help but smile at the thought that her hero was a sixty-three-year-old, balding, chubby guy, but he was and she felt better.

– 23 –

Serious

Mildred had been up about twenty minutes when she received a text from the casino. **Call me when you can – Bud.**

Immediately Mildred dialed the direct line. "Hey, boss, what's up?"

"I have to meet with the new casino attorney and I need to talk to you first. Can you come over? I'll buy breakfast."

"I'm not in any condition to meet a human being. I couldn't get there for a while."

Bud dropped his voice. "I'm worried about your computer and any connections it has to our network. Did you download any of the recent upgrades?"

Mildred whispered back. "No. Nothing since the expansion. The only thing I do is my reports."

"Sorry, I have just been in a panic about who may have stolen the computer and what access they may have gained." She could hear the relief in his voice.

"We talked about an upgrade," Mildred said. "But never got around to it. I had no need. They have my folder of evening reports and my solitaire lifetime scores, but not much more. Oh, and little old man pornography."

Bud's tension seemed to break. "Meeting with this new guy again."

"The attorney? He seems to be digging into a lot of things," said Mildred.

"I'm getting paranoid. Everything had been so smooth in our system that I started to get worried. Do they have any clue of who broke into your place?"

Mildred settled into the limited information she had. "I'll check back with Elton, but they aren't sharing much information. They had a fake search warrant and I don't think there was anything to find. I didn't go back last night. I put my son on notice, just in case."

"Well, G-ma, be sure to check with me when you come in and I'll have the new laptop for you. We'll stick with a stripped-down model and a new password."

"Okey-dokey. I don't need anything more complex, anyway."

As Mildred ended the call, she heard a huff and turned toward the cats' bowls, finding Arnie standing there looking at her. "Okey-dokey? You are full of those phrases. What's going on?"

Mildred shook her head and poured him some of the fresh coffee she had just made. After a quick review of the conversation with Bud, she finally admitted that fear was starting to penetrate. There was a new concern beginning for her son and his family.

"We found the box of cold cases at Richie's and I need to talk to him."

With a quick gulp, Arnie finished his coffee. "Get dressed. I've got a hinky feeling about all of this too. Is he working from home?"

"Hinky? And you have the nerve of giving me guff about *okey-dokey*," Mildred mocked him as she gathered both cups into the dishwasher. "We can get something to eat as we go."

Within an hour, they were in the pickup truck and on their way. They went to Richie's first with a small bag of carry-out treats. He had heard nothing. While they waited, he called the storage company and they checked the unit. Shortly there was a callback. The lock was cut and hung back in place on the door. Mildred called Elton and he promised to leave immediately with the promise of a team. *There has to be a leak somewhere.*

They followed Richie to the storage unit. Elton had already arrived. The security guard was with him and she noticed one of the FBI operatives with some other officers. They were checking the lock and adjacent area for cameras and prints. She learned that the manager wouldn't let them open it until Richie was there.

"We'll open it in a second. It was obvious that the lock was cut."

Silently they watched the forensic team do their work. Waiting for it to open seemed longer than it was. Richie was second to enter the mess. Photos, old report cards, sports memorabilia and baby clothes were tossed around the room. Whoever had been there was thorough and Mildred recognized the feeling of violation on Richie's face. She listened as her son assured the officers that he was confident that there was nothing other than personal belongings and old furniture. She heard Richie confirm that a thorough search had been done after they had found the original box of cases his dad had stored. He was certain there was nothing left besides personal belongings.

With her arm around her son's waist, Mildred promised to help clean the mess and he nodded. His career as an engineer had fit his need for precision and organization. He could never tolerate any mess.

"Don't worry, Mom. Glory is home, so I have my girls to help. Besides, so much of this is just stuff and it needs to go." Mildred could see the tears challenging his demeanor.

Elton was making notes as he spoke. "Whoever broke in was a pro. They wore gloves and left nothing behind. Agent Moreno went to the storage office and is waiting for the manager to isolate the video. I don't have many hopes as the one in this aisle has been sprayed with paint." He turned to Richie. "Mr. Petrie, do you remember the last time you were here?"

"I'm sorry, but it has been a few weeks. I picked up a box of toys to send to my brother." He turned to his phone, then added, "It was on the 16th at three in the afternoon."

"That helps a lot. We know when to start checking the video in the office." Elton walked away and talked to one of the investigators.

Mildred pulled Richie closer and whispered. "Honey, I'm so sorry. I feel responsible for all of this."

Richie stepped back a half step. "You're sorry! This..." He waved around the room. "...has nothing to do with us. This is bigger than we are. It was those cases Dad was working. Amelia was right. This has to do with his murder!"

His words and anger were true and silenced everyone as the investigation continued. It was nearly a quarter hour before Mildred spoke. "Officer Block, when can I go home?"

Block held up a single finger and whispered to the forensic team. He turned back and spoke, "They haven't turned up anything yet. They found disconnected and spray-painted cameras and no prints. They are reconnecting and cleaning the..."

Mildred interrupted. "Could they leave a wire hanging loose, so it looks like we didn't catch it?"

"Pretty clever." With a nod, Elton turned back to the team. "Done. I doubt they will be back."

"Don't tell Arnie, but I'm a little frightened to go home. I feel like every gangster in the county knows my address," said Mildred.

"I'm standing right here, Mil. I can hear you." Arnie had his hands on his hips and shook his head. "You have a place to stay and you know it. My job is to keep you safe."

"I know they don't want me. Whoever they are, they want Dick's files and I don't know why."

Richie looked up from the pile of little girl clothes he was folding and packing into a box. "You know why. Dad was on to something big. They know it. I know it." He turned to Elton. "Detective, go back to the beginning. There is more to the original case with Judge McCaffie. I can see it and I'm just an engineer."

"And a heck of an engineer," sang Arnie. His weak attempt at humor broke the tension, but the truth had been spoken and was very clear.

Richie smiled and checked his watch. "Do you think they may try my home too? I've got to think of my wife and girls."

Elton answered immediately. "I'll get someone over to watch your house right away. These are pros and desperate to find something." He tapped into his phone. "I don't think we will find anything here. I do need you to see if anything is missing, then you can go."

"Hell, like I said, there was nothing here. I've got things to do and will come back to clean-up. Call me with any questions." Richie handed a business card to Elton and left, with Mildred and Arnie right behind.

Arnie went to the car, and Mildred hugged her son for a quick goodbye. She whispered in his ear. "Who did you tell about the box?"

He whispered back. "No one. I told Lindsey we found some of his old stuff, but no details. No mention of any files. You?"

"No one. I didn't even tell the police. I just gave up the entire box once Elton saw I had it. I never mentioned it to anyone." Then she spoke louder. "Love ya. Hugs to all the family."

Mildred walked to the car and got in the passenger seat. Once they left, they drove to her condo to gather clothes and a disguise. Arnie cleaned out the freezer and refrigerator. She didn't turn on any lights as she waded through the piles of clothes thrown on the floor. It didn't take long and after setting the timers on the lights, they were gone.

– 24 –

Fortune Cookie

G-ma on the floor.

> **10-4 good luck – already busy.**

Mildred's alter ego, Bambi Hunter, burned-out biker, slid the phone into her leather pants and started her first tour leaving from the hotel lobby, passing restaurants with waiting lines and busy gift shops. *They weren't kidding. 7 o'clock and people everywhere – good thing I wore the comfy boots.* Once she arrived at the first bank of slot machines, the noise filled the areas. There were players on every row, and 70s rock music played in the background. The hypnotic punch, roll, wait and punch dance was in full action.

Mildred made the turn to the gaming tables when she heard Perry Block check-in. **Como in-house.**

With a quick text, she advised of her location and that he could pull the first shift watching for the counterfeiters. With a glance, she saw her tall partner dressed in his balding, old guy with cargo shorts outfit. As he passed, she spoke. "How's it hanging, Mr. Cane?"

"Ahhhh, Miss Hunter. Good to see you," Perry answered as he walked past, continuing toward the new gaming area. "Talk later."

It was nearing nine when Mildred decided to break for dinner. It was American night and a big bowl of chicken noodle soup was calling her. She sat down at her favorite table with a view. Three spoons into it, her earphone beeped.

"Your suspected cashier, is her name Kathy?"

Mildred took one more bite and then answered, "Yes. With a K, I'm pretty sure. She is middle-aged with short, dark graying hair. Can't tell you about height. Only saw her behind the window. The third window last time I saw her."

"She just passed a rack with a green sticker. Not our sticker, mind you. Looks like something from the office supply store."

"Arnie should have signed in; let him know. Easier if I do it."

A third voice came on. "I heard you. We did a workstation check yesterday. I'll have the supervisor do a follow-up. We'll take over from here. I'll keep you posted."

Perry spoke, "I'll amble on down the hall later."

Mildred heard the line click and decided that she better not mess around and get some pot roast and mashed potatoes. 100% comfort food filled her plate. Mildred couldn't help wondering if the corn was fresh. Then Chef Mike slipped a fortune cookie on top of her apple pie.

Fed and ready to get back out there, she bit the cookie before she beeped. "Where are you, Perry?"

With an obvious slot clanking, she listened to his answer. "Taking a turn to the south, and through the nightclubs. Looks clear right now."

Mildred joined in. "Good I'll go to high rollers."

With a quick look around, Mildred paid the cashier and turned to the back elevator and the upper floor. The sports venues were packed with a majority of men. They were very animated, watching football, and next to that, the horse racers broke into an excited shout. This was one of those nights when the casino made much more than they paid out. Every venue was active. Past the poker rooms, she noticed a man stand quickly to confront a dealer. There were no chips in front of the man's chair, and it was obvious that this could escalate. Security was present, but had his back turned, talking to the bartender.

Quickly, Mildred walked to the bar and tapped the officer on the shoulder. "Trouble brewing, left center."

He spun around and went directly over as the player escalated and pushed the small woman dealer.

"Ma'am, would you like a drink?"

The bartender startled Mildred. "Ahh, yes. I'd like a vodka... no, Miller Lite." *That was close. I almost ordered the wrong character's drink. I need to get back into focus.*

Mildred paid for the beer and stood to the side, trying to disappear into the activity of the room. She sipped the beer when necessary as she slid from the room. Once she arrived at the balcony, there was a view of the lower section. Arnie was escorting the questionable cashier toward the investigation room. Taking the stairs down, Mildred spotted Detective Hampton watching the proceedings from the front roulette wheel. *If all of us undercover operatives* went home would the casino still be busy? She couldn't help but chuckle as she entered the lower gaming area.

After a couple of uneventful hours, Mildred finally threw the bottle of warm beer in the trash and started a northern patrol. She recognized a large, well-dressed man at the crap table. She tapped her earphone. "Hampton, if you are on, scratch your ear."

It was only a moment later when he scratched his ear and ran his fingers through his hair.

"Brenda, are you on?" There was no answer. "See the big guy in the navy windbreaker? Back two tables." Hampton picked up his chips and moved causally. "He blends in and is to the right of the shooter." The detective started toward the busiest table. Mildred continued to talk. "I think he was one of the fake FBI agents. No, I could be wrong. Damn, I know him from somewhere."

Mildred walked over to the women's restroom, concerned about being recognized if he hadn't already made her. *No, I know now. He is the second guy with the unmarked rack of chips. He looks like the faker, but isn't.* She quickly returned to the floor and noticed Hampton walk up and start a conversation with the suspect. Mildred could only assume what was said. Then she saw Hampton lean forward and place a bet. There was a win on the pass. He reached for his winnings and dropped some on the floor. The suspect shook his head in disbelief and then helped picked up the chips and handed them to Hampton. They laughed and she watched manly back patting, then the detective walked toward the men's room.

Mildred stepped out as he was about to pass, and mumbled, "You could have a career in security."

He didn't answer, but she could see a smug expression on his face.

The overhead speakers announced that the Blue Collar Comedy Tour would be starting their show in ten minutes. Mildred started toward the entertainment venues, expecting a big turnout. The crowd was lined up for the main stage. Since Perry was near the entrance, Mildred continued to the pizza stand and checked out the offerings. With a slight delay, she turned back to the older section's main floor. Mildred approached just in time to witness an elderly woman throw her drink at the Jewel of the Nile slot machine. As she was raring back to throw her purse, Mildred took her arm and spoke gently.

"Can I help you?"

Frustration was clear on the woman's face as she sighed. "I need to go home. Can you find my husband?"

Mildred asked about games of choice and a brief description as she walked her over to the customer service counter, where they took over. Mildred continued the patrol and heard a page for housekeeping and Samuel Albritton to report to customer service.

Unsure of Perry's location, she continued through the gaming tables and finally back to the new section to watch for bad chips. The third cashier window was still closed, there was no expectation of them being stupid enough to pass off much. The man in the navy jacket was gone and everything seemed to be moving smoothly. Mildred took a seat with a view of the pit boss station and picked at her nails as she watched.

As per usual, after two o'clock the shows were over and the nightclubs were closing. The slots stopped singing for the night and the hardcore gamblers stayed settled into the tables. They were always the last to head home; often leaving just in time for the retirement village buses to arrive. Mildred was tired, and her thoughts were searching for too many answers.

G-ma out.

Employee exit – walk u out.

Mildred smiled as she leaned against the post at the exit. *Arnie has walked me to my car most nights since I started, almost two years now.*

— 25 —

Pancakes and FBI

Click, beep. "Hi Grandma, I've been home for almost a week and haven't seen you yet. I was wondering if you wanted to go for breakfast? Oh, this is Glory."

"Hello, don't hang up, I'm here. I'd love to do breakfast, sweetie. What time are you thinking?" said Mildred. They proceeded to chat for a while when they agreed on an hour at The Egg Nest. As Mildred started to hang up the phone, she heard another girlish voice in the background begging to go too. Ready with fifteen minutes to spare, Mildred left a note on the kitchen table for Arnie, fed and cuddled the cats. She was first to arrive and, on a hunch, she got a table for four.

Mildred felt relieved to not worry about counterfeiters, liars, and cheats as happiness took over. With barely enough time to order coffee, she heard the gaggle of Petrie girls come through the front doors. The guess had been right. All three granddaughters were there and looked hungry. Mildred couldn't imagine anything more complimentary than the girls arguing over who would sit next to her in the booth. The server had to come back twice as they were so busy talking to make any decisions on food. Once they ordered, the conversations began to settle. Izzy continued to chatter about a new class on computers, using terms Mildred had never heard of or imagined.

The server delivered platters of eggs, bacon and way too many pancakes. The girls went silent as they dove into the feast, with only a slight struggle over the syrup. It was Glory who set down her fork and broke the frenzy.

"Grandma, I want to catch up with you. Since I'm not twenty-one yet, I'm taking some criminal justice classes at the university. I'll have better opportunities after my birthday."

Mildred looked up from her plate. "You are very wise, my love. You are getting close. Have you submitted any applications yet?"

"Not yet. I want to have the cyber investigative and crime and society classes first."

Mildred could see her granddaughter blush ever so slightly. "You know I have connections. So I could introduce you around."

"I hate to do that, Grandma. I want to succeed on my own."

Mildred smiled. "There is a lot of competition and you should use what you have to get in. Then you prove your worth."

Glory brightened up. "I do like the idea of having a letter of recommendation from Officer Millie, McGruff's helper." Even Izzy laughed with a mouthful of pancake.

"That was some years ago. Do you really remember?" asked Mildred.

"You betcha. I used to brag in grade school that McGruff was my grandpa."

"Seriously, a letter from your grandmother doesn't add a lot of credibility. Why don't you get your resume together, along with your class results and I'll introduce you around? Can't hurt." As she spoke, her cell phone buzzed.

Mildred checked. It was a text. "Speaking of connections, here is one now. Detective Block wants me to come by the station in a half hour. Why don't you come with me?"

They settled down, finished eating and paid the check. They walked to the parking lot and by then Glory had agreed to go. "I drove the girls, Grandma, so I have to go home, but I'll come by and pick you up as soon as I drop them off."

"The hell you will, I can drive," announced Amelia. "But you have to include me if there is anything on Grandpa's investigation."

They agreed on a plan. Mildred and Glory waved as the other two girls pulled from the parking lot. "Makes me feel old, seeing you three mature and dash into adulthood." Glory reached across the front seat and patted her grandmother on the shoulder.

During the drive to the station, Mildred shared the details about the investigation into Granddad's possible murder. Glory was very curious about who broke into the storage. She had helped her dad clean up the mess. She giggled as she pointed out that it took a criminal act to get her dad to get rid of the boxes of girly baby clothes.

They walked in together. The desk sergeant was busy when he waved Mildred through. There was a quick wink and salute at Detective Hampton as they passed through the bullpen to Elton's office. The FBI agents were with Elton, standing at the whiteboard. Mildred tapped on the door and waved. He motioned for them to enter. The two agents turned the board toward the wall, but both Mildred and Glory saw Dick Petrie's official photo near the middle.

One of the FBI agents approached them. "Mrs. Petrie, so glad you could make it in so quickly."

Mildred had to scan the ID around his neck. "Good to see you, Agent Moreno." Mildred introduced Glory to the agents and Detective Block. Mildred mentioned Glory's recent graduation and the men nodded approvingly. "Has there been any progress?"

Elton spoke. "There was a mother lode of information that deals with a lot more than Captain Petrie's death. We are calling in more support to hand off some of the other investigations."

Agent Franklin interrupted. "We are focusing on your husband's case and would like to take a supplemental statement. Do you have time now?"

"I'll make time. Is that okay with you, Glory?" Glory nodded her head and Elton motioned for her to sit in next to his desk. Mildred could almost hear her granddaughter's mind gathering information.

Elton assured Mildred they would be alright and made a call for some soft drinks to be brought in. The two FBI agents took Mildred to the small interrogation room. The interview didn't take long. She affirmed the police had found Dick's body in the car, parked in an abandoned lot near their home. Mildred had been taken to the station and didn't see him until he was processed and ready for identification with the

Medical Examiner. It had all been handled like other officer suicides. The sadness returned, but Mildred continued.

"As sad as my loss was, I had noticed he had pulled away and would isolate himself. I had accredited his death to depression and loss of the daily challenges. He seemed to fit the pattern for so many officer suicides. Even though we were moving and downsizing, he would disappear for hours. It fit the usual checklist."

Mildred noticed that the questions became more detailed and repetitive. If she didn't know better, it would have felt accusatory. They didn't seem to believe that it was a relatively happy marriage of over forty years. She explained that they both worked for the same police agency and added a mention of outreach as Officer Millie and McGruff the crime-fighting dog.

Franklin was the one to ask, "Where is his gun?"

"His service weapon wasn't returned. I assume it should still be in evidence. He had a second Glock that I have locked in a safe in the back of the closet." Mildred had a sudden thought, "I wonder if those imposters took it? It's in a metal gun safe. I don't use it and don't even think about it." She stopped and then added, "Both of our prints would be on it. I had it out last year for one night. Then I relocked it and stuffed it away. Never wiped it down. In fact, I never even cleaned the darn thing."

The agent scribbled some notes and inquired after details of the gun. When Mildred returned to the office to pick up Glory, her granddaughter was chatting with Elton and Detective Hampton.

"Sorry about breaking up the party, but I need to get this young woman home before I have to feed her again."

Both men stood as Glory gathered her sweater and bag. "It was great seeing you again. You have an amazing grandmother, Miss Glory. I'll do a reference letter for you this week," said Elton.

Hampton added, "I will too. Let me know if you need anything else. Mildred, I'll see you later tonight."

"Mildred, do you have just a moment before you leave?" asked Elton.

"Sure." She watched Hampton and Glory walk into the squad room. She sat down at the chair directly opposite the detective.

"They have completed the secondary autopsy on Captain Petrie. The FBI used a specialized team. They are ready to release his body for reburial. The reinterrment will be next week back at the original burial plot."

Mildred was momentarily stunned. They had had his body for so long, she had tried to dismiss the next step. "Yeah, sure. Let me know exactly when so I can be there."

She started to tear up as Elton spoke. "It will be Wednesday about eight in the morning. That is when the cemetery is the quietest."

"I'll be there." Mildred rose to leave, and Elton came around the desk, hugged her and walked her out to join Glory who was waiting in the outer office.

– 26 –

Next

Seven a.m. came earlier than expected, but it was important to Mildred to be there for Dick's reinterrment. It was comforting to think of it in those terms and not "buried." She was stunned by her numbness and memories of when they had met on the bus, and how he had gathered up her broken mess of youthful disappointment.

Mildred had planned to watch from the sidelines, but when she arrived at the cemetery, Richie and his entire family were already there. Each girl held a small bouquet. With barely time for greetings, a backhoe roared up and began to dig. The casket arrived shortly afterward and was left next to the bewildered family gathering. Mildred waited for the equipment to back away before she approached the casket. She was silenced by the feeling of loss, overwhelmed by how it felt so new. Every one of the family members took a moment as the workers paused before returning Dick to his resting place. They left the flowers on the casket as it dropped out of sight.

Mildred was touched how Izzy behaved; she had only been seven when Dick had died. Mildred stepped back and recognized the wonder of the girls that lived because she had met that incredible man. It broke her heart for what her love had missed.

Mildred hadn't been home other than to pick up things since the faked search of her condo. Glory asked to go with her to see damages and if anything was missing. When she unlocked the front door, it was clear that the two searches had left a disaster. The drawers were pulled out, and most were dumped. The forensic team left a bigger mess than the intruders. Every drawer and the floor around it had fingerprint powder. The mattress was pulled off the bed and was cut open. The closet was stripped and things were thrown all over the bedroom. Mildred started to cry.

Glory put her arm around Mildred. "Don't worry, Grandma. I'll take care of it for you. I have nothing planned tomorrow."

"I'll pay you whatever you want."

"You don't have to pay me. You do so much for us. This is the least I can do. We're family."

Mildred took a deep breath and looked directly into Glory's eyes. "I will pay you whatever I want then. No more discussion. Do you still have your key?"

Glory reached into her purse and pulled out a key fob. "Yes, ma'am. Here it is."

"Be sure the place is empty when you get here. I can't imagine any problems, but be careful. I can only guess what they were looking for," said Mildred. She picked up a slip of paper from the floor and wrote on it. "Here is the code for the alarm system."

"I can guess. When I helped dad clean up the storage, he told me about the boxes of cold cases you two found. He didn't even tell Mom. I wonder who knew about them."

"Now you mention it; I didn't tell anyone either. I gave the boxes to Detective Block, but I didn't mention to anyone where they were found. I must have told Arnie, I don't remember doing that, but he has mentioned it. Like they say, no such thing as a coincidence."

"Somebody has information. I don't know who to trust other than you and Dad."

Mildred worried as she picked up some mail from the floor. "I agree with you; I'm rethinking everyone." Pulling out her key ring, Mildred continued. "I'll be right back. I'm going to check the mailbox." She stopped and stared at the key ring.

Glory slid a drawer back into the cabinet. "Do you have storage here? These places usually provide that."

"I never thought about that and Grandpa never said anything about it. The manager should be in; we can walk over. Let's see what there is. I could use a place to put some of this stuff."

The manager was available and seemed aggravated that Mildred was unaware of the storage rooms. They were sent to the rear of the complex community building and entered a code he provided to a door marked Residents Only. A light came on, and they could see it was a long hall of numbered doors. Mildred checked the extra key. It said 119. As they walked through the hallway, lights would come on as they searched for the corresponding door. Everything was silent. Not even a breath could be heard as she turned the knob. The door opened to what appeared to be an empty room until the light clicked on. In the back of the deep narrow room was a rickety card table with files, a camera and Dick's old tape recorder. His dress uniform was hanging on the back wall. Mildred recognized Dick's writing on the folders. There were two more file boxes covered in dust.

Glory approached and took Mildred's hand. "We best not touch anything. Do you have someone you absolutely trust at the police station? How about the FBI agents?"

"That's the trouble. I trust all of them. I'm frightened there seems to be so much going on that I am oblivious about. I did some amateurish background checks last year and everyone seemed clean. There is something else. Grandpa was on to something, and I think he was killed because of..." She waved her arm around the room. "This. Dick and his obsessive investigations."

Glory sighed. "Dad must have got that from Grandpa." Mildred was unaware that her face was covered in tears until Glory tried to dry her eyes with her shirt sleeve. "Grandma, I want you out of this. Don't tell anyone, not Mom, not Dad, not Arnie, no one. I'm taking over, so give me the key and tell me who you trust the most."

With a big intake of breath, Mildred spoke. "You are right, but I don't want to pull you into this. It's dangerous stuff."

"Grandma, I'm trained, remember? Also, I'm an unknown. So who do I contact?"

Mildred pulled her phone out of her pocket. "Elton. Here is his private cell number. Just remember we don't know what's in the boxes. It could be Grandpa's books or baseball cards. We have no idea."

"Baseball cards? That could be worth something. From this moment on, you don't know anything. This is on me and Detective Block. I will only report anything to you in person, not by phone or text. Okay?"

"Okay. Does this mean you won't be cleaning my house?" asked Mildred.

"Yes, I will, but I have to go home first and change. I'll use that as my excuse for how I found this. Just remember, this room does not exist." Glory led her Grandmother out of the storage room and the light went off as they closed and relocked the door. They walked back to Mildred's condo silently. Glory instructed, "If you don't need anything from inside, get your bag, lock up and take me home. Then go to Arnie's, get your nap and go to work like usual. Take this completely out of your thoughts and tell NO ONE."

"Are you taking a bullying class at the university or something?"

"This isn't bullying. It's leadership and decisiveness. Get used to it." Glory took Mildred's keys from her hand and unlocked the car, getting into the driver's seat. She then tossed the keys to Mildred. "Now set your alarms, lock up and no more discussion. I've got things to do."

They pulled into the driveway at Arnie's house and Mildred was relieved that the truck was gone.

Fully aware she needed some quiet time to put things into perspective, she entered the side door, where both cats greeted her. She filled their bowls with food and, after a quick snack, the cats followed Mildred for a needed lie-down. The purring and headbutting helped calm her conflicted emotions. As Mildred drifted off to sleep, a decision to keep Dick's memory as her main focus and, as per Glory's instructions, let the discovery go for now.

– 27 –

Churros

Awake with two hours before work, Arnie still wasn't home. Mildred showered and decided to go as Grammy Crumpet. Her new disguise consisted of the curly blue-gray wig and she added a shiny blue tracksuit, pairing it with an Ivory Winds Casino Tee-shirt. After scrubbing off all of her make-up, she added a dark shadow under her eyes and donned the no-correction glasses from the dollar store. Mildred was ready. She hadn't eaten lunch and the missed meal had caught up with her.

G-ma on the floor.

Early?

Hungry.

Como in – at Berbere. I'll buy.

Mildred made a quick turn. She was not someone to turn down a free meal. She was thrilled at the opportunity to try the Ethiopian restaurant. Scanning the dining area, she didn't see Perry right away, but finally, in the rear corner booth, he waved with the menus in hand. Mildred slid into the opposite bench, smiling at his bald, old man persona.

"Peter Cane, I presume?"

Perry nodded and answered, "Two nights in a row. I like the shoes and the fanny pack. You're new.

I wouldn't have recognized you right away if I didn't know better. It looks like you tacked on an additional fifteen years."

"I'll take that as a compliment. Have you ordered yet?" Mildred opened the menu and scanned the pages. "I haven't eaten here before and I don't know what things are. What do you suggest?"

"Wat for a beginner."

"That is what I asked. What should I order?"

Perry smiled and shook his head. "Wat is a wonderful stew. They have the Doro Wat tonight. It is my favorite."

They settled into a quiet conversation about the unique food and descriptions. She learned that Perry ate there almost as often as Mildred went to the buffet.

The injera bread came first and as they tore off sections, Perry asked, "Are you alright? You haven't seemed the same."

"I'm so sorry. With the counterfeiting and the distraction with the stuff we found with that key, I'm not myself."

"G-ma... ah, I'm sorry, let me know when you name this character. I only know a little about this and I understand."

"They brought in the FBI and did an autopsy on my husband,. He was reinterred this morning."

Perry looked deep into her eyes. "Oh, I didn't know. I would have come."

"Thank you, but you didn't have to do that. It was at eight this morning, not our finest hour. I meant to go alone and was surprised when my son and family beat me there. Even though we already had a funeral. I just had to be..." Mildred's eyes started to mist. "Well, you know."

The food arrived. After only a few bites, Mildred promised herself to come back. The flavors were complex and still basic.

Perry changed the subject to the counterfeit chips and the cashier they took in. He didn't have any information, but discussing suspicions helped. They shared concerns about many of the same suspects which convinced them they were on to something. Mildred would take the first shift in the gaming area.

The rotations had been smooth when she received a call from Perry. "I've got a suspect on the floor."

Mildred turned toward the wall to hide the conversation. "Where is he? I'll tag along for a while."

"Big 6. Moving. Gotta go."

The next rotation was close, so Mildred had already worked her way that direction. She was able to walk directly to the new game area. As she approached, she recognized the suspect walking toward her and Perry was visible a short distance back. With a lazy turn toward a gift shop, she was able to track back around and get behind the target. Perry rolled off and she took over. This guy seemed intent on his path direct to the tables in the original game section. Craps? No. Blackjack? No. Roulette? Yes.

Mildred settled into her favorite slot machine with a good view. He didn't have the usual rack but pulled chips from his jacket pocket. He started to bet. She noticed Arnie was on the floor behind the craps tables. She clicked on the main communication line.

"Chip suspect on the roulette wheel in the original section."

"Which one?" Belinda answered.

"Tall, older guy in dark blue windbreaker."

It was only a second or two when Belinda answered. "Got him." There was some background talking, and then she continued. "Robin will continue to follow. Hampton got his fingerprints back."

A third voice spoke, "Thought we used channel six? I'm on my way over. I have a warrant. This guy is connected. Stick with him until I get there then roll off."

Mildred saw Arnie's attention change to a direct focus as he shifted position, turning towards the game in question. Mildred spoke. "He doesn't have a rack, but is pulling chips from his pocket."

Mildred switched to channel six and brought Perry up to date. Perry advised he would move on to the upper-level card rooms with a standard patrol. Not ready to roll off, Mildred reinserted her player's card, made a small bet, and watched as Detective Hampton moved in next to the suspect. Hampton took the suspect's arm and whispered into his ear. Arnie appeared on the other side, taking the other arm. The three men walked away from the table toward the hidden door toward the interrogation room.

She calmly played a couple of pulls on the slot machine, won seven dollars and walked toward the hotel and gift shops. She texted the office.

Follow up, Clanton pit boss just walked in and turned back out.

10-4

Within a couple of minutes, the answer came. **Clanton scheduled – no sign in.**

No matter how curious she was, Mildred was fully aware that she wouldn't know much of anything for a while. *Note to self, follow up on Clanton. Report suspicions to Hampton.* Her usual patrol continued toward the restaurants when she passed Perry. They didn't speak or make eye contact. Mildred turned toward the nightclubs. The music was beginning to blare from the entrances while the bars filled. There was a shout that appeared to be coming from the Sahara. Mildred turned towards the sound. The lights were dim so she couldn't see through the two-way glass. The entry was blocked by a large, young man who had obviously been drinking. He was yelling and grabbed at the server.

Mildred called in using her earpiece. "Security, Sahara ASAP."

With no time to wait, Mildred stepped into the trouble and held onto the man's arm as he was trying to shake the server. The woman's fear and anger were clear on her face as she struggled to maintain a hold on her tray.

"Hey, bitch, this isn't about you!" and he knocked Mildred away. By the time Mildred hit the floor the bartender was involved in the melee. Pulling out her Taser, Mildred held back to be sure she had a clear shot. The troublemaker wouldn't let go of the waitress. "I want my money, you thieving whore!"

The waitress was struggling to break free and screeched. "Sir, you didn't pay me anything."

Mildred jammed her feet into the back of the irate customer's knees and he went down, meeting her on the floor. A security guard entered at that moment and threw himself on top of the man. A second guard was right behind and secured the belligerent customer.

The waitress reached for Mildred and took her hand, helping her off the floor. "Thank you. Why did you step in? He could have hurt you."

"I don't know," answered Mildred. "Guess I just hate bullies and violence."

A sob escaped the young woman's lips. "I forgot to ask, are you alright? Did he hurt you?"

"Honey, I'm fine. How about you?" Mildred brushed off her backside and straightened her wig.

"I don't know. I wouldn't serve him because it was obvious he was impaired. Then he wanted the money back. It was all so fast." The bartender directed them to an empty table and then returned to the bar. In moments, he brought two glasses of water.

Mildred pushed the tray aside, then told her, "You will probably hurt tomorrow, just pay attention. Better yet, go over the clinic when you get a break. You need to be checked out."

"Okay. Can I buy you a drink or something?"

Mildred stood up and kissed the young woman on the top of her head. "No, honey, I'm on my way to dinner with my friends. You take care." The bartender tried to get her attention before she left, but Mildred chose not to notice, passing the on-duty nurse rushing in through the main door.

Almost immediately her earphone buzzed. "Where did you learn that takedown? Not in the security handbook."

Mildred snickered. "Learned it from Popcorn, my cat."

"We will need him to do a training film. Oops, gotta go. I'm saving that tape."

"Later, Larry."

Mildred walked straight to the churro stand and ordered the *mas grande* order and a Champurrado. Settling at the empty table, Mildred sat facing the window to the parking lot. The adrenaline was still surging and she knew something would ache tomorrow. Staring at the crowds of people entering the main door, they seemed excited and ready for a great adventure. This wasn't the first, nor the last time she would celebrate the Mexican treat in an African themed casino. Try as she might there were no African desserts she knew of at this moment. Maybe tomorrow.

Her reverie was disturbed by a familiar voice. At the table directly behind her, Arnie had slipped in and whispered as he held a paper cup to his mouth. "Are you alright? I heard on the radio and rushed to find you. Have you been checked out?"

Mildred swallowed and took a sip of the hot drink. "I'm fine. Probably won't know until my butt bruises come out tomorrow."

"Why don't you go home? We have a full shift of security and Perry is here."

Mildred signed. "I still haven't recovered from reburying Dick. I feel as if he is with me."

His voice raised. "He probably is. I'm still upset that you didn't tell me? I would have gone with you."

"I know, but it was eight a.m. and you were barely home." Mildred bit a churro in half and swallowed with only minimal chewing. "It isn't any big deal."

"It was a big deal. I don't care how many times you have to bury someone, it's tough. Even more if you loved them. Promise from here on out, you will keep me informed. I've worried all day. Hell, all week something has seemed off."

"I thought I'd be back before you woke up, but Glory went home with me and helped with the clean-up. I didn't realize that I, ah..." Mildred caught herself, almost said too much.

He murmured, "Realize what?"

"That I had kept so many of Dick's things. She lectured me about cleaning out that darn closet." In this moment, Mildred realized that silence would be difficult. She was used to telling him everything. Finishing her Champurrado, Mildred stood. "I have to get back to it. Liars and cheats need to be wrangled. Later, Romeo."

Mildred walked away and could feel his eyes on her. She began to sway her hips in her best impersonation of Mae West, confident that she could throw him off until she could settle her concerns.

The night settled down to just busy and Mildred decided to take Arnie's advice. It had been a painfully long day. She checked with Perry, who was fine taking over. Mildred started toward the back door.

G-ma out.

There was a quick response. **Walk u out, usual spot.**

Mildred sped up slightly. There was no telling when Arnie would arrive at their usual spot. She was about to pass the hidden door to interrogation when it opened and Arnie walked out. He didn't notice her being slightly behind. Then she saw a young, well-dressed man pulling the door closed from behind Arnie. Their eyes met and held for just a second as if they recognized each other. Mildred continued to the usual exit and met Arnie by the post under the camera.

"Glad to see you are taking my advice. You look tired," said Arnie.

Mildred giggled. "You have already told me this is part of the disguise." She took off the glasses and stowed them in her bag. "Who was that guy you were with in the back hall?"

He hesitated. "James Ivans. He's the new board member, the attorney. He came in to meet management."

"Management? Pretty late for management, unless he meant you?" asked Mildred.

"Don't forget Belinda and Larry. He seems like a sharp guy. I don't know anything about him. In all these years, never has a board member made that effort."

"I felt like I knew him. He must look like someone from back in the day."

Arnie waited as Mildred unlocked her car. "Yeah, he's the only one of the new board members I've met one-on-one. I mean he came to us and we weren't sent for." He leaned in to kiss her. "Where are we sleeping tonight?"

"Your house. You have my cats and I need a cuddle, a rub and a purr." Mildred kissed him a second time and started the car. He pushed the door closed and waved goodbye.

– 28 –

Open Eyes

Mildred had disturbing dreams through the night. She noticed it was nearly five a.m. when Arnie crept into the room. Not completely awake, she was in a near-dream state as she watched him gather pajamas and tiptoe into the bathroom. With barely any noise, the light went out and he moved the cats to the foot of the bed. She felt the weight of the bed shift, then his CPAP machine started. Mildred rolled toward him and kissed his forehead, away from the sleep mask and whispered, "Goodnight." Without a word, he cuddled next to her and they both relaxed and fell deeply asleep.

Mildred woke around one in the afternoon, but couldn't garner the energy to open her eyes. It was the insistence of Louie and his message of empty bowls that moved her. A quick stop in the downstairs bathroom, she washed her face and went to feed the cats and make coffee. Almost mesmerized, Mildred leaned on the counter and watched the dripping liquid filling the pot. She heard Arnie enter the kitchen when he stopped to talk to the cats before wrapping her in a giant hug.

"Want to go to Denny's for breakfast?"

Without turning around, Mildred could tell he was still bare-chested and in his pajama pants. "Tell you the truth, I don't want to go anywhere. Let's put something together here."

"Deal! I had to ask." He immediately went to the refrigerator and pulled out eggs and some frozen sausage links.

Mildred opened the bread box and pulled out the half loaf. "We've got this covered even better than I expected."

In less than a half hour, they were seated in the matched recliners with TV tables and a movie playing. The day stayed calm with little talk of work. When it was time to get ready for the night, Mildred finally got showered and dressed. She decided against a disguise and arrived exactly on time.

G-ma on the floor.

10-4

Her earphone beeped and it was Larry. "Mildred, have you talked to Hampton yet?"

"No, just had a quiet day. What's up?"

"They found our pit boss, Paul Clanton. Looks like a suicide."

"A WHAT!" Mildred surprised herself with her outburst and looked around, but no one seemed to notice. *Old woman invisibility pays off again.* "Do you have any details?"

"Not yet, except the basic fact. I was hoping you knew. Can't talk now." Larry disconnected the call.

Mildred almost collapsed onto the stone bench near the main door. *I just saw him last night. He must have been escaping more than just from us.*

Her mind went back to Judge McCaffie and the connections he had with organized crime. *I thought we had cleaned it up, but it must go deeper than we imagined. I need to reinterview the judge. No, not me, but someone. I've got to talk to Hampton.* She felt as if she had sat for hours, but it was only a few minutes. There was so much demanding her attention, and it was getting difficult to separate work from home. After a deep breath, she stood and started a patrol of the north end of the casino.

Como in-house.

10-4

With no particular plan, Mildred tapped on her phone. **Meet interrogation.**

His answer was almost immediate. **Be there in 5.**

Mildred was in a gift shop and purchased two packs of M&M Peanuts and exited directly toward the hidden door. The door was open when she entered the back hall and Perry was sitting at the table with two lattes. He pushed a paper cup over to her and she threw a pack of candy to him. Perry's face lit up as he tore open the package.

"What's up, boss?"

"We need to check in with each other. Did you hear about Paul Clanton?"

Perry shook his head. "No. I know that he cut out after we started gathering up the suspect."

"They found his body last night, possible suicide. Larry couldn't tell me any more than that. Did you hear anything from Elton?"

Perry pulled out his cell phone and made a call. Mildred sat quietly as he spoke to, she assumed, his son, Detective Block. He rose from his chair and paced the room as he acknowledged what was being said. It was obvious he was getting a serious report and she was anxious for details.

He finally said something she could understand. "Lunch tomorrow at Jake's, your turn to pay. See you then."

He walked out, but before the door closed, he was back in. "This was supposed to be a quiet little retirement job. Here is the dope. This looked like a professional hit, hastily made to suggest suicide. There were certain signature clues that the FBI operative recognized. The M.E. has the body, and there is an autopsy in process. The shot was from under the chin and a Glock 22. The gun only had Clanton's prints and was left on the floor of his car at the scene."

"Stop! That was the same as my husband death. This is too much." Mildred was shocked and getting angry. "Do you think that's possible?"

Perry waited before he spoke. "Elton didn't mention anything about that, but I'll bring it up. He said that Hampton was handling this because of the casino association. I guess someone found him out. His car was found back behind the parking lot near the woods. Some kids found him when they went out there to smoke."

"Oh, my gawd, kids. Did they see anything?" Mildred reached back to the counter for a notepad and pulled out a pen.

"Elton didn't know. He isn't officially part of the investigation and only did a quick briefing with Hampton. He's concerned about you being a common denominator and wants me to watch out for you."

Mildred couldn't stop the blush. "So you end up being an under-undercover guardian? Don't worry about me. I'll stay alert and try not to be goofy."

Perry's face lit up as he responded. "Not be goofy! Please don't take on more than you can handle. Let's keep in closer touch, by cell privately. I'll walk you out when you leave,and we need to meet more. How about a code?"

"Onomatopeia – Banyon Tree? We might want to think about this further. Arnie usually walks me out; has since I started working here, but I'll let you know if he is busy. It isn't a hundred percent. I agree about working closer together. You need to learn that I refuse to live scared, but things are tense." Mildred tore the page off of the notebook, folded it, stowed it into her jeans pocket and stood to leave. "Oh, one more thing. Did Elton tell you about the storage?"

Perry thought for a second before he spoke. "No, I don't remember anything about a storage unit. He is a professional, you know. He doesn't discuss all of his cases with the family."

"True enough. I seem to have lost that skill. I'm working on it though. There's just something I'm missing. Guess I'll kick up my vitamin D. With the counterfeiting possibly contained, it could help. I'll pull the first game room shift."

He dug into the package and pulled out the last M&M and slid it to Mildred. "Here is some extra vitamin M, hope that helps. Now get out of here. I'll clean up."

– 29 –

Tuesday So Soon

"Do you want me to let the cats out of the carriers?"

"Thanks, Arn. They will love seeing everyone again. If you put up the groceries, I'll get the turnovers in the oven and make the coffee."

Mildred was running late since she had had to stop at the store before returning to her condo for the weekly meeting. The oven timer dinged as Bud looked through the door and announced himself.

Arnie went to the door and helped with the insulated food carriers. "Hey, Bud, what is the surprise today?"

"I'm not sure. Chef Mike wouldn't let me peek. He had it packed and ready when I walked in." Bud unzipped the first carrier and pulled out a huge casserole dish filled with breakfast burritos. The other was huevos rancheros.

Arnie looked like a vulture ready to strike. "That is a lot of food. Do I have to wait for the others?"

Mildred shook her head, rolled her eyes and opened the oven to hold the dishes. "Calm down and answer the door."

No one had knocked, but Arnie knew to do what Mildred asked. When he opened the door, the rest of the crew were approaching, with bags of donuts and muffins. Mildred looked at Bud and could almost read his mind. This group was family, and everyone carried part of the weight, but Mildred was sure there was a weak link somewhere and that might have been what got the pit boss killed.

After serving up the food and all of the polite conversation, they settled in for business around the dining table. The front door opened slightly and Detective Hampton stuck his head in.

"Everyone here? Have room for one more?"

Arnie waved him in and gave up his seat while he moved to the stool at the counter.

"Hampton! Fill a plate. We are anxious to hear about any reports you may have." As he poured a mug of coffee with a touch of creamer, Mildred dished up a plate. "Eat and then talk. We are all waiting."

As soon as he sat, the questions started to fly about the possible suicide, counterfeiting and the two that were arrested. Hampton chewed for what seemed like a week. He gulped coffee and put his cup down. "Much of this is still under investigation. We are hoping to get one of the suspects to talk, but I really can't share anything yet. Have you had any other bad chips show up since Saturday?"

"No, but I've met with the supervisors in accounting and scheduled to attend their meetings," said Bud. He held up a fresh muffin. "But they don't have near as good a team as security."

"Remember, Bud, they don't have a secret team," said Perry as he shined his nails on his shirt, looking smugly at the group.

"True enough. Mildred, Perry, Robin, please take a bow," said Bud. "We wouldn't have solved this so quickly without you."

After Bud made the announcement, the meeting went back to socializing, drinking more coffee and discussing plans of a few days off and regular hours again. It was suggested and agreed to start meeting every other week unless there was a problem.

With no major issues staring at them, the group broke up earlier than usual. The leftovers were wrapped and moved to the refrigerator. Arnie started up the dishwasher while Mildred began gathering the cats for their yearly vet visit. Popcorn was in the carrier, but Louie wasn't nearly as compliant. There was a knock at the door when Mildred was on her hands and knees after the cornered cat. She was relieved to hear Arnie greeting her granddaughter, Glory. With two hands full of wrestling cat, Mildred entered the living room and tried to hug her.

"Am I too late for the donuts?" asked Glory.

Arnie left the room immediately to get a plate. Mildred smiled. "You are in the nick of time. Sweetie, what's up?"

"Oh, just hoping to see you and I know on Tuesdays there are usually extra treats in the refrigerator." Then Glory looked toward Arnie, putting a plate in the microwave. She whispered to Mildred, "I need to talk to you in private."

Mildred nodded and spoke loudly. "Can you get that other pet carrier open before this monster draws blood? Hey, Arnie, I'm letting you off the hook about the vet. Glory will help me."

They could hear him clanking around the kitchen. "Sure, Cinnamon Bun. I need to do some work around the yard at the house, so I'll head over there."

Mildred winked at Glory, as she walked into the kitchen. "Kiss me, old man. We've got to go. See you later."

Glory ate quickly and then picked up the heaviest pet carrier. As soon as they had both cats loaded, Mildred started the car and didn't speak until they cleared the parking lot. "Now you wanted to talk. What's going on?"

"I don't know how to tell you, and I don't know what any of it means. It has to do with the stuff in the storeroom?" As Glory sat quietly waiting, Mildred could see contradiction on her face.

"I met him and the FBI agents and let them in. They were gathering the materials. And ah, ah... I don't know what to say exactly."

"Glory, just tell me."

"You know I like Arnie. He has been so good for you and he's kind. Well, I stayed back and watched as they gathered the papers and file folders. You know Elton didn't let me dig through stuff."

Mildred stared at her granddaughter, trying to read her intention. "Yes, sweetie, I know. What does that have to do with anything?"

After a deep breath, Glory reached for her grandmother's hand and squeezed it while she spoke. "Grandpa had a picture in a folder on the table. It fell out as they were packing things. It was unmistakable who it was. He was younger than today, but on the back was the name Arnold Baghetti." Glory kept talking quickly, not allowing her grandmother to ask any questions. "I didn't say anything, but Elton looked at me and shrugged his shoulders. He looked stunned too. I had to tell you."

Mildred could barely speak, she whispered her questions. "Is there anything else? Any reasons?"

"Nothing yet Grandma. He could be a good guy working with Grandpa, or, I don't know. All kinds of possibilities. I made Detective Block promise to keep me informed. He said not to act hastily before they can dig into the information. Please give him some time. He said it's a priority and will call as soon as he has anything at all."

"But, ah, hell, I don't know."

"Pay close attention and don't jump to conclusions, Grandma. Leave that up to me. I'm very good at making things up."

"I need to think about this. I trusted Arnie explicitly. I've told him almost everything, except about the new storage unit." Mildred's voice choked on the words.

Then she went mum, set her shoulders, and shut off the car. She gathered Popcorn's carrier and Glory followed her grandmother's lead with Louie. They entered the veterinarian office. Mildred was friendly but reticent as she took care of her pets.

When back in the car. Mildred looked at Glory before she started it. "I truly love who I think he is. I don't know what to do."

"Grandma." Glory hesitated for a moment before beginning again. "We don't know what any of this means. Maybe he was working with Grandpa. Maybe they knew each other another way. I'm going to follow up with the detective and I'll be sure you know everything as soon as I do. For now, I think you should continue like there is nothing different. But please, please, pay attention."

"I don't know if I can. I believed in him. If he knew Granddad, he would have said something, and the different last name, I just don't know if I can go back. Love and trust are the same thing and I'm feeling foolish and used."

"I can stay with you. I'm turning twenty-one in three weeks and starting to get applications out to the police departments. Arnie knows that, no big surprises."

"Okay, this gives me a plan. Arnie knows that I've taken reburying Grandpa hard. We can use that. You're staying with me until you find a job and know where you will be located..." Mildred drifted off in thought.

Glory picked up the suggestion. "Because they are turning my bedroom into a game room, er, an office."

"Thank goodness I have the cats out of his place. We will need to pick up more food. Supposedly he's at home working in the yard. I'll start developing my story for you staying here."

"At least for a day or two. Once we get you and the cats home, I'll go see Elton and pick up some things from home. Do you need me to anything else for now?"

"I have a lot of food there from the meeting. I think we're good for a few days. All of my female disguises are at his place, but I still have some hats and Oliver, so I should be good for a few."

Once a plan started to manifest, Mildred was able to put her emotions on a back burner. She could decide later if she was frightened, mad, or overreacting to nothing.

— 30 —

Guesses

G-ma on the floor.

   Hungry?

Mildred nodded to the camera just past the main entrance and kept walking. It was nice to realize that Belinda was still in and their dinner plans were on. Continuing into the first bank of slots, Mildred texted Dr. Q and received a confirmation. The night was starting perfectly as she entered the Nairobi café and saw Dr. Q already had the back table. She had a quick flash of memory of when she had first met Qaseema, still in housekeeping, cleaning the floors and saving a choker. In the past two years, she had finished her medical recertification and been promoted. *How things change and time flies.*

Belinda entered the restaurant about five minutes later and the three friends re-bonded over salads and nightly specials. It was a surprise to Mildred how much she missed spending time with them. Mildred wanted to talk about her concerns, but stuck to her plan of secrecy, at least for now. They gossiped and laughed and talked about Belinda's twin babies and Dr. Q's new husband, Detective Hampton. Mildred asked if either had ever met Arnie's dad. Neither had. She then diverted the conversation away from her questions, staying evasive.

Mildred was reading the dessert menu when Belinda blurted, "Qaseema, you are pregnant! I can see it now. How far along?"

They both watched as Q blushed and bowed her head. "I have yet to take a test. What caused you to say?"

"Remember I just had a couple of them. I can see it on your face."

Mildred laughed and reached over to hug Q, who was usually shy around public displays, but this time she hugged back. "Now that you mention it, I can see it too. Does Hampton know?"

"I will tell him when I know for sure." Q covered her mouth as she giggled and blushed a deeper color of red. The conversation slipped into stories of pregnancy humiliations and promises of used baby clothes.

Mildred checked back in as she left the restaurant, filled with hope. She was able to still her constant query into why her husband would have a photo of Arnie and who the hell Arnie could really be. Since it was Wednesday and Perry was off, she started a patrol from south to north. Stopping from time to time, Mildred would play a slot and watch a spin or two.

As the night clicked on, Mildred avoided Arnie's usual patrol patterns. There was a minor issue in the large gift shop with a talkative older woman walking out with sunglasses on. It was easily resolved with a nervous laugh and twenty dollars. A wet chair at a winning Queen of the Nile slot machine and a minor confrontation in the Sahara Nightclub as the band was starting were the main problems. The night would stay slow and Mildred decided to check out at midnight.

G-ma heading out.

As expected, there was an immediate response. **Out front by circle drive, walk you out.**

Mildred was not surprised as this was their habit. She tapped in a response, **C U.** Not sure how long he would be, she waited by the large column just out of view of the valet parking station.

She stared at the stunning display of a clear night when she noticed the new member of the board walk past the other side of the post, toward a red T-Bird in the reserved parking. *Wait, Arnie said he was the new board member.* She finally placed where she had seen him before. *He was the attorney at Tim's office that arranged for the sisters' release in the sex traffic ring. What the hell is the connection?*

Mildred almost jumped when she heard, "Cinnamon Bun, I've missed you." Arnie gave her a quick kiss as he stepped out of the line of sight from the entry. "I can hardly wait to sneak into bed with you again."

"I'm sorry, but it was more upsetting than I expected. I realize Dick has been dead for several years, but I was with him over forty. I still love you, but I feel like I'm cheating."

The tears of frustration began to sneak from her eyes and Arnie comforted her as they walked to the car. "I do understand. Take the time you need. I have no intention of going anywhere. You call, I'll be there. Got it?"

Mildred nodded as she started the car. He wiped her tears with his shirt sleeve and closed the door.

Mildred watched as Arnie stood in the parking until she had pulled away. Arriving home, Mildred noticed the light was on in the living room. She was surprised how happy it made her to have Glory there and awake. Inside, the fold-out couch was open and Glory was sitting there with her tablet. One of the late-night talk shows was on, but the sound was low.

"How did it go, Grandma?"

"Fine. It was a quiet night and I avoided Arnie until it was time to leave. He usually walks me out so when I told him about my feelings about Grandpa, the tears started. He was so supportive and said I should take it easy. But I think I've got something." Mildred picked up her laptop and sat in her favorite chair. "I have to email Tim Selkirk, an attorney I know. Just realized that the new young board member at the casino was the guy that helped get the two sisters back home to the Ukraine or Russia, I don't remember which. I knew them and..."

"Is that the pimp shooting in the parking lot last fall?"

"You have it. I knew he looked familiar but when waiting for Arnie, I saw him again and it suddenly dawned on me where I'd seen him before."

"Wow, do you know his name?"

"Yes. Ah no, I forgot." Mildred stopped typing.

"I've got it." Glory made a couple of quick taps on her tablet. "Here is the list of board members. Do you see one that fits?"

Mildred reached for the tablet and scanned the line of names. Most names were familiar, but there were two she didn't know. "These two are new. Let's search and see if there are any photos of them." It was only a moment before Glory had something on the first one. She couldn't find anything on James Ivans. It was as if he appeared out of nowhere until recently. "This has to be the one. Hopefully, my friend can identify him." After a few searches and guesses, they found James Ivans in the Bar Association directory and Mildred recognized him. She started an email when Glory spoke up.

"Grandma, stop. We have to talk to the detective and the team. I'm going over tomorrow. I'll set up a real appointment in the morning."

Mildred's computer pinged and she was stunned as she looked. "It's from Tim Selkirk. I didn't expect him to be up this late. He confirmed the name." Mildred answered right away, teasing about losing sleep and asked for a meeting. Mildred closed the computer and stood to go to bed. "Lunch tomorrow, Glory. Better get some sleep."

Glory broke into a hearty laugh. "Right, Grandma, you eat more than anyone I know. I'll try to sleep, but it won't be easy."

She shut off her tablet, turned up the volume on the TV and snuggled down into the blankets. Mildred kicked off her shoes and scooted in next to her. They watched a black and white movie with only vaguely familiar actors. They woke up to a news show. Neither spoke until Mildred checked the time.

"We have an early lunch meeting. Do you want to skip breakfast?"

Glory flipped off the television. "I'm good with just a cup of coffee and a shower. I'll make coffee and you get the bathroom first."

Mildred rolled out of bed, still dressed from the night before, and ran to the bathroom. "How did you know?" Within a few minutes, she came out to gather clean clothes. "Do you need the bathroom before I get in the shower?"

That was when Mildred realized Glory was on the phone. The girl walked in, continuing her conversation, and shut the bathroom door. She was still talking when she exited, explaining their work from the night before. With her hand over the phone she mouthed *Sorry I didn't flush.*

Once Mildred was ready, she came out for coffee and to allow Glory time to get ready. Glory walked to the bathroom and before she closed the door, she said, "Your guy Elton will meet us at Lilly's Diner and he won't be alone. I also called your attorney friend, and he will be there too. Why did every one of them insist you are paying?"

Mildred laughed. "Because it is usually the first one there pays."

She made sure that she had her credit card just in case. They were off to lunch twenty minutes early, and, as luck would have it, they were the first ones there. Elton had called ahead to reserve a private dining area. They left the door open to watch for Tim, who came in with Elton and the FBI agents.

Tim was the only one who didn't already know Glory. He walked directly to the women, hugged Mildred and introduced himself to Glory. "Has your Granny told you how we met yet?"

Glory looked confused. "No, it was for the Russian women, right?"

He laughed quietly and winked at Mildred. The group settled into a polite conversation until the food arrived. As soon as they were served, Special Agent Franklin stood and closed the door. "Time to get serious. The information you provided, Mrs. Petrie, is extremely broad-reaching. I'm glad you brought your attorney. The coding in the school books, as well as the zip drive, have years of information on organized crime. The only way you could have gathered this was from the inside."

Mildred looked at Tim and then answered. "First, I don't have an attorney. Mr. Selkirk is my friend."

Tim put down his fork and looked at Mildred. "I'm her attorney now."

Mildred nodded and continued. "I was sent a note and had a phone call directing me to the information. Elton was informed and involved at every step. I had nothing to do with gathering it. I don't even know what is there."

Elton stepped in and confirmed everything. He appeared aggravated. "I explained this to you before. I have worked with this woman with other issues, and I guarantee with my reputation and my right arm, that she has been cooperative and open every step of the way."

Glory interrupted. "I understand that you have questions. We all do. But we called this meeting with our questions. Gran, did anyone tell you what was involved with the books you were given?"

"No, I only got to touch them to hand them over. I relinquished the key within the agreed twenty-four hours. I don't know who sent it. Everything was unsolicited and unknown." It was obvious Mildred was angry.

Glory and Tim each reached for Mildred's hands. Glory spoke first. "We are here with questions." The agent started to speak, and Glory turned to him and hushed him. "We are talking about my grandfather's cold cases files. When you confiscated them, I saw a photo of my grandmother's boyfriend... no, that sounds stupid... her lover."

Mildred gasped. "Ewww, Glory, let's use partner, no, that isn't it. My close friend. Yes, there, friend."

Elton began to chuckle. "Arnie is also a good friend of mine. I have worked closely with him. I was even at his father's funeral." He stopped and looked at Mildred.

She nodded and added, "At least I think it was his father."

Elton continued. "Anyway, we are working on a background. It looks like Arnie appeared about ten years ago when the casino opened. We are searching for records with both names and have found a minor arrest record for a young Arnold Baghetti that would be about the same age, but nothing definitive yet. He inherited the house with the death of his father, Anton Arneson. I'm even working on the old man's background. At this time, it is too early, and I don't have more to add. Mildred, I don't think you are in any danger and if there is anything shady, I will drive to his house and kick his ass myself."

There were a couple of half-hearted apologies and Tim made it clear if they wanted to talk to her again, it would be through his office. The rest of lunch was quiet and as they prepared to leave, Mildred excused herself. When the rest of the group exited, she had already settled the bill. Mildred rejoined the group as they left.

"Hey, Elton, I almost didn't pay for the FBI guys. But seriously, I'm suspicious and trying to find out if anyone at the casino met Arnie's dad before he passed. Nobody yet. I'll talk to Bud and keep you posted."

Elton looked at the FBI agents and hugged her while he whispered. "They seem like asses, but I've been watching and they are really good. So much I can't tell you, I'm sorry. Something's about to come down."

Mildred nodded and walked over to Glory and Tim. "First of all, Mr. Selkirk, thank you for stepping up to be my attorney. I hope you aren't expensive."

He smiled and said, "You can ply me with salads and pie."

Mildred said, "Now the real reason I called. The attorney who helped the two prostitutes involved in the shooting of the pimp. Do you know anything else about him? I've wondered how that agreement was accomplished, with no charges or court involvement."

He thought for a moment and finally answered, "I don't remember off the cuff how they processed this through, but I assumed they greased some wheels to take care of a potential problem. These women had nothing and were the true victims. He suggested they didn't want the attention right then. I jumped on the chance to help them get away. I did double-check where the tickets were to, then we cashed them and changed the location to add a layer of protection."

"I think I've seen that lawyer around the casino. I'm not sure, as I only had a glimpse of him at your office and maybe at the courthouse when I sent for that darned key." Mildred hesitated only a second. "Do you remember his name or have any information?"

He looked thoughtful. "I haven't worked with him, before or since. I know he is new to the area. Aw, hell, he is young, probably new to practice. His name is James Evans, no, Ivans. I'll pull the file and see who he is associated with."

Mildred waved for Glory and turned back to Tim. "What can I do to learn more?"

"Penny has dinner plans tonight at the Berbere dining room at the Ivory Winds. What's a good time to talk?"

Mildred's face lit up. "I'll go to work early, about six-thirty, before it gets busy. Let me know when you are there and I'll look for you at the restaurant. They don't know me there and it's dark."

"Let's make it at one of the clubs. They are dark and not really busy that early, but noisy." Tim made a note on a small notepad that seemed to appear from nowhere. "She will be at the Sahara at eight, so I'll meet you around an hour before. I won't be able to dally."

Mildred giggled and Glory looked suspicious. "You know damn well Penny dillies and dallies any time she wants."

He waved and walked away, "Oh, how I know."

"Come on, Glory. I need to go pick up my Delilah disguise."

— 31 —

Moving Along

G-ma on the floor.
> Looking – oh there you are. My fav.
> Quick meet Sahara.
> 10-4

Mildred found the rear booth empty. Only a couple people, mostly at the bar. This place wouldn't start hopping for a couple of hours. Mildred/Delilah parked her walker next to the wall. She had to lean out to peek at the door. She was about to sit back upright for a break when the energy in the room changed. That always happened when Penny Dumple entered a space.

"Penny, back here."

"Oh, my darling, I wouldn't have known you. Rocking the red. You will have to give me the recipe for those breasts."

"Water balloons, now sit down. The butt is doll pillows and granny panties."

Penny nodded in approval. "Good to know for my later years. I have to be quick. Plans have changed and I need to be across town by eight." Mildred leaned in as Penny continued. "James Ivans is a relatively new attorney. He is part of a powerful firm, but not a partner. I, personally, have questions about the firm.

They are known to defend high profile criminal cases and some of the upper echelons of organized crime."

With a quick hush, he was giggling when the bartender approached to take their order of two iced teas, one Long Island and the other unsweetened.

Penny continued, using her regular voice. Mildred found it unnerving to see the beautiful, flashy woman being discreet. "Ivans has a couple of little things on his sealed juvie record as a kid. Both parents are deceased and his dad did time for the murder of his mother. He has a fascinating background. If I ever do a book, it will be about this kid."

Mildred/Delilah smiled. "That's a relief. I worried you would write about me."

The boisterous Penny's laugh filled the booth. "Now, Mildred... I'm sorry, I don't know what to call you... turning you into fiction would be unbelievable."

"Delilah Hopper. You can call me Delilah."

"Delilah, perfect. Anyway, I couldn't dig too deep. I didn't want to flag anyone who may be paying attention."

Mildred added, "I parked in valet, and his sports car is here. I was hoping he would show up while you were here. I want to be sure."

"That would be handy, but I trust you and seeing the law firm he is with, any answers only pose more questions." The bartender brought their drinks and they both simply sipped. Penny/Tim's phone buzzed. "Shoot, I have to go. My Lyft is here."

Mildred waved and reached for her orange handbag in the walker basket. "I'll get the bill as part of my attorney fees."

Penny/Tim's face lit up as he stood and leaned in to kiss Mildred on the forehead. "Damn right. If I get anything else, I'll be in touch. These are tough dudes. Be smart."

Mildred watched Penny sashay out of the bar as she drank more of her unsweetened tea. It was time to go to work. Mildred left money on the table and waddled out, pushing her walker into the first patrol.

It was nearly ten when Arnie caught up with her in the off-track betting room. "I got your note. Sure wish I hadn't missed you. Is Glory doing alright?"

Mildred held her betting sheet up to block her face. "Yes, she is alright. They are remodeling her room. You know, paint, carpet, that kind of stuff. She noticed I was having an emotional time, so she is staying with me for a little while."

Arnie walked over and checked the betting window and walked back. Mildred continued, "I do miss you."

"I know." Arnie looked at her briefly. "We have something special. I plan to walk out with you every night. As long as the creek don't rise."

Mildred smiled and started to scoot her walker forward. "Don't you mean roll me out?" She continued to leave to check on the high limits card rooms. *Whew, that went well.*

Her earpiece clicked. "I love you."

Mildred tapped to answer. "Who is this? Clark Gable, Rock Hudson?"

The earpiece almost lit up with a variety of voices, only some familiar, all saying, "It was me." The last one sounded like Robin.

"You guys are hilarious." Mildred turned down the volume and continued.

Perry's voice came on. "And you assume the message was for you? I'm lovable, too." Mildred's laugh caused several card players to turn and look at her.

"You aren't scheduled to work tonight." She continued through the mezzanine.

Perry continued, "Anywho, I'm in for a computer date in the showroom area. Didn't go well. Where are you going next?"

"I'll continue upstairs and work down to the hotel and restaurants." They worked out a loose route, and he would wink as they passed in the big slot area.

The evening was well behaved with only one call for housekeeping to clean-up after a drink was thrown at a cash machine and a drunken slip and fall in the west entry.

G-ma out.

Meet you at back door.

I'm parked in valet.

Out front.

Mildred was seated near the front door when she saw Arnie rushing toward the doors. She stood and started pushing her walker out. He held the door for her and then walked ahead. The valet approached.

She gave him her ticket and $3. "I'm close. Take care of the others; I want to walk."

The valet offered to help with the walker, but Mildred waved him off. Once clear of the bright lights, Arnie slid in next to her from the shadow of the pillars.

"There you are, Cinnamon Bun. I wondered why you parked here. I forgot about that damn walker."

Mildred started talking about the events of the night when Arnie interrupted. "I came by for brunch late this morning, and you weren't there. I folded up the hide-a-bed for you."

"Oh, I didn't notice. Thank you so much. Glory and I met with Elton for an early lunch."

He put his hand around Mildred's waist. "Did he have any new information about Dick's death?"

Mildred knew she had to think fast. "No. Glory is almost twenty-one and I was making sure she was introduced, trying to get reference letters. Luckily the FBI agents came along and she had a great meeting."

"I didn't see you at Denny's."

Mildred gave him a quick hug and answered. "Note to Arnie, there are other restaurants in town. We went to Lilly's. I haven't been there in years."

She kept the conversation going about what she ate and how good the service was until they were at the car. He helped her wrestle the walker into the trunk and suggested she consider getting a new one that would fold easily.

As usual, Mildred got into the driver's seat and started the car. He kissed her passionately and closed the door and watched her drive away. Mildred sighed, relieved that Glory would be at her home. She was confident that the more truth her stories contained, the better.

Unlocking the door and pushing it open quietly not to disturb her granddaughter, Mildred noticed the TV was off and Glory was asleep with cats cuddled on both sides. Mildred locked up and carried her laptop computer into the bedroom. It was a relief to take off the wig, bra, and shoes, as she set up the pillows at the head of the bed so she could do her report.

Once finished, Popcorn had joined her and was sound asleep. Mildred noticed how bone-tired she felt with the cat where her legs belonged and wondered why she didn't want to disturb an animal that slept sixteen hours a day. She was about to shut down the computer when, on second thought, Mildred sent a private email to her boss. **Bud, did you ever get to meet Arnie's dad?** One more trip to the bathroom and she turned the light out, squeezing her feet between the cat and the edge of the bed. There would be more to think about in the morning.

— 32 —

Changes

"Oh! Sorry, Grandma, I didn't know you had company."

Mildred jerked awake as Glory covered her face on her way to the bathroom. Her eyes went to the other side of her bed. Arnie was there, completely dressed, and sound asleep. Her first question was *how* followed by *why*. A brief second later Mildred realized she hadn't dreamed that kiss goodnight. *After all, he does have a key.* Glory came out of the bathroom while Mildred tried to sit up. Glory made a grimace, wrapped in an apology, while she tiptoed back to the living room. Mildred checked the clock. It was nearly ten. She moved carefully, covered him with the throw blanket and crept to the bathroom. Then, wrapped in her bathrobe, she closed the bedroom door behind her on the way to the kitchen. Glory had already started the coffee and was sitting at the counter.

Mildred poured a cup and sat down. "Guess I didn't dream that goodnight kiss. I didn't even realize he was here; did you hear him come in?"

"I didn't hear either one of you. I took an allergy pill last night and they knock me out. Didn't you invite him?"

Mildred could feel a flush creep up her neck to her face. "We both have keys to each other's place and stopped inviting months ago."

"Don't be embarrassed, Grandma. You are an adult and he has always seemed to be a great guy who loves you to the moon. Something you can't fake. Tell you the truth, I don't want you to ruin a good thing because of unsubstantiated suspicions and I'm here for a while, so there is that."

"I like you living here. Are you as hungry as I am?" Mildred started to get up.

Glory smiled as she finished her first cup. "I have no idea how hungry you are, but I'm ready to eat." Mildred filled both cups as Glory went to the refrigerator for eggs and anything else that might make a meal.

"There is a ham slice in the freezer."

Glory opened the freezer and found it full of Pepperidge Farm turnover packages, but after a quick search, she found the ham. "My dad tells stories about the turnovers, but I never dreamed it was as bad as this.."

"Oh hush, those are for the Tuesday meetings. Even those folks tease me about them, but 'Katie bar the door' if I don't have them." Mildred got out possibly the world's oldest waffle maker and a box of pancake mix.

They didn't talk much as they prepared different specialties. The food was ready to serve when the bedroom door opened and Arnie walked out. His hair was all pushed to one side and his uniform was wrinkled. "Good morning, beautifuls. You two don't have to make me a tray. I'll eat out here with you."

The women looked at each other and laughed. There was no hint of a tray for him. Glory quickly cracked three more eggs, adding them to the ham scramble, and Mildred filled his favorite mug with coffee.

They all took a stool at the counter and talked of last night's casino adventures and Glory's resume and her plans for a future. Once finished, the young woman shooed them out of the kitchen with a promise to handle the clean-up. Mildred turned on some music and folded up the couch while Arnie went to the other room. A short time later, he appeared all dressed and brushed.

"I have to head home. Another doctor's appointment this afternoon and I need to get a shower."

"Wait a minute. I did a load of clothes and I have a basket with your stuff in the laundry room." Mildred left him standing at the door. "You could get ready here if you are pushed for time."

Arnie took the basket from her and leaned over kissing her lips. "Thank you, Cinnamon Bun, but I have errands to run. I'll see you tonight." Mildred held the door open and watched him leave, waiting to wave as he pulled out of the parking lot.

"Cinnamon Bun? Grandma, that is so cute. Why does he call you that?" Glory was watching from the dining area.

"I wouldn't let him call me baby or sweetheart. Told him that if he was going to go the nickname route, it better be an original," said Mildred.

"I had never thought of it that way. Hayden better watch his P's & Q's."

"Hold it, Missy. Who is Hayden? You better dish some details." Mildred plunked down on the couch.

"Oh, ah, nobody. Just a guy I know in my college courses. Speaking of which, do you mind if I take the bathroom? I have a class at two-thirty."

"Sure, but you aren't getting out of this so easily." Glory brushed her off, picked up her small suitcase and went to the other room. Mildred called after her. "Details, I want details, maybe a photo." The bathroom door slammed. "And a background check."

The door reopened and Glory called out. "Don't touch the coffee mug on the counter. I'm taking it in for fingerprints."

Mildred turned immediately to the kitchen and saw Arnie's mug in a ziplock bag. That image brought her back to the nagging insecurities that she had let slip for a few hours. She retrieved the laptop computer from the side of her bed and plugged it in. Lifting the screen, she signed in and checked email. There were four ads, something from LinkedIn that she didn't understand and one message from Bud Moses.

> **Now that you mention it, I never did meet his dad. He had Alzheimer's, and there was mention of nurses, but I never met the man. – Bud.**

Mildred began a search of nursing services and sent emails when Glory came out of the bathroom, all showered, dressed, and full make-up. "Is Haybarn in the class today?"

"Hayden, H A Y D E N, and yes, he is. We aren't dating, just a couple coffees and ice cream, but he is really smart and," Glory stammered. "I really like him."

"You are out of his league and he is damn lucky. You are amazing, and please let him know that I might be seventy-two, but I can still kick very high."

They laughed and continued to straighten the kitchen. Glory broke the silence. "I'm going to run by the cop-shop, so I'm leaving early. I'll be back by four or six."

"Call me with any problems, but otherwise I trust you. Do you have any money?" Mildred reached for her bag and pulled out forty dollars.

Picking up the coffee mug, Glory answered. "No need, I'm okay."

"Take it for later. It is a babysitting fee. Or better yet, hush money."

She took the mug, money, and kissed her grandmother goodbye.

Mildred didn't plan on researching Arnie's stories, but that was exactly what she did. It started with nursing providers, cremation services, and then to the ownership records of the house. They showed that Anton Arneson was still on the deed, with no record of his death. The questions expanded as things didn't line up. After a few hours, Mildred changed her password and slammed the computer closed. She went to lie down so she would be ready for work and noticed her cell phone had moved from the charger and was on the floor next to the bed. She plugged it back in as the cats began to nudge and headbutt, demanding attention. Once they settled, the purring helped Mildred calm down and, surprisingly, sleep.

Mildred was struggling into her elastic waist pants when Glory came home. Adding the blue-tinged curly wig and glasses, she came out to welcome her back. "You hungry? I'm going over to the buffet."

"No. Pardon me. I don't know your name."

"Grammy Crumpet, glad to meet you."

"Charmed, I'm sure. I've already had dinner."

"With Haystack?"

"Yes, Mrs. Crumpet, with HayDEN."

"Cool beans. I changed the password on the laptop. I was doing some deep diving on Mr. Arneson. So, if you need to sign on it is..."

Glory interrupted. "I don't need it. I have my tablet. Did you find anything?"

"Surprisingly little. Bud has never met his father either, so I got digging. I called nursing companies, telling them I wanted to make sure the bills were covered by insurance and if they had any remaining balances. Couldn't find any accounts. Property taxes and stuff."

"I'll work on it some more. What is that password? Just so I don't duplicate any efforts."

"Frankensteen-244-Hat."

"What?"

"It had to be something that no one would hack. I loved *Young Frankenstein*, and the numbers mean nothing they just jumped into my head."

"Hope you wrote those down. Detective Block is supposed to get back with me tomorrow on the prints. I'll see what else he might have. You better get going. It is almost seven and I have studying to do."

G-ma on the floor.
10-4

Buffet first.

Have the rollatini.

Mildred walked into the buffet and claimed her favorite table when she saw Perry at the salad bar in his bald, old man disguise.

She crept up behind him and whispered "Caprese."

He swung around quickly, with cherry tomatoes flying off of his plate. "Funny!" He put his plate down and picked up the tomatoes when a buffet server came around and took over the cleaning. "Are you at your regular table?"

Mildred grimaced. "Well, that suggests I need to change things around when I have a regular anything."

"Elton called and he has a bad feeling."

"Bad feeling? I know what you mean."

Perry continued to build the salad. "Why don't you join me? I've got that table over there." He pointed. "In the middle of the action."

"Will do, Mr. Cane. An old couple is less noticeable than two odd singles. We can talk about bad feelings," said Mildred.

He grinned in agreement and picked up a second, larger plate, moving on to the entrees. Mildred designed her dinner, starting with the eggplant rollatini and a spoonful of fettuccine alfredo. She left her plate at his table and walked over to pick up her drink and receipt. After too much pasta, two panna cottas and a shared tiramisu, they started the first patrol as a team. They worked together and occasionally split off. It was getting late when Perry went to the sports betting while Mildred policed the slots. They rejoined for a lite beer and a Shirley

Temple at the MozamBeat. Double teaming helped stop Mildred's obsessing over truth and lies.

It was the end of the night and Mildred had noticed that Arnie hadn't pulled a patrol.

G-ma out.

Como out.

There was no answer and Arnie didn't rush to respond about walking her out. *He is probably busy.* They both tend to park in lot G, outside of the cameras, so the new – old – couple walked out together.

Perry held her car door open and said, "Grammy, don't forget this weekend is the Miss Universe Reunion. I think you can blend in, so don't worry about a disguise."

Mildred couldn't help but laugh. "Maybe you should come as your alter ego Lola Finesse and teach those beauties how it's done."

Perry joined in the laughter. "Don't think I have time for the pedicure and the wax. How do you women keep it all up? Good night, Mildred. See you tomorrow."

He shut her car door, and she watched him walk over to the other lone vehicle in the clearing lot. She started the engine, and before she pulled away texted Arnie's phone.

Missed you. Everything alright?

Pulling away from the parking space, Mildred sat at the stop sign and decided to make a quick check. His pickup truck wasn't in the employee lot.

Looking at her phone, no answer. With a quick drive past Arnie's house, she discovered the truck wasn't there either.

— 33 —

Room 431

Mildred's first thought when she awoke in the darkest part of the night was of Arnie. She checked her phone. He hadn't responded to her text. The clocked continued to click off minutes slower than usual. Mildred caught herself manufacturing reasons why she hadn't seen his truck. Finally, she settled on the assumption that he was busy, but that only helped her sleep in short fits. Petting Popcorn as she drifted deeper into fear, her phone beeped with a message. Nearly jumping straight into the air, Mildred was shocked to see light entering the room as she ran to her charging phone on the dresser. It was from Elton.

A trip to the bathroom was followed by a plan to call him when she was ready for the day. The hot water was running over her head when Glory knocked on the shower door. "Grandma, Detective Block is here. Hurry up."

It took a few minutes for Mildred to rush into the living room, fully dressed with wet, dripping hair. "Good morning Elton. No pictures, please." She could see the concerned look on his face. Turning, she also greeted Agent Franklin, but a deep feeling of dread swept over the room. "Sorry to keep you waiting." She looked around. Glory was pouring a line of mugs with fresh coffee.

"I called to let you know we were on our way." Elton opened a folder and looked at the agent. "This is an update on the information you provided."

Mildred was initially confused by what he meant. "With the key? Is that the stuff you're talking about?" Elton nodded. "I was wondering what was there."

Elton continued and was much more serious than she had ever seen before. "Arrest warrants went out last night and this morning. Several big cases have opened up and it goes very deep. They brought in the Baltimore mob boss late last night. There is an indication that his influence was more extensive than we expected. All hell is breaking loose as they are searching for and arresting people all over the east coast."

Glory spoke first. "How does this affect my grandmother?"

"We don't know, but we found a contract had been put out on Captain Petrie over seven years ago," said Agent Franklin.

Mildred nearly dropped her cup of coffee. "What the hell? Is this why you had your dad stick with me all last night?"

"I couldn't say anything," Elton said. "And I didn't know how deep this would go."

Mildred's face contorted in thought. "That was before Dick retired, but not by much. Any idea why?"

Elton looked at the agent and back to Mildred and Glory. "I don't have anything substantial yet, but the department is in disarray. Some officers are implicated in different departments. Don't forget Captain Petrie's cold cases are moving in on them. I can only guess that someone somewhere used you to turn on them."

Mildred pondered. "You took the cold cases. I only looked at a couple of them. Do you think that Judge McCaffie was in deeper than we thought? Dick had a bunch of dirt on him."

Elton continued speaking to the agent. "The Judge did prove to be dirty, and his wives were taking payoffs from the same group. He has been under house arrest for a year."

Franklin interrupted. "Special Agent Moreno is to meet with him today for a statement."

Glory repeated her question, only louder. "How does this affect my grandma?"

"We don't know. Somehow you are caught in the middle of this," said Agent Franklin. "Do you have somewhere else you can stay?"

Glory looked alarmed. "Grandma, we can go to my house."

Mildred responded, "Sweetie, we don't want to place the family in danger."

"I'm here to suggest the safe house," said Elton.

Mildred brushed away the suggestion and faced Glory. "How about you and I get a suite at the casino? It's public and I have friends around 24-7. Don't forget room service."

Both men seemed resistant, but finally agreed. Franklin spoke first. "Keep it secret, please. We don't know what is what."

Mildred held her finger to her mouth. "Oh, and by the way, I haven't heard from Arnie since yesterday around noon."

Elton dropped his eyes to the folder. "Thanks, Glory, for the prints yesterday. The forensic team noticed that they appeared to be burned, and there was a juvenile record that was sealed. We did scare up three other aliases, but nothing serious or violent. I'm sure his real name is Baghetti and we are working out the transition to Arneson. The research was interrupted by all of the other warrants and high-profile arrests."

Mildred looked at her granddaughter. "How soon can you move?"

Glory took a deep breath to answer. "As soon as I pack a few things and I get these cats in a carrier."

"While you do that," said Elton. "I'll call Hampton and have him check you in. He is supposed to be over there already. Text him when you are ready and I'll have him meet you with the door cards."

"I'll call Bud and have him check me in and Hampton can pick up the cards from him. I get a discount."

Glory stood up and turned back. "I have class today. Do I have to miss it?"

"No, we don't want anything to look suspicious. There is no threat that we have heard of." Elton looked at Franklin, who nodded in agreement. "Just a bit of over-caution. I'll let you know if anything changes."

Agent Franklin stood to leave. "Let us know if you see Arneson and for now don't be alone with him."

At one-fifteen, Mildred unloaded two suitcases at the casino and noticed the red T-bird drive past slowly a row away from where she stood. Not wasting any time, Mildred went directly to room 431. With a single tap, the door was opened. It had been arranged for Glory to meet with Detective Hampton at one o'clock for the room cards. That way Mildred could avoid the front desk. Mildred stood and looked around the double room. "Damn, if I had checked us in, we would have a suite."

Glory shook her head, then answered, "We are in hiding, not on vacation, Grandma. This is nicer than my single bed at the Petrie manse, not to mention the fold-out couch. I talked to Dad and he understands. He agrees I need to stick with you. He promised to keep everything secret. Well, other than talking with Mom."

Mildred rolled in two suitcases, one filled with cat food, supplies and a small bag of toys. Glory had brought the large cat carrier with both cats. Not wanting to be stopped, Hampton had carried them up. There was a flush and Detective Hampton walked from the bathroom. "I was searching to be sure the room was clear."

"Thank you for your service." Mildred rolled her eyes and continued. "I'll go ahead and work my regular shifts. Have you found anything about the death of Paul Clanton?"

"No, everything is hush-hush. I'll be here more, at least while the arrests are underway. Did Elton give any other instructions?"

"No, he hopes this might be a little overreaction, but I feel better not being at the condo. It seems like everyone and half of their families know where I live." She lifted the suitcase onto the rack and the cats stood at her side as she opened it and took out their bowls. "Glory, don't you have school this afternoon?"

"Yea, I'm ready and leaving in a few minutes. I'll get there a little early so that I can finish my reading assignment."

"Let me know if you will be staying after class for Hayburner. Please."

"Will do." Glory proceeded to gather her book bag and kissed her grandmother. Detective Hampton left to walk Glory down to the car.

Mildred flopped on the bed, surprised how stressed she felt, even though they were only being cautious. Popcorn pulled away from the bowl and laid down next to her, followed by Louie. She stroked both cats and the calming purrs hushed her fears. Any time a police officer said *this is probably not necessary* that told Mildred it was. She drifted off to sleep and didn't wake up for two hours.

With a slight movement, Mildred turned on the television, and a news channel was already on. About to flip the remote to the usual afternoon fare, she saw Agent Franklin in the background at the police station. The reporter was standing on the street, microphone in hand, discussing newsworthy arrests. Mildred knocked the remote to the floor and as she struggled to turn up the volume, they posted a list of names and pictures of men she hadn't seen before. The story ended with the message that this was broad-reaching into police, courts, and government. Unable to move initially, she finally was able to hit search and she found the story was on every channel. Mildred sat up and rewatched the story on national news. She assumed she was the unidentified source. Only a few knew that she was simply the conduit for the real source.

Her first thought was for Glory, then her phone beeped. It was Arnie. "Where are you? I'm at your place. Were you kidnapped?"

Mildred knew she had to keep everything quiet even from him. "I'm with Glory. We went to lunch and are thinking about a movie."

"...and the cats?" She could hear the angst in his voice.

"I had to take them back to the vet for follow up shots. They are keeping them overnight." *Aw, hell, Arnie.*

"What is it, the movie or the vet?"

"Oh, my. The vet is on the other line. I'll call back." Mildred's heart sank and tears flooded her face as she stared at the phone. *Arnie, I can't lie to you. It should only be another day or two.*

She opened a text and tapped. **I love you. Talk soon. <3**

266 Mildred Raising the Ante

− 34 −

The Usual

G-ma on the floor.

10-4.

Meet interrogation – Como.

Mildred walked directly to the secret door and down the hall to interrogation. When she arrived, Perry was already seated and pushed out the chair next to him for her to sit. Neither was in disguise, but dressed casually to blend into the usual weekend crowd.

He leaned in to whisper, "I talked to Elton today. He wants us to keep close. Guess we are doing Mr. and Mrs. Cane again."

Mildred made an almost unnoticeable nod in agreement and whispered back. "We met. I've been briefed with an accent on *brief*. Learned more on the news than talking to your son."

He stood to leave and spoke in a louder voice. "That's the plan then. We will check out the fifty years of beauty queens and runner-up reunion."

Mildred waved into the camera as they turned off the light and left for the patrol. They started at the north slots and gaming tables and around to the event venues. It was stunning the number of well-dressed, thin women standing around waiting for the next speaker or workshop.

Perry took her hand and leaned down to whisper. "Damn, I haven't seen so much make-up since Max Factor and Merle Norman had the knife fight at the mall."

Mildred coughed, trying to stifle her laugh, and squeezed his hand. "You should have worn your strappy gold sandals."

He continued. "None of their foreheads move. Can't tell if they are angry or bored. Should we worry?"

"Naw, they can't run. They are too busy looking stunning..."

Perry interrupted. "And solving world peace."

"Well, at least they care. I'm sorry, I have to sit down for a moment." Mildred was shaking with restrained laughter, so they turned toward the gift shops. "Did you notice them staring at you like you were the last donut in the desert?"

"Did not." Perry silenced his routine.

Mildred had almost forgotten how handsome Perry Block was until she noticed the beauty queens taking slow, hungry, looks at the 6'2", fit, silver-haired man who was whispering and laughing.

It took twice as much time to rove through the gift shops. They were full of conference attendees. The team made up time with the nearly empty restaurants. Finally reaching the hotel, they took a break in the overstuffed chairs by the fireplace. Mildred put her feet on the hearth and felt the warmth inch through her soles and up her legs. Perry followed suit after kicking off his shoes. They sat silently scanning the room and then staring into the flames.

"Mildred, are you alright? Something seems wrong."

She was quiet for a moment. "You mean more than being in hiding because of the possibility of a mob hit, or something else?"

Perry's chuckle was mostly a snort. "Well, that and anything else."

Mildred spoke in a sigh. "I haven't seen Arnie. This is the second day. I talked to him when he showed up at the condo, but I wasn't there. I hung up because I didn't know what to say. I'm not sure if he has lied to me and if so, how much. I miss who I thought he was."

Perry scanned the room as he slipped on his shoes. "This sounds like a conversation for the privacy of a car. Hold on, I'll be right back."

He calmly walked away toward the front desk. He reached out and caught a young man by the back of his coat. Mildred watched Perry whisper to the guy. She watched him hand a credit card to Perry. Perry then led him back to the front desk and gave the credit card to the clerk. They both talked to the teen, then Perry escorted him to the door.

Perry returned to where Mildred was seated and rejoined her. This time he kept his shoes on. "Damn, Mr. Cane, nice catch. I need to clear my head and get back on task."

"You'll back me up when I need it, too. Remember there is a reason why we have four eyes. Next one is yours." Mildred noticed that when he sat back, he looked proud of his quick catch.

"Wait, wait, hold on. I might be up. See that thin guy over there?"

"The one in the black shirt?"

"No, the one ahead of him. I recognize that guy, but I don't know from where. My spider senses are clanging. I'm going to follow him. Wanna come?" Mildred stood up slowly but kept her eyes locked on the target.

"Yeah, I'm with ya."

They stayed quiet and a reasonable distance from the target. The man slowed as he approached the Sahara nightclub when Mildred tugged at Perry's sleeve. "I've got it! He was my first puker."

"Good gawd, Mildred. None of us ever forget our first puker." The target stopped to talk to someone, and Mildred and Perry slowed to check a gift shop window.

Mildred's voice stayed low and Perry leaned toward her. "He was smuggling party drugs in his mouth and swallowed the plastic bag. I met Q that night when she was still working housekeeping. I've got a feeling he didn't learn his lesson."

"Well, no evidence yet." Perry glanced over just as the suspect turned toward them. Perry moved to block the view of Mildred. "Here we go, looks like events."

"Shoot, we have our beauty queens and DJ Spin Doctor is playing?"

"Sure is. Let's stay close."

Mildred sped up closing the gap, noticing the guy had on pants with multiple pockets. "If he is carrying, he has options." The music from the DJ blared into the lobby. "Hold on, Perry. Keep with him, I'll be right back." Mildred walked to the entry and briefly spoke with security at the door and then entered the venue.

Perry continued to follow the suspect and watched as the man appeared to case several venues. They were turning back to the music when Mildred tapped his arm, causing him to jump. "Calm down, Mr. Cane. I have help." Off to the side was a young woman with a half-shaved head of purple hair. "May I introduce you to Melody, no last name." Mildred pulled him down to whisper, "PD vice."

He stood up to his full height and winked at the tiny young woman. He then coughed, pointing at the suspect and walked to the elevator for the upper-level games. Mildred took a turn through the crush of beauty queens, not seeing anything of concern. *The only thing they could smuggle in here is Botox and diet pills.* It was about fifteen minutes later that she followed Perry to the upper levels.

She walked directly to the staircase, and she made a quick tap on her earphone. "Heading down to slots and tables." She saw Perry tap his ear and continue his patrol. She then clicked to the main channel and asked, "Is Arnie on tonight?"

Larry's familiar voice answered. "He is scheduled, but I haven't seen him yet."

Mildred's heart thumped with an indescribable fear as she continued to walk the slots until she found the Hungry Hippos and sat to watch the comings and goings.

Nearly a half hour later she spotted Perry and walked over to join him. "Lots of single old men. Do you think it is the Miss Universe event?"

Perry smiled. "I can't say for them, but that is why I'm working tonight."

Mildred coughed, covering her mouth. "Bull-caff! You always work on the weekend."

Perry answered, "Yeah, we both took these later in life jobs to meet beauties and…"

Mildred interrupted. "And old dogs in polo shirts."

"Touché. Now back to creeping around. I'm thirsty. How about you?" Perry took her hand and started for the open bar near the transition of the original and new gaming rooms. It was busy, but it only took a few minutes before they were seated on the bench near the entrance with two glasses of wine and a pack of peanuts.

Mildred was scanning the various characters when she saw Glory walk toward her. She was with a handsome man, who appeared too old for her. "Grandma, I want you to meet my friend, Hayden."

Perry stood, and offered them his seat. Hayden shook his head no and then reached out to shake hands. "We are going to the bar that has the R&B group."

Mildred greeted him shaking hands and then, "Maybe you better try something else. Glory isn't of age for another week."

Hayden looked surprised and turned to Glory. "I'm not drinking, don't worry."

He looked at Mildred and said, "I think we will go to the restaurant with the pizza instead."

"I like that, Haybail. I'm impressed."

He started to correct her when Glory squeezed his hand. "Can't change her, so you have to accept my grandmother's quirks. What was the name of the Ethiopian pizza place?"

With a few more words and instructions the young couple left toward the restaurants. Perry looked at Mildred. "How old was that guy?"

"I don't know, but he seemed surprised to hear about her age. Funny, Glory wanted to get into law enforcement and was going to a club underage."

"Undercover. It skips a generation." Perry gathered the empty glasses and motioned for Mildred to join him.

By two a.m. when the clubs were clearing, the duo had spotted a cash machine assault and one panic attack in the men's restroom. There wasn't any more evidence of Glory and her date.

G-ma out.

Como out.

She waited a few minutes, and there was no response from Arnie when Perry spoke. "Let me walk you to your car."

"I didn't drive, but could you take me past Arnie's?"

"Sure thing. I didn't see him tonight. I assume you still haven't heard?"

"Not a peep."

They walked to his SUV and the ride was quiet as Mildred fought her imagination. Arnie's house was dark and his truck was still gone. Perry took her back to the casino and Mildred made an excuse about needing more desserts to avoid searching for her car. Glory had used it last and Mildred had no clue where it could be parked. Mildred then walked across the little bridge and the blocks to home. The light timers were working, but there was no evidence of Arnie anywhere. She picked up her mail and walked back to the hotel in the silence of the night. Realizing that she hadn't obsessed the entire shift and sent a silent thank you to Perry Block.

Mildred used the back stairs from the lobby to the second floor, then took the elevator to the fourth floor. Quietly, she entered the room as it was after three and Glory was sound asleep. Books took up half her bed. The black cat and Glory took up the rest of it.

Mildred prepared for bed and, as she was about to lie down, she tapped another text. **Who is Arnold Baghetti?**

− 35 −

Day Games

The light was creeping through the edges of the blackout curtains and Mildred rolled to the side to check her phone. No missed calls, no messages. She looked over to Glory's bed. It was smooth and empty. Mildred struggled out of bed with the usual morning aches that had come with every birthday since turning sixty. The walk to the bathroom was a huge help in getting her knees and hips loose again. She flipped on the overhead light and there was a note written on the mirror.

> **G-ma, Interview this morning. I'll meet you at the brunch buffet – noon. Luv ya – Glory**

Checking the time, she discovered there was an hour to get ready. With no drive, Mildred had time for a hot, leisurely shower in a place with a never-empty hot water tank. No matter how much she wanted to luxuriate, Mildred couldn't stop the nagging worries and outlandish scenarios. She inched up the heat to almost too much and the steam helped erase the tears. All dressed and polished, Mildred had a twenty minutes before breakfast, so she called Detective Block and left a message. After unplugging the phone charger, Mildred double-checked to be sure there were no missed calls or texts and decided to walk slowly to the buffet.

Seldom had Mildred been at the casino when the sun was shining through the skylights. Most of the customers seemed excited, not in the usual hypnotic state. The buses were still there from the retirement villages and the bingo hall was packed. It was a day game with a large older following. There was a bench near the entrance to the buffet and she sat to watch and wait for Glory. It was only a few minutes when Mildred spotted her granddaughter walking down the grand staircase with the young man she had noticed before at Tim Selkirk's office and with Arnie. Once they reached the bottom of the stairs, they shook hands and he turned toward the main entrance of the casino. Glory walked directly to Mildred as she stood to greet her granddaughter. Mildred was warmed as Glory's face lit up with recognition.

Filled with questions, Mildred decided to wait until they had full plates and a private table. It worked out that Mildred didn't have to ask anything. As soon as they entered the buffet, Glory opened the conversation.

"Talk about coincidence. I submitted an application hoping to get more dope on Arnie, and I was able to wrangle a meet with that James Ivans from the board. It was easier than I thought. As you could see, I met with him this morning. He said that they need another security director and with my training, he wanted to interview me personally."

Mildred found this suspicious. "That is amazing. I never heard of any directors doing interviews. Did he say someone was leaving?" asked Mildred.

Mildred watched Glory's face glow as she spoke. "No suggestion of replacing anyone, but he said they were short on the swing shift. They had enough patrol officers. With the police academy and the extra courses I'm taking, he thought I might be an interesting choice."

"Is this what you want?"

"Hell no. I've been helping Detective Block and that is more my direction, but I don't want to close any possibilities. Besides, I've heard you mention that guy and I took a chance on checking him out."

Mildred smiled. "Oh, my gal is a natural."

Glory shrugged. "I need a job as soon as possible. I can take any extra classes online or try to work it around whatever hours I have. Darnedest thing, he said he recognized my name and said he saw your name and wondered if we were related to Grandpa."

Mildred was momentarily stunned. "Oh, that is interesting. What did he say about him?"

Glory chatted on. "I guess Grandpa gave him a ride when he was leaving for college or law school." She didn't appear to notice the difference in her grandmother. "He said that he overheard them talk about what a great investigator he was."

Mildred interrupted, "Them? Any idea who that could be?"

Glory looked cocky when she answered. "Yes, he said he had been staying with his Dad's boss while finishing school." Mildred watched Glory's reaction closely. "He said he was always grateful for the ride. When I said I was related to both of you and he suggested that it was as good as any reference letter. Now, don't worry, he hasn't made any offers but wants me to think about the possibilities and get back to him the first of the week."

"Oh honey, I've heard about some big arrests going down, so don't rush into anything. You can stay with me and don't worry about money. Wait for the right job to come along."

"Thanks, Grandma. Do you want more fruit?" Glory turned to the salad bar.

"I'll get my own when you come back." Mildred's mind was reeling and she wanted to learn more about James Ivans. Something about him was nagging at her, and now he had involved Glory, who was already on her way back to the table with a small plate of bananas and grapes.

Mildred took her turn and picked up a dish of bread pudding with hot caramel sauce. They laughed and joked about health and figure changes as aging takes control.

After finishing, they walked back to their room. They both giggled at the bevy of aging Miss Universe contestants. Many were still wearing sashes with countries and states on them. Mildred decided she needed to go by Arnie's to get her wig and biker costume for the night shift. Together they went to the car, and there was a broken heart drawn on the dusty rear window. The two women looked accusingly at the other and then laughed out loud as Glory rubbed it off with a wrinkled napkin from McDonald's.

Not long after that, Mildred pulled into the driveway. Arnie's truck was still missing. Using her key, they entered the front door of the deathly silent house. Climbing the steps to his bedroom was almost spooky. Mildred felt a chill. Nothing looked like it had been touched and yet it was different. She went into the closet and gathered her disguise. It was this moment that Mildred decided to collect all of her things. She called for Glory to help. Her overnight bag was missing. That was when she noticed his toothbrush and CPAP machine were also gone. Then, checking drawers, Mildred found they were half empty. Mildred went to the top of the stairs and called for Glory a second time.

"Pack all of the cat food and everything of interest in the freezer." Something was very wrong. "Let's make it quick. I'm calling Elton."

Mildred sat on what used to be her side of the bed and noticed her fuzzy pink socks sticking out. She stuffed them into her pocket, and then dialed Elton Block's private number.

With only one ring he answered. "Hey, lady, what's up?"

"I haven't heard from Arnie. I'm at his house and it is weird. Only a few things are missing, but it feels abandoned. I also asked at work, and he hasn't checked in for two nights. He never misses."

"Calm down. I'm at home, but I'll come over."

"I'm going back to the hotel. I don't want to hang around here. I'm packing up some of my things and getting out of here."

"Good idea. What room are you in?"

"Arnie's bedroom, or do you mean 431? On the fourth floor."

"The hotel. How much time do you need? Mildred, calm down. Things are moving forward. I'll call the other agents to keep things coordinated. Say about an hour. If longer, I'll call. I also have had a call from Glory and I need to speak to her too."

Mildred stuffed things into a case and hauled it downstairs. Glory was finishing loading groceries into a large garbage bag. "We scored a lasagna, veggies, three ice creams and some frozen pork chops. What's going on?"

"I'm not sure. We'll talk in the car. Let's get out of here."

They drove directly to Mildred's condo to unload the groceries and pick up the new tattoo sleeves for work. Back at the hotel with a little time to spare, Mildred started a name search for Arnold Baghetti. There was a quiet knock on the door and Glory answered, greeting Elton and Agents Franklin and Moreno. Popcorn started to weave through Agent Moreno's legs. Glory pulled the chairs and small table over to the couch and moved Louie to finish his nap on the bed.

There were no niceties and they went straight to work. Elton confirmed what she had heard on the news. Multiple high-level members of organized crime had been arrested, with possibly more to come. They had kept her name out of the files and were being careful that she wouldn't be implicated. The investigative material that Dick had gathered was with the State Prosecutor and would not be released until the cases moved forward. Elton went on to discuss their probe into Arnie's background. They promised things would move quickly now that the prints had been processed and an FBI background search was underway.

Elton called the station and asked for a search on Arnie's cell phone and home numbers. Both cats were lying on Agent Moreno as he tried to work around them, taking no effort to push them away gently. Mildred decided that he was her favorite agent, even though Franklin usually took the lead.

Mildred looked at Glory and they nodded in agreement. The agents agreed with Elton that Mildred and Glory could move back home Sunday afternoon. Laughter filled the room as Mildred pointed out it was imperative to score the free Sunday brunch for hotel guests. When they left, Mildred overheard Franklin suggest as long as they were there, the buffet sounded good to him.

It was nearly an hour later when there was another knock on the door. It was Elton. "I thought you should know. The cell phone isn't operational anymore. He may have destroyed it. The background check confirmed Arnie's real name is Arnold Baghetti, from Trenton, New Jersey. He does have a record."

"You mentioned two other names the other day. What were they?"

He opened his notebook, and read. "He had an unlicensed arms charge and fake driver's license as Antwan Barker and something like..." He studied the page. "I can't read my notes here, Albert Blackmon. We also found that there is no Arnie Arneson. It appears that he may have moved into the house after the fatal car accident with his claimed mother Althea Carson Arneson and Charlotte Baghetti. His story was true, but Charlotte was his sister, not a fiancée. I assume he moved into the Arneson house, changed his name and made a survivor's claim. There was an Anton Arneson who had died when he was a kid. It is true that Anton Arneson had Alzheimer's, but no evidence that Arnie knew him. Looks like your boyfriend combined just enough truth to support his stories."

Mildred almost collapsed with the information and Elton walked her to the couch. "Everything was a lie; I trusted him completely. Hell, I fell in love with him and we slept in the same beds. There are so many questions. Like whose ashes were in the canister for the tree that we buried at the cemetery?"

Elton added another note to his list. "Good point. I'll get another warrant and find out. Mildred, will you be alright? Do you need anything?"

Glory had been silent, but she walked over to her grandmother, put her arms around her and answered. "Don't worry, Detective, I'm here and will stick with her." She reached for his notepad and pen, wrote her name and number. "Please call me with anything else. The more she knows, the better."

Elton went to the bathroom and brought Mildred a glass of water. "I'm sorry for all of this. There are more questions than answers, but I'm working on it." He hugged her and left.

In a very small voice, Mildred spoke. "I know there is more to this. Nothing is simple. To hell with the buffet, let's go home."

A half hour later, Mildred pulled into the condominium parking lot. They unpacked the car and last in was the crate of cranky cats. Taking care of the most important issue, Mildred went to the kitchen and filled Popcorn and Louie's dishes. She heard Glory unfold the couch and turned on the television. With two bowls, some yogurt and a box of cereal, Mildred walked back to the living room. She noticed Glory looked stunned as she handed her a bowl.

Glory squealed, "Grandma, you have to see the news." She turned up the volume and there was a series of photos of arrests.

Mildred was confused until Glory started explaining. "They have arrested crime bosses in six different cities."

The two women watched as Detective Block came on the screen. He pushed past the crowd of reporters and a myriad of questions. He repeated the same answer, "No comment."

Dumbfounded, each holding empty bowls as they watched the stories from late last night. Glory was the first to speak. "This is bigger than I thought. Do you think it was the stuff that was sent to you or Grandpa's files?"

It was difficult for Mildred to speak. "You know it is. It could be another case, but you know what they say about coincidences."

Together they said, "There is no such thing as a coincidence."

Mildred sat down on the couch and put the food on the table, staring at the television in disbelief.

Mildred started to call Elton but stopped when she realized he wouldn't be available at a time like this. The rest of the afternoon they spent searching a variety of names and news channels trying to follow the increasing stories.

Missing the usual nap, Mildred went to get ready. She texted Perry that she would be Bambi Hunter, tonight. As she was pulling on her last set of tattoo sleeves, her phone beeped with a message.

10-4 see ya front door at 7.

– 36 –

Joy to the World

G-MA on the floor.

OK.

There was a gentle tap on her shoulder. Mildred was startled and jerked around. It was Perry, in a beat-up biker disguise which matched Mildred's Bambi Hunter. The sight of him released some of the tension and she could deal with the evening's patrols.

She offered a fist bump and spoke, "I have a quick errand. Which way are you going? I'll catch up."

Perry smiled and Mildred noticed he had his front teeth blacked out. "Since the Miss Universes are gone, I guess I'll walk through on the way to the upstairs high-rollers."

Mildred nodded. "When I'm done, I'll take the south end."

"Ah, nope." Perry adjusted his bandana, "Elton said to stay as a team at least one more night. He has a B.O.L.O. out on our friend."

"My friend, right? The news suggests he has warrants for every seedy character in the free world. I'll text when I'm finished."

They walked toward the grand staircase. He waited as she rang for the elevator off to the side.

Once the door slid open, they parted ways. Mildred punched the private button that took her to the top floor office suites.

Greeted by a receptionist that faced the elevator, Mildred spoke, "It's surprising to see anyone in the office this time of night. I'd like to see Mr. Ivans, please."

"Do you have an appointment?" Her voice was stilted and reminded Mildred of a truly bad actor.

"No, I do not. Please tell him Mrs. Petrie is here."

The woman made a call and spoke low. She looked up and Mildred could see the judgment on her face turn to surprise. "Go to the last office down that hall. He will meet you."

Mildred walked to the door and knocked. The handsome young man she had been noticing on the periphery of her life was standing there.

He looked shocked as he spoke. "Welcome, Mrs. Petrie, it is nice to meet you."

Mildred walked in, then noticed her reflection in the large window and was surprised. Mildred had forgotten she was dressed as Bambi Hunter. She had to remain focused on what was needed. "Oh my! Sorry, I'm in character for work tonight." Mildred smiled and reached out to shake his hand.

"You aren't who I expected for sure. Good work."

He walked her over to a small couch by the window with a stunning view that included Mildred's condo community and the adjacent nature trails. He took his phone from his pocket and turned it off. He motioned for her to do the same. Mildred shut down her phone, turned off the earpiece and took it out.

With a nod, he began to speak. "How can I help you?"

Mildred was suspicious, but recognized his caution. "I have noticed you around the casino and saw you at Attorney Selkirk's office. Yesterday you were with my granddaughter and she mentioned you said something about my husband. That was when I decided we need to talk."

Ivans leaned back, turned up a radio and then spoke softly. "I'm sorry for all of this. I'm being extra cautious. I'm glad to meet you, Miss ah... I don't know, do you have an alias?"

"Bambi. Bambi Hunter, biker extraordinaire."

He nodded. "Welcome to the Ivory Winds Casino." His voice dropped, "I don't think there are any mics or cameras, but it is best no one sees us together."

Mildred answered with a hoarse whisper. "There is so much going on with the news and I want to know if it is about my husband, er, ah, ex-husband. Shoot, that's wrong too. My husband passed about five years ago, and ah, I need to know what is happening."

"I only met Captain Petrie briefly. But I'd heard his name mentioned back when I was in college."

"What college? Was it another student, professor, or what?"

His voice went even lower, "I stayed with some people back then and I still owe. So I have nothing more I can say."

"Did you take philosophy, by chance?" Mildred stared at his face while he answered and she read the truth in his eyes.

"Yes, that's a required course where I went." At that moment, Mildred was confident she knew who had provided the coded book and the zip drive. He continued in a normal tone of voice. "I have a dinner engagement in a few. Is there anything else you would like to discuss?"

Mildred answered in a similar tone. "I want to see if there is anything additional you need for my granddaughter's application?"

"No, nothing at all. I have copies of everything. We are good." He stood to dismiss her.

Mildred prepared to leave, then leaned back over to him. "Are you part of the nightly news? Do you know where Arnie Arneson is?"

"No, Ms. Hunter." Then his voice dropped, "He may not be who you think he is. I know of some of his contract work. We can't meet again, things are changing. Be careful."

"Back at 'cha." Mildred slipped back into her Bambi persona, offered him a fist bump and left.

Mildred rang for the elevator to the second floor, turned on her phone and earpiece, then texted Perry as it went down. The door opened and Perry was standing there.

"Hey, Bambs. Where you been?"

"Ol' man, heard there was a shorter line for the can upstairs." Perry did his best tough guy nod and entered the elevator, pushing the main floor button. As the doors closed, Mildred whispered. "Something is going on. I think it's big."

"Find out anything about Arnie?"

She shook her head no as they exited to the cacophony of the main floor's slot clangs, music, shouts and crowd.

"Let's go check out the event center and the Three Dog Night."

Mildred's eyes perked up. "The real ones?"

"Guess we'll find out. This is the only night and we would be remiss."

The show hadn't started and they were able to score tickets. It was concert, seating with a large dance area in the front. As soon as the first piano notes rang out, the lights came up to *Momma Told Me Not To Come*. The dance floor filled with excited white-haired and balding fans. Mildred and Perry joined in the group and took turns between singing along and making the rounds. There was very little security and Mildred chose to ignore a slight whiff of pot smoke.

The concert was going into encores when they slipped out; the casino security was now in evidence as they checked out the tables of Tee-shirts, records, and CDs.

"Ol' man, is this one of the few groups of fans which still has records available."

"Oh, where? Stop, I see them." Mildred chuckled as she watched Perry pull out cash to buy an album and the matching Tee-shirt for *It Ain't Easy*. "What are you laughing at? This might come in handy in the future for my work uniform."

As she continued to giggle, he shopped. He was moving to the next table when Mildred spoke. "Catch up with you when you're done. I'm going to walk the gaming room and grab seats at the MozamBeat if we aren't too late. I've got a feeling this crowd might want more drinks and music."

He shook his head yes and waved her away as the crowd started to emerge and join him.

Mildred decided most of the gamers were at the concert. She found one seat at the bar and ordered two lite beers. She had hers half gone when Perry walked in. He had a bag in each hand.

"Oh, thank you, Bambs." he stowed the bags on the hook under the bar and downed the beer.

"I've never seen you drink like that, ol' man."

"Being a rock fan of the 60s and 70s is thirsty work." She scooted her stool over and he squeezed in standing at the bar. "WOW, you were right. The crowd followed me." He held up two fingers for the bartender.

Mildred realized that the familiar music and dancing with strangers had soothed her angst.

They traded off on the barstool and checking the gaming areas. Most of the activity was at the slot machines. It was around midnight when the throng seemed to leave in mass. Mildred had a full beer when she took her turn on the stool. He stood next to her. "Nice thing about a middle-aged crowd is they go home early."

Perry nearly spit out the last of his second beer. "You crack me up. Middle-aged!" He laughed some more. "Do you think this group plans on living to a hundred and forty-four?"

Mildred scanned the retreating people and noticed through the window behind the band that there was a line of retirement village buses waiting. "Well, I do, and I won't look a day over a hundred when I do."

"I wouldn't be surprised. I hope to be there for that birthday party." He patted her arm, put down his beer and took his turn on the walkthrough.

He was back in about ten minutes. "Overall quiet night and no problems. Why don't we head out?"

Mildred didn't speak and simply texted the office. **G-MA out.**

Como out.

See ya; sleep well.

Perry walked her to her car. "Well, Bambs, I'm going to hate going back to working solo."

"Yeah, me too. You have made work fun." Mildred said as she unlocked the car.

"See ya Tuesday for the meeting." Perry started for his car when he turned back and threw one of the two bags to her. "A happy hundred and forty-third birthday." He then rushed away.

Mildred shook her head as she opened the bag to find a size medium *Suitable for Framing, Three Dog Night* Tee-shirt. He drove past and flashed the lights as she laughed.

She sent a quick text to Arnie, but her phone flashed *unavailable*. She turned the radio up and started for home.

As she parked, Mildred noticed the light was low through the living room window. As soon as the song finished on the classic rock station and the announcer came back on, she shut off the car and started in. She was surprised how spending the shift with Perry had erased much of her angst and questions. With a quick flip of the key fob, she locked the car and was about to unlock the front door.

"Mildred!" There was a soft whistle. "Mildred." She knew the voice and exactly who it was. She turned toward the whisper and Arnie was approaching from the darkest part of the parking lot.

"Arnie, it's you! Where have you been? Are you alright?"

"Hush. Cinnamon Bun. Stay back; I'm so sorry for all of this mess."

Mildred settled herself with a deep breath. "Who the hell are you? You have been lying to me."

"I'm sorry. I had taken the job at the casino trying to get away from my old life. They found me and they offered a deal that if I made one more contract, they'd let me out." She could hear the angst in his voice. "They left me alone for nearly five years. I believed that the agreement was good. I never planned on falling for you."

"You realize that lying by omission is still lying. With the news today, I need to know who you are and who you work for." Mildred backed up slightly which triggered her motion detector light to come on. With the sudden brightness, she could see he was holding a gun.

His answer was clear. "I think you have figured it out."

Mildred's concern was replaced by anger. "You are a hit man! I know too much about blood spatter for you to lie to me. Answer me, did you murder my husband?"

He didn't answer and Mildred was hopeful that the exterior video was working. She glared at him as he raised the gun slightly. She listened as he spoke.

"I'm sorry, but never forget I really love you and always will. Everything I do from now on is for you."

With strength and resolve, she didn't realize she had, Mildred didn't beg and stared into his eyes. There was a swift, almost invisible, movement and a shot.

Stunned, Mildred stood staring, unsure of what had just happened. She started to search for a wound when lights started coming on around the complex. Arnie was on the ground and Perry was on top of him. Unsure of who was moaning, Mildred approached.

"What happened?"

Perry pointed at the gun that was under the window of Mildred's condo. Glory had rushed out and kicked the gun further away. "Grandma, are you alright?"

"I'm fine."

"Excuse me, ladies," said Perry. "Could someone please call 911. I need backup and an ambulance."

Bolted to action, Mildred dropped to the ground and noticed the blood on both men. "What can I do?"

Perry moaned. "911, please."

"Already done," said Glory. "Who was hit?"

Perry answered, "I was. But I don't dare move; I've got him pinned."

"Is it bad?" Mildred started to search for a wound.

"Hell, I don't know. I'm not a doctor, but it hurts like, ah..."

That was the first she noticed that Arnie had been stunned, probably by the Taser that was still in Perry's hand.

She heard Glory speak. "Stay still, I'll get my cuffs and clear the crowd. Okay, folks, we will talk about this at the next homeowner's meeting. Better go home now." A few left, but the others just moved to the sidewalks as the sound of emergency vehicles came closer.

Mildred knelt to the two men. "How did you know, Perry?"

He took a deep breath. "I recognized his pickup truck a row behind where you were parked. Once you pulled out, he followed with his lights out." His voice shook with pain. "I decided to fall in line to be sure you were alright. I didn't know anything. In fact, I still don't know what was happening. Just when your light came on, I saw the gun."

The ambulance arrived a few feet in front of the patrol car. Mildred rose to help Glory, who had taken charge. Arnie was starting to come back around. The officer pulled Arnie to his feet and started repeating the Miranda warning.

"Hold on, guys," Mildred spoke briefly with the officers, then with Glory. That was when she climbed into the ambulance next to Perry.

– 37 –

Late Night Emergency

There was no concept of time. Mildred held Perry's hand as the medic tried to stop the bleeding in the rush to the hospital.

Mildred had to drop her head down next to his face to be heard over the siren. "I can't believe you took a bullet for me."

"That's what we do," Perry whispered.

"You aren't a sheriff anymore, ol' man. You are an Ivory Winds Casino security guard. We aren't supposed to get shot."

She removed his black wig and stroked his hair. She watched as he started to lose consciousness. A quick look at the medical technician confirmed that it was the drugs taking effect.

Once at the hospital, they ran him past the people in the waiting room into the trauma unit. They had an admitting clerk talk to Mildred and take her away as they went to work. Time clicked past with no thought until Glory showed up and, shortly after, Detective Block. He was immediately ushered to the treatment rooms.

A disheveled Bud Moses arrived. It was obvious that he had been asleep when the call came in.

"Nice jammies, Bud."

He sat down in the uncomfortable plastic chair next to her. "I had to start wearing pajama pants after we hired you, Miss. Nice to see you in the waiting room for a change."

Mildred's smile was stressed. "I think it is easier on the other side of the swinging doors."

Bud nodded. "Time for an update. You must stop getting your helpers shot."

Glory excused herself while Mildred retold the details of the night. She returned with drinks.

The three had a view of the skyline as the sun lit the horizon. No one had slept when Elton came back out with an update. He nearly collapsed in the chair next to Bud.

"He is alright. It was deep, but nothing that can't heal. I know he won't be sitting for a while."

Mildred looked at him questioningly.

Elton looked directly at her. "I can't believe you got my dad butt shot."

"Butt shot!" Mildred exclaimed. "I'm sorry, there was so much going on, I didn't realize."

With a shake of his head, Elton continued. "I should have expected as much. It could have been worse. He is in recovery and will be out for a while. I have to go to work in a few, so I'm going to head out. I think you can go and get some rest." He looked to Mildred and continued. "I'm going to need a statement from you. Any idea of what time?"

"Much of this happened in front of my place, so hopefully the video activated."

"I'll send a tech over to pick it up."

He waved as he started to walk away. Mildred called over to him. "Don't you ever sleep, Detective?"

"Not much, since I met you, Mrs. P."

Glory interrupted. "I'm taking her home first. Maybe sleep a little and to get out of that disguise." Glory gathered the cups and wrappers and all three dragged to their homes.

Four hours and a shower later, Mildred and Glory arrived at the hospital to check in on Perry on their way to the police station. Perry was lying on his side eating a hamburger. Elton was sitting next to him, eating the hospital meal. They both looked guilty.

Mildred looked at Glory and asked, "What is wrong with this picture?"

The women looked on disapprovingly as Elton tried to explain.

"I brought something so that I could have lunch with my dad, and he took it."

Perry said nothing as he enjoyed another bite and held up the order of fries as if to share.

Mildred sat on the ledge by the window. "How are you doing, ol' man?"

He swallowed before answering and put on an exaggerated sad face. "They cut off my tattoo sleeves."

"Why? Your arms weren't anywhere near your wounded cheek. I'll order some more, the least I can do for a certified hero." Mildred smiled. "How long are they going to keep you?"

Elton spoke up. "Not long. There were a bunch of stitches, some muscle repair. The bullet didn't lodge, so we are going to your place to see where it may have ended up."

"Ended up!" Glory laughed. "Sorry, but as bad as it is, it's kinda funny."

Perry looked her straight in the eyes. "I'll laugh about it when I can sit."

Elton joined in with her laughter. "Dad, you have to admit it is funny."

"Not today and not in this room." Mildred tried to look harshly at the two. "I'm so happy to see you, Perry. Is there anything you need?"

"No, Mil. I think I'll be out of here soon. I might need some help when I'm home, but we will see then."

Mildred turned to Elton. "What is happening with Arnie?"

"He is doing fine. Franklin and Moreno are interviewing him today. He has been pretty quiet. Only gives his name, which we know is an alias, and asks about you. He has already called for that young attorney at the casino."

"Ivans?"

"Yeah, that's him. I didn't talk to him, but the prosecutor told me Ivans said he would find someone else to show up. He refused to represent him," said Elton.

Mildred pondered for a moment and then asked, "Do you think it would be alright if I visited him?"

"Best not," said Elton. "We don't know if he was planning on killing you or what. It isn't safe or smart."

Perry wadded up the paper wrapper and tossed it to the trash. "Not to interrupt, but, Mildred, your boyfriend is an ass."

"You don't need to be all butt-hurt about it, Mr. Block," said Glory.

Even Perry grimaced due to an obvious posterior ache. "Stop, you're cracking me up," he howled.

Glory yelped, "Crack up!" which caused them to all to lose any semblance of control until a nurse came in to quiet them.

Since Mildred's planned a trip to the police station was off, Glory suggested they stop for a couple of those giant burgers that Perry had eaten. While they waited, Mildred excused herself to the restroom and called Tim Selkirk. His office put her through, and after a quick update he agreed to go over and talk to Arnie. He promised to check back in after the visit.

Mildred called back and spoke to his secretary providing her newly paid-off credit card number and set up billing information. She stood at the sink and stared at her reflection. Surprised by conflicted feelings, *I loved him so; it must be the lies. There is something deeper and then I'll understand.*

— 38 —

Self-Investigation

"Grandma, wake up. There is a woman at the door," Glory called from the living room.

Mildred was momentarily confused. "Who is it, dear?"

"Penny."

"Oh, ask her in. I'll be right out." Mildred leaped as high as a 72-year-old woman can and dashed to the bathroom. Two minutes later, Mildred joined Penny and Glory at the table. A hot cup of tea was already poured. "I'm so sorry to keep you waiting."

Mildred started to do introductions when Penny interrupted, "No need, darling. I have already explained to Glory and she understands." Glory grinned and winked at them. Penny/Tim continued, "I'm sorry to be so early, but I have a group meeting today and I didn't want to wait." Penny took a deep drink and continued. "I met with Arnie last evening. He was very open and worried about you. He didn't want you to think the gun was for you. He didn't go into any details and would only talk to me off the record. Thomas Conner showed up to be his attorney and he said you would remember him. Guess he has connections."

Mildred nodded. "Yes, he represented Judge McCaffie and he often defends the high-profile criminal cases."

"Yes, that's the one. There has been gossip around the bar association about his..." Penny made air quote signs around the last word. "Connections. Arnie said that young attorney, Evans..."

Mildred interrupted, "Ivans."

"Yes, that's him. I arranged for Conner to meet with him. The private message to you is he had withdrawn from his previous associations and had built a new life in the casino. He wouldn't give me any more information, but I'm to tell you how much he loves and owes you. He added he knew it was impossible to make it up to you."

Mildred could feel the emotion welling up and nearly spilled over. "I, ah, I don't know."

Glory reached over and patted her grandmother's hand. "I have the private number for James Ivans. I'll call him."

Mildred was shocked. "I thought he was a job interview?"

"Well, kind of. But we met at the police station and talked there. No offense, Grandma, but I don't want to go into security first. He said he would do a reference letter, but to keep things quiet for now."

Mildred's head spun to face her. "Are you dating him!?"

"No. We are kinda friends, right now. We'll talk later."

Penny stifled a smile. "Well, he is a cutie, you can't deny that, Millie, old gal. Anyway, back to my report. I did contact Attorney Conner and explained that a friend of Arnie's had sent me and we hadn't known of his involvement. I offered to help if it was necessary, but he dismissed me. I don't have anything to support my suspicions, but this all seems tied to the arrests from the information you presented. I never mentioned your name. They are very closed-mouth about what is going on, but some heavy-hitters are showing up."

"Thank you, Pennnnn...ah, Tim. I truly appreciate your help. I expect a bill for this," said Mildred.

"Yeah, okay. I'll expect payment in water balloons, cocktails and dinners. Honey, we are friends, and it was one visit in suit pants." Penny rose. "I have to go now. My support group meets this morning and it's my turn to bring cookies."

Mildred reached out. "If you want, sit down for more tea and I'll heat the oven to knock out some cherry turnovers."

"Deal! Those glams would love that."

Penny went to refill the teapot, and Mildred rolled out three packages of turnovers. The room filled with teasing and laughter as Glory put the warm baked goods in the insulated carrier. There was no more discussion of the new information. Mildred needed to process what she had learned and the other two recognized and respected her need.

Glory handed the icing packets to Penny for when the turnovers cooled a little. Mildred stood at the door and waved as Penny loaded everything into her sports car. His bright red lips smiled as he waved and called out to them. "Paid in full!"

Glory closed the door and started for the kitchen. "Eggs?"

Mildred went directly to her computer, "Yes, that would be great. Would you rather go out?"

"No, I'll throw us together an omelet. More tea?"

Mildred sat at the counter and started to search. "I'm still working on that last name Baghetti. Was I spelling it right?" Mildred started tapping and searching.

"Like spaghetti only with a B." Glory quieted as she made a simple breakfast and then carried the plates to the table.

Time passed before Mildred went back to her bedroom. "Glory, the jail visiting hours are soon. I'm going over to see if I can get in."

"Is that a good idea?" Glory put down her book and started gathering the breakfast dishes.

"Probably not."

"I'm going with you. Do you want the bathroom first?"

They were out of the door and on the way before Glory asked. "Is this alright with the FBI?"

Mildred kept driving. "I've decided to go with the plan of better to get forgiveness than permission. I have to see him. I need answers."

"I hope you get them."

The ride was quiet and they entered the reception area. It was only a few minutes before Mildred was called up and Arnie refused the visit and added to the message. **Please don't come back. I don't want you in this.**

When they reached the car, Mildred nearly collapsed and Glory led her to the passenger side. "I trusted him. I love him. Who the hell is he?"

"I don't have answers for you. We have to trust Elton and the investigation. You know in your heart that they will find the truth. For now, you need some sleep and to think about something else. Buckle up. Are we going to the hospital and visit Perry?"

"Sure, it's handy that the jail and hospital visiting hours are the same. They are, aren't they?" Mildred picked up her phone and started a text. It was only a few minutes later there was an answer. "Well, Perry has been released and is staying at Elton's. Guess you are right. Let's go home and take it easy."

"Now you are making sense." Glory made a right turn at the next intersection, and they went home.

− 39 −

Tuesday Again

TODAY'S MEET CANCELED – BUD.

Mildred was up and had a large pot of coffee brewed and four packages of Pepperidge Farm turnovers were baking in the oven. She stared at her phone screen for a moment before she called to Glory. "Sweetie, you can stop cleaning the bathroom; the meeting is canceled."

Glory entered the kitchen with an armload of towels and laid them on the washer in the linen closet. "What's going on?"

"I don't know," said Mildred. "A text from Bud just came in. Guess we are having turnovers and ten cups of coffee."

Glory pulled out a stool at the counter and pulled two cups over. "I'm ready to give it a try." Before she could pour, there was a knock at the door, and the knob turned. The two women looked at each other as the door opened.

A familiar voice spoke. "Well, maybe not completely canceled." Bud Moses came in with James Ivans. He put a two-pound egg casserole on the counter. "Elton called and wanted a select few. I can't tell you any more."

James Ivans took off his hat and extended his hand. "Nice to meet you, Mildred... or should I call you Bambi?"

Mildred smiled. "Mildred, Millie, Dred, all are acceptable."

Ivans turned to Glory. "Miss Petrie, very nice to see you again."

Glory smiled and Mildred would swear that the girl darn near curtsied. "Would you like some coffee?" She led them into the dining area where the meetings usually occurred and started pouring.

Almost immediately there was another tap at the door and Elton Block peeked in the door. "You still don't use the lock on that door nearly enough." He then held the door for Perry to limp in, along with Special Agent Franklin, who handed her a bag of muffins.

Mildred said, "Hold on." She grabbed a pillow off of the couch and rolled her padded office chair into the meeting for Perry. "We were going to the hospital to visit yesterday. How's your ass?"

Elton spoke first. "I usually call him Dad, but you can ask him directly."

Mildred rolled her eyes as she stifled her giggle. It was obvious that Perry was still in pain. "Well, Como, you are out and around sooner than I expected."

"Me too, but Elton thought this meeting was important and wouldn't let me sit this one out."

They worked in tandem. Glory set around full mugs and plates to each of them. Mildred removed the turnovers from the oven and plated them, along with the other offerings as the men spoke in low voices. Once they settled, Elton took over.

"This isn't our usual meeting and we have left out some of the others from the casino. I'm not sure if everyone has met Mr. Ivans." Handshakes and nods went around the table. "As you all know, he is a new board member at the Ivory Winds."

"Please call me James. I was sent to the casino to help with a covert ownership takeover. I have a history with a *business* based in Baltimore. They specialize in questionable businesses and practices."

Mildred started piecing things together. "Wait a minute. You helped get the young prostitutes back home. Did you have anything to do with getting Arnold Arneson that attorney, Conner?"

"I didn't get Thomas Conner in to defend him. That was, as we shall say, above my pay grade."

Agent Moreno looked at Elton and Franklin. "This is off the record, but Arneson has fired Connor and asked for the prosecuting attorney. We don't know what he has, but he's been moved to an isolated location. It appears he has some information."

Mildred turned to Ivans. "Do you know what it is?"

"I'm sorry, no. When my dad was in prison, I was a homeless street kid. The boss took me in and he groomed me into law. He wanted me to be a part of the business, but I avoided as much as I could. I was as much a prisoner as a houseguest, but as time passed the boss began to trust me."

Mildred was so full of questions she could hardly contain herself. "The key? Was that you?"

He shrugged his shoulders and everyone at the table was silent. "I met with Mr. Baghetti and he doesn't want an attorney." Ivans turned to Franklin. "He intends to testify in the cases against four of the dons you have arrested." Ivans continued, "Now, Mildred, I will need to speak to Special Agent Franklin privately."

"I'm sorry to interrupt, but how does Arnie know these guys? What is the connection?" Mildred looked directly into Ivans' eyes.

Agent Franklin interrupted. "He did some specialized contract work. I can't say anything further."

In a tiny voice, Glory spoke. "Did Baghetti murder Captain Dick Petrie?"

Ivans was silent for a breath or two. "I don't know. It was a contract that went to several specialists, but I don't know for sure who handled it."

Mildred asked, "Not for sure. But do you think it is possible?"

Franklin sat up straight in his chair, took out his phone and tapped something onto the keyboard. "Will he want witness protection?"

Ivans bowed his head momentarily. "First of all, Glory, I don't know. He handled some contracts, but I have no proof." He then turned to Franklin. "Depending on the charges and any deals that might help, it's still bad. Even if he goes to prison, he'll need deep protection for the rest of his life."

Franklin seemed to go cold and turned to Ivans. "You can't go back to the casino or your home from here on out. We don't know who else may be involved in this."

Ivans continued the conversation. "I know most of the dirty details. I'll be fine. If it gets dangerous,

I always have a go bag in the car. Baghetti tried to bow out, but they found him working at the casino and were pushing him to come up with numbers. He was tasked with researching Captain Petrie and any other information. When he stopped cooperating, I was put in place to push his assignment. I was also to finalize the stock transfers and clear out any known roadblocks for them to take over the Ivory Winds."

Franklin responded. "Did he take care of Paul Clanton?"

"The old man was really steamed about some punk trying to steal from him. He demands a very high level of loyalty. As for Clanton, it seems to match Arnie's signature, but I wasn't privy to the details. I've spent my years primarily in a place of overhearing."

"Do you need a safe house or someplace to go?" asked Agent Moreno.

"No," said James. "There isn't any place you know of that is safe enough. I've been prepared since high school for this day. I'm good. I'll give you a contact number if you need any further information."

"Will you be available for testimony?"

James Ivans shook his head. "No. I will be gone after I walk out of here."

Mildred didn't hear the rest of the conversation. She served food and poured coffee but had no memory of the actions. She continued to build uglier and guiltier scenarios. Glory took over and asked questions and offered information. Mildred marveled at the young woman who had been a child playing on the floor days ago.

Finally, Mildred heard her name and noticed everyone was standing and that Bud had cleared the table. Perry's voice broke through her consciousness. "Glory, if you can give me a ride, I'll stay for a little bit. Elton needs to head back to work."

"No problem." Glory fixed him a place on the couch so he could lie back.

Mildred went to the kitchen, and it was already clean. She turned to see Perry and Glory watching the news channel. In a low voice, Mildred asked, "How did this happen? I fell for my husband's killer." She sobbed. "I slept with a damn murderer."

Perry hushed Glory as she started to speak, then she helped him stand. He limped to Mildred's chair and spoke softly. "We don't know anything for sure. He may have been in that business, but that isn't the man he is now. You changed him. Arnie is putting his life at risk and it is for you. Not for the casino, society in general or justice, it's all for you. Now take your time, have a deep cry, scream if you wish, swear and yell, then sleep. We're here for you. I am here for you."

"Thank you." Mildred found her grief was so deep that tears wouldn't come. Hours later, she remembered the steps of grief and knew that she would recover. She decided to accept anger for now and let it stay as long as necessary. She watched Glory help Perry towards the door to go home.

"Glory, get my Delilah walker for Perry. It might help."

He smiled, noticing her change in mood. "No need. The insurance company is giving me one that isn't red and folds up without help."

"Wait a few minutes, and I'll ride along." Mildred turned to the bedroom. She was confident that the demands of her job, friends and family would help make it alright. Scheduled to cover for Perry tonight, she put on her elastic waist pants and a glittery casino sweatshirt. She called from the bedroom, "Anyone hungry?"

Perry was the first to speak. "I could eat. Oh, and by the way, I wanted to tell you, the doctor said I'd be fit and on my feet before the Elvis convention next month."

– Other Books by Toni Kief –

FICTION
Old Baggage, Never too Late for a New Beginning
https://www.amazon.com/dp/1530424887/

MILDRED UNCHAINED SERIES
Mildred in Disguise with Diamonds
https://www.amazon.com/dp/154495669X/

Mildred, Romancing the Odds
https://www.amazon.com/dp/B07CQ873N5/ref

WRITING
Dare to Write in a Flash
https://www.amazon.com/dp/1731244746/

SHORT STORIES
Detours & Transformations
https://www.amazon.com/dp/B07454JCYC/ref

All available on Amazon and www.tonikief.com

– About the Author –

Toni Kief never planned to write a book, until she was sixty. Born in the Midwest, lived in Florida, she presently calls the great Northwest home. She continues to resist writing an autobiography because of her odd incarnations and the tendency to catch a bus and leave town. Much of her creative  energy goes into women of certain age. Toni calls her work OA, Old Adult, as she focuses on the ability to grab life full force and face unidentified dreams. Working with the Writers Cooperative of the Pacific Northwest, she has started her next book.